Wild Card

BOOKS BY STUART WOODS

FICTION

Wild Card[†]

A Delicate Touch[†]

Desperate Measures[†]

Turbulence[†]

Shoot First[†]

Unbound[†]

Quick & Dirty[†]

Indecent Exposure[†]

Fast & Loose[†]

Below the Belt[†]

Sex, Lies & Serious Money[†]

Dishonorable Intentions[†]

Family Jewels[†]

Scandalous Behavior[†]

Foreign Affairs[†]

Naked Greed[†]

Hot Pursuit[†]

Insatiable Appetites[†]

Paris Match[†]

Cut and Thrust[†]

Carnal Curiosity[†]

Standup Guy[†]

Doing Hard Time[†]

Unintended Consequences[†]

Collateral Damage[†]

Severe Clear[†]

Unnatural Acts[†]

D.C. Dead[†]

Son of Stone[†]

Bel-Air Dead[†]

Strategic Moves[†]

Santa Fe Edge[§]

Lucid Intervals[†]

Kisser[†]

Hothouse Orchid[*]

Loitering with Intent[†]

Mounting Fears[‡]

Hot Mahogany[†]

Santa Fe Dead[§]

Beverly Hills Dead

Shoot Him If He Runs[†]

Fresh Disasters[†]

Short Straw[§]

Dark Harbor[†]

Iron Orchid[*]

Two-Dollar Bill[†]

The Prince of Beverly Hills

Reckless Abandon[†]

Capital Crimes[‡]

Dirty Work[†]

Blood Orchid[*]

The Short Forever[†]

Orchid Blues[*]

Cold Paradise[†]

L.A. Dead[†]

The Run[‡]

Worst Fears Realized[†]

Orchid Beach[*]

Swimming to Catalina[†]

Dead in the Water[†]

Dirt[†]

Choke

Imperfect Strangers

Heat

Dead Eyes Grass Roots[‡]
L.A. Times White Cargo
Santa Fe Rules[§] Deep Lie[‡]
New York Dead[†] Under the Lake
Palindrome Run Before the Wind[‡]
Chiefs[‡]

COAUTHORED BOOKS

The Money Shot** (with Parnell Hall)
Barely Legal[††] (with Parnell Hall)
Smooth Operator** (with Parnell Hall)

TRAVEL

A Romantic's Guide to the Country Inns
of Britain and Ireland (1979)

MEMOIR

Blue Water, Green Skipper

*A Holly Barker Novel
[†]A Stone Barrington Novel
[‡]A Will Lee Novel
[§]An Ed Eagle Novel
**A Teddy Fay Novel
[††]A Herbie Fisher Novel

STUART WOODS

Wild Card

G. P. Putnam's Sons
NEW YORK

G. P. Putnam's Sons
Publishers Since 1838
An imprint of Penguin Random House LLC
penguinrandomhouse.com

LIBRARY OF CONGRESS CATALOGING-IN-PUBLICATION DATA

Names: Woods, Stuart, author.
Title: Wild card / Stuart Woods.
Description: New York : G. P. Putnam's Sons, 2019.| Series: A Stone
Barrington novel ; 49
Identifiers: LCCN 2018057955 | ISBN 9780735219281 (hardback) |
ISBN 9780735219304 (epub)
Subjects: LCSH: Barrington, Stone (Fictitious character)—Fiction. | Private
investigators—Fiction. | BISAC: FICTION / Action & Adventure. | FICTION /
Suspense. | FICTION / Thrillers. | GSAFD: Suspense fiction. | Adventure fiction.
Classification: LCC PS3573.O642 W55 2019 | DDC 813/.54—dc23
LC record available at https://lccn.loc.gov/2018057955
p.   cm.

Printed in the United States of America
1 3 5 7 9 10 8 6 4 2

Book design by Francesca Belanger
Title page photograph by dibrova/Shutterstock.com

Wild Card

1

Stone Barrington and Jamie Cox had spent an idyllic month at Stone's estate, Windward Hall, in the south of England, on the banks of the Beaulieu River (pronounced *Bewley*, if you're British). The weather had been surprisingly un-English, with only occasional showers. They woke early each morning, made love, and then, after breakfast, took horses from the stables and galloped across Stone's acreage.

After that, Jamie went to work on her book, based on her *New York Times* story, in which she and her team had investigated a family-owned investment bank called H. Thomas & Son, exposing deep roots of organized crime going back generations. They had also investigated hundreds of millions of dollars in illegal wire transfers, money stolen from the international banking community by the Thomases. She was nearing the end of her final draft of the book.

Then, in the late afternoon, Stone's friend Dino Bacchetti telephoned, and everything went to hell.

"What are you telling me?" Stone asked, trying to slow down his friend, who was the police commissioner of the City of New York.

"I'm telling you, the FBI has closed its investigation of the

Thomases' computer crimes. The explosion and resulting fire in their computer control center destroyed everything and melted fifty interlinked computers into a solid lump of metal and silicon."

"They're not prosecuting that guy, Rance Damien, who constructed the whole thing?"

"If you remember, their software used in the wire transfers erased all trace of itself when they were done. And that software was destroyed with the computers. Which means the FBI has zero evidence against them."

"What about the copies of their software that Huey Horowitz, the *Times*'s computer whiz, downloaded onto computers in my upstairs guest room?"

"That was erased, too. All Huey had left was a blank hard drive."

"Jesus," Stone said, "can this get any worse?"

"It can," Dino replied, "and it has. Rance Damien was one of the two survivors of the fire—the building was empty except for three people, and one of them died later in the hospital. We were hoping Damien had burned to a crisp. But not only is he alive, he was discharged this morning from a private clinic, after extensive work on his face. Oh, did I mention that he is very, very angry with you?"

"At *me*? I didn't set the guy on fire."

"Sources at the FBI tell me that Damien remains unconvinced of that. While he doesn't think you set and pushed the plunger on the explosives, he does think that whoever did it works for you. Am I getting through to you?"

Stone was alarmed that Rance Damien believed this—

because it was true. At least, the part about the bomber, Bob Cantor, working for him was true. However, Stone had neither ordered up the explosion nor known anything about Bob's actions, until he saw the results on TV.

"Okay, I read you," Stone said. "What do you propose I do about it?"

"I propose that you keep your ass out of New York," Dino said. "That shouldn't be too hard because, having visited your property there, I know that you are as happy as a pig in shit— and getting laid regularly."

"I cannot deny either of those contentions," Stone said. "So I'll stay longer than I had planned."

"I am relieved to hear it," Dino said.

"But only if you and Viv get on an airplane and come visit me. Otherwise, I'm leaving for New York tomorrow."

"Okay, you've convinced me," Dino said. "Viv is due back tonight from Hong Kong, or somewhere, and I'll run it by her." Vivian Bacchetti was chief operating officer for the world's second-largest private security company, Strategic Services, and traveled widely for her work.

"I want a confirmation tomorrow," Stone said.

"Okay," Dino replied. "But watch your ass until I can get there to watch it for you. Rance Damien knows how airplanes work, and the FBI tells me he has a passport."

"I'll keep that in mind," Stone said.

"Where is *your* airplane at the moment?" Dino asked.

"It's over here," Stone said. "Faith and her copilot are ensconced in one of the cottages on the estate."

"Maybe we can hitch a ride on a Strategic Services flight."

"Free is always the best choice," Stone replied. "Call me." He hung up.

When Jamie finished work in the little basement office Stone had arranged for her, they met in the paneled library for drinks, where her vodka and his bourbon were kept in stock. He told her the news.

Jamie was appalled. "Oh, God, just when I thought this was all over, Rance Damien rises from the dead? Did somebody forget to drive a stake through his heart?"

"I would have done it myself, if I had thought of it," Stone replied.

"I finished the book about twenty minutes ago," she said. "I was looking forward to getting you drunk and taking advantage of you."

"You needn't let bad news deprive you of either of those pleasures," Stone said.

The phone rang, and Stone picked it up. "Yes?"

"Mr. Barrington," Kevin, the butler, said, "Dame Felicity Devonshire is calling for you. Shall I put her through?"

"Yes, thank you," Stone said, then waited for the click. "Felicity?"

"Yes, Stone," she replied. "How are you?"

"I'm very well, thanks. Where are you?"

"I've just arrived at my house, back from dealing with the Muddle East"—which was what Felicity called any place east of the Mediterranean—"and my housekeeper told me there was a rumor that you were in residence, but keeping to yourself."

"I am in residence," Stone said. "My lady friend has been working feverishly on a book, but she's just finished it, so why don't you come for dinner?"

"I was hoping you'd ask," Felicity said, "and I accept. I've been gone five weeks, and there isn't anything in the house that's thawed."

"Drinks at seven?"

"Perfect, and who, may I ask, is this one?"

"Jamie Cox—I'll introduce you."

"I shall look forward to meeting her," Felicity said. "May I bring someone? He owns a dinner jacket."

"Of course. See you at the dock." Stone hung up.

"Are we having a guest for dinner?" Jamie asked.

"Yes, does the name Dame Felicity Devonshire ring a distant bell?"

Jamie cupped a hand to her ear. "I believe I hear something. Intelligence, is it?"

"She's director of MI6, the British foreign intelligence service."

"Ah, yes, and how did you come to know her?"

"That memory is lost in the mists of time, but she's my neighbor across the river. She's bringing someone, but I forgot to ask who."

"I love a surprise."

"We'll see about that. He's probably one of her father's contemporaries and will harrumph and bah a lot."

"Oh, swell."

"On the other hand, it's black tie, and we can rely on Felicity to dress to kill, so you can have a shot at that, too."

"I knew there was a reason I brought those dresses."

2

Stone and Jamie met Felicity at the dock and took her lines. Her companion looked familiar, Stone thought. Jamie actually gasped when she saw him. He was a little taller and a little slimmer than Stone, and movie-star handsome. Stone hoped he wasn't a little smarter, too. He introduced Jamie.

"Stone, Jamie, this is Craig Calvert," Felicity said, with just a tiny note of pride in her voice.

Calvert was, of course, a British movie star, though Stone hadn't seen him in anything. Calvert revealed spectacular dental work as he shook their hands, and his voice was a little deeper than Stone's.

"How do you do?" Calvert said, rather formally, but he looked only at Jamie.

"We do very well, thank you," Stone said, choosing his pronoun carefully as a small shot across his bow.

Felicity enveloped Stone in her buxom embrace, reinforced with a tiny pelvic thrust—to make sure he was paying attention. "How wonderful to see you," she said, clinging for a moment.

Stone got everybody into the Range Rover, then drove the ninety seconds to the house, where the butler, Kevin, awaited them on the steps with the front door open. Half a minute later,

Stone was playing bartender, pouring martinis for everyone but himself. He kept martinis and vodka gimlets, premixed and in the freezer. And when he had poured himself a Knob Creek, he sat down and let Felicity take over the conversation, since not doing so would have been fruitless.

"Craig is about to begin shooting a grand new film at Pinewood," she said. "He has been our guest at the office for a couple of days to soak up a little intelligence atmosphere."

"I'll bet Felicity made you sign the Official Secrets Act," Stone said, mentioning the draconian document that hijacked the right of free speech on anything to do with intelligence.

"She did," Calvert replied, "so I can't even tell you where the men's room is at MI6 without being jailed."

"Fortunately, I know where the men's room is," Stone replied, in an attempt to restore a level playing field. "What's your new film about?"

"A spy thriller, of course."

"Are you playing the role of spy or spy catcher?"

"Both, as it happens. I should get paid twice."

"I'm sure you're worth every shilling," Stone said.

"Stone," Felicity interjected, unable to contain herself. "I understand that you and Jamie have been involved in a very big story in the States."

"Jamie has been," Stone said. "I'm just a bystander."

"Not an innocent one, though," Jamie added. "I just finished my book on the subject this afternoon and delivered the manuscript via e-mail."

"Then congratulations," Felicity said.

"I suppose you'll have some time on your hands now. You

should come up to Pinewood and see the fabulous sets that have been built there," Calvert offered.

"I'd love to," Jamie replied, with a little more enthusiasm than Stone would have liked.

"So would I," Stone said. "May I come, too?"

"Of course," Calvert said, with a little less enthusiasm than Stone would have liked. "We start principal photography a week from Monday, so any time before then, unless you'd like to be bored rigid by watching actors speak the same lines over and over."

"Stone," Felicity said, a little reprovingly, since she had lost steerage of the conversation, "I understand your big story ended in tears."

"Not my tears," Stone said, "nor Jamie's. The subjects of the investigation shed a few, though. One of them committed suicide, and another was injured in an explosion that the FBI thinks may have been of his own making."

"Sounds like there's a film in there somewhere," Calvert said. "I'd love to read your manuscript, Jamie."

With his head in her lap, Stone thought.

"I'll have my agent send you a copy," Jamie replied. "We have to go through channels, you know."

"Craig might be very good as the villain," Stone said. "A very nasty character. He should be fun to play. Don't actors all say that villains are the best parts?"

"Some do," Calvert replied. "Is there a hero?"

"Well, there are two choices, I think," Jamie said. "One is a nineteen-year-old computer whiz, and the other is Stone."

Calvert's face fell a bit.

"Oh, come now, Jamie," Stone said. "Bystanders can't be heroes, unless CPR or the Heimlich maneuver is involved."

"Perhaps you should play yourself, Stone," Felicity offered.

"I'm not an actor, Felicity," Stone replied. "And if I tried, I'd be a very bad one. I don't have that certain twinkle that a leading man must display." He smiled at Calvert, who kept his dental work to himself.

Kevin entered and announced dinner, indicating a table set at the other end of the library.

"We're not enough for the dining room," Stone said.

"I love this room," Felicity said, gathering herself for the trek. "I've spent so many lovely evenings here." That one was aimed directly at Jamie.

"I'm sure you've spent lovely evenings everywhere," Jamie replied, without quite adding *on your back.*

Stone seated everyone, with himself facing the door.

"The gunfighter's seat," Calvert said.

"Facing the butler," Stone replied. "It saves ringing a bell."

Jamie quickly fell into conversation with Calvert, who seemed to have rung her bell, while Felicity commandeered Stone.

Stone turned his attention to tasting the wine.

"What is it, old chap?" Calvert asked, sniffing his glass.

"A Mouton-Rothschild '78," Stone replied, glancing at the label. "Sir Charles left me some very nice bottles when he sold me the house."

"Ah," Calvert said, nodding. "One doesn't see much of that anymore."

"A case turns up at auction now and then," Stone said.

"I don't like auctions," Calvert said. "One ends up paying what things are worth."

"Oh, Craig," Felicity said, "you're a film star. You can splurge."

"Stardom doesn't last a lifetime," Calvert said, "but the money must. I'll turn forty this year, so I have to start thinking more about investing and less about drinking."

"You're a wise man, Craig," Felicity said. She turned toward Stone. "So, what's this I hear about your villain leaving hospital this morning?"

"I heard that, too," Stone said.

"You're not going to have people shooting up the neighborhood, are you?"

"I hope not."

"Well, it's happened before," Felicity said.

"Your hearing is too sharp," Stone said. "And your memory, too. Tell me, Felicity, how are things in the Muddle East these days?"

That diverted her long enough for Stone to breathe more easily.

Dinner finally ended, and cognacs were downed. "Oh, by the way, Stone," Felicity said, "I wonder if Craig could make use of your gym for a few days. He has to be in top form for the new film."

"Of course," Stone said reluctantly. "Just present yourself to Kevin, and he'll show you the way."

Kevin drove them back to the dock.

3

Stone and Jamie crawled into bed, too tired to make love. Jamie, however, was not too tired to talk about it.

"You've fucked Felicity Devonshire, haven't you—and often?"

Stone sighed. "I recall that, early in our relationship, you placed your past sex life out of bounds."

"I did," she admitted.

"Is that not a two-way street?"

"I suppose it is. I apologize."

"Thank you."

"How many times, approximately, have you fucked Felicity?" she asked, enjoying the alliteration.

"I decline to answer that, on contractual grounds."

"'Contractual'? We don't have a contract."

"Certainly we do," Stone replied. "We have a spoken agreement limiting our areas of discussion, and you have crossed the lines of that agreement."

"Oh, come on, Stone, this is just pillow talk."

"It encompasses the whole bedroom, including the furniture."

"You fucked her on the furniture?"

"I didn't say that."

"You implied it."

"Do you know who Felicity would really like to fuck?"

"Craig? Who could blame her?"

"You."

"*What?*"

"Felicity occasionally expresses an attraction for someone of her own gender—and you're just her type."

"I . . . ? 'Her type'?"

"Ask her, if you don't believe me."

Jamie lay back in bed and thought about that. "I wonder if she's my type."

"Oh? Do you also have the occasional attraction to someone of your own gender?"

"Well, not since college, and then just once. Maybe twice." She sat up in bed. "Wait a minute, you're violating our contract. No judge would allow that."

"I would tell a judge that you opened the door, making it a subject for questioning."

"'Opened the door'? Is that a euphemism for sex?"

"Sometimes."

"Why do you think Felicity is attracted to me?"

"Did she place her hand on your knee at dinner?"

"I thought that was Craig."

"That would have been your other knee."

"There were hands on both my knees."

"Then you are very popular."

"I have an awful lot to think about," Jamie said.

"Sweet dreams," Stone replied.

• • •

Stone was already in the basement gym the following morning when Craig Calvert arrived with a short, muscular man in his fifties with a broken nose and short-cropped gray hair. "Good morning, Craig," Stone said.

"Good morning, Stone," Craig replied. "May I introduce Mick O'Leary?"

Stone shook his hand. "Good to meet you, Mick. Are you Craig's trainer?"

"He's more of my restrainer," Craig said. "I tend to get a little too enthusiastic at times, and Mick is here to see that he can deliver me to the set, undamaged, on the day."

"Dat's right," Mick said.

"You're not Irish, are you, Mick?" Stone asked. Everybody laughed.

"Well," Craig said, "Mick and I had better get to work. Just ignore us." The actor stripped off his sweat suit to reveal a physique that, while trim, Stone found intimidating.

"How much time do you spend in the gym, Craig?" he asked.

"Ordinarily, two hours a day, but the month before I start a film I do four hours a day."

"God, I'm glad I'm not an actor," Stone muttered. He went to the weight system and started his routine of lifts, pull-downs, curls, and sit-ups. It didn't last very long.

Mick put Craig through a long regimen of stretching, then Craig got back into his sweat suit. "We're going to do a little run before I start on the weights," Craig said. "Join us?"

"Sure," Stone said, retying his shoelaces.

They left the house and Stone pointed them toward a route away from the country hotel next door that would keep the guests from hanging out the windows, staring at Craig. Mick followed in one of the estate's golf carts. Every couple of minutes, Craig would run a hot sprint, and then return to Stone and Mick. "I'll have to do a lot of that in the film," Craig said, having rejoined them. "These days, there are as many chases on foot as in cars."

"Well, you never have to run more than thirty yards," Mick said. "It's in your contract. More than that, they have to bring in a stunt double."

"For which I am grateful," Craig said, "especially when it's over rooftops. I'm terrified of heights." He pointed ahead. "Is that an airstrip?"

"It is," Stone said. "It was originally built during World War II as a testing ground and a runway for light bombers carrying explosives or Special Air Service commandos to France. The ancestral owner of the place kept it up for his airplanes after the war, and I land my own airplane there." He pointed at the open hangar, where the nose of the Latitude could be seen.

They were almost at the hangar when Craig yelled and fell to one knee. Mick drove alongside and pushed him all the way down as he jumped out of the golf cart to cover Craig's body with his own.

"Shit!" Craig yelled. "I've been shot!"

Stone got down on the ground, too, and looked around. "I didn't hear anything." Half a mile away, an unmarked van crossed a meadow and left the estate. Stone got out his phone. "I'll call the police and an ambulance," he said.

"You'll call neither," Mick said. "I'll handle this."

Stone took charge of the golf cart, while Mick hustled Calvert onto the rear seat.

"I don't think we'll be shot at again," Stone said. "I think the shooter was in the van that just took off in such a hurry." They got Craig into the house gym through a back door.

"I'm going to need a first-aid kit and some light," Mick said, helping Craig onto the massage table.

Stone hurried to the office of Major Bugg, the estate manager. "Where's your medical kit?" he asked.

The major took it from a closet and followed Stone to the gym. "What's happened?"

"One of our guests has had a mishap." They entered the exercise room where Mick had Calvert lying facedown on the massage table, his pants and shorts stripped off. There was a bleeding trench running across Calvert's right buttock.

Mick opened the case and began removing things. "Lidocaine, good. Penicillin, too. And here's a suturing kit."

"Do you need a doctor's help, Mick?"

"I'm a licensed physician's assistant," Mick replied. "I can do suturing." He injected lidocaine around the wound and cleaned it carefully, then he trimmed the edges with scissors, threaded a suturing needle, and completed a dozen stitches. "There," he said, "that'll hold him. He'll need a tetanus shot, though." He found the vial and used a fresh syringe. "You'll be fine, Craig, until the lidocaine wears off and you have to sit down."

"Who the hell would want to shoot me?" Craig asked nobody in particular.

"I think the shooter was likely aiming at me," Stone said. "You just happened to be in the way."

"Felicity said something like this would happen, and it has."

"For God's sake," Stone said, "don't tell her she was right."

4

S tone found Craig another pair of sweatpants and tossed his bloody ones into the trash, while Major Bugg returned the medical kit to its home.

"You're sure you don't want to call the police?" Stone asked.

"Don't even think about it," Mick said. "Somebody at the police station will leak it to a reporter and by cocktail time it will be all over the news. You'll have two dozen photographers crawling all over your estate trying to snap a photo of Craig Calvert's ass. And we don't want that, do we?"

"I don't want Felicity to know, either," Craig said.

"Where is she today?"

"At her office. She left early this morning."

"Go back to her place, pack your bags, and leave her a note saying you've been called back to London for a script conference. Then come over here, and we'll put you up for a few days. You're not going to want to answer anybody's questions about why you're limping or sitting funny."

"Stone is right," Mick said. "If the insurance company hears that you've been shot, they'll put you in hospital for a whole new physical. That, and the resulting publicity, will screw up the shooting schedule. It will also increase the insurance pre-mium, and your producers won't like that."

"Thank you for the offer, Stone," Craig said. "I accept. Let's go pack, Mick." He hobbled out of the house and, with Mick's help, headed for the dock in the golf cart.

Stone told Major Bugg to have rooms prepared for Mr. Calvert and Mr. O'Leary—but not too close to his own. Then he went upstairs and found Jamie drying her hair.

"Well," she said, "that was a long workout."

"Shorter than planned," Stone replied, "and you're going to envy me."

"Why?"

"Because I've spent the last half hour gazing at Craig Calvert's bare ass."

"You're right, I envy you. How did he come to expose him-self to you? I may want to try myself."

"Someone took a shot at us when we were out running—at me, very probably—and Calvert's ass got in the way. He's moving in with us—rather, with me—for a few days while he heals up."

"Where is he sleeping?"

"You don't need to know. Let's go down for some lunch."

"Just a minute," Jamie said, "did you say someone shot him?"

"It was only a flesh wound, as they say in the movies."

"I take it that it wasn't a passing hunter."

"Craig's ass does not resemble a grouse."

"Are we in danger?" she asked.

"Isn't that why we left the States?"

"It's not why *I* left the States," Jamie said.

"Well, you can add that to your list." He hustled her to lunch.

. . .

They were having sandwiches in the kitchen when Dino called.

"Hey," Stone said. "Are you on your way?"

"We'll be there in the morning the day after tomorrow," Dino replied.

"Good. We've had some action here. Is Viv listening in?"

"I am," Viv said.

Stone told them what had happened. "Viv, will you call your London office and get some people down here?"

"Sure, they know the drill by now. So there's going to be a movie star in the house?"

"I'm afraid so. I may have to sit on Jamie the whole time."

"You may have to sit on me, too," she replied. "That Calvert is a dish."

"I'll do whatever sitting on you is required," Dino said.

"Call me on the satphone when you're an hour out," Stone said, "and I'll have you met at the landing strip."

"Okay," Dino replied, then hung up.

Mick and Calvert came into the kitchen with their bags. Stone spoke to the cook about them. Calvert lowered himself gingerly into a padded chair and tried to get comfortable. "The lidocaine is wearing off," he said.

"Anything I can do?" Jamie asked.

"Yes," Stone replied, "go write another draft of your book."

"You don't want me near a computer," she said. "I'm itching to write a story about what just happened to Craig."

"Oh, Stone," Calvert said, "I hope you don't mind if my

girlfriend joins us. She's my leading lady, too, and bringing her down here is the only way I can keep her quiet."

"We'd be delighted to have her," Stone replied, and with real feeling.

Back in New York, Rance Damien entered the penthouse office of Henry Thomas, the patriarch of the Thomas family and the real power behind everything that happened at H. Thomas & Son.

Henry peered at him closely. "You almost look like yourself," he said.

"They tell me I'll need three or four more surgeries before that will happen," Damien replied sourly.

"Are you ready to come back to work?"

"I've been back since early this morning," he said.

"We're going to have to turn our attention to Mr. Stone Barrington," Henry said, "if we're ever to have any peace."

"I have already done so," Damien replied. "I gave the orders last night, and a team was down at Barrington's place early this morning, their time."

"Did they get a shot at him?"

"Yes, but he was running with another man, and I'm not sure which one they hit. They got him back to the house, but they didn't call the police or an ambulance."

"That's good news," Henry said. "They may get another shot."

"What do you want to tell Hank about this?" Damien asked. Hank Thomas was the old man's grandson—formerly a congressman from New York and a candidate for the presidency, until his father's suicide, after which he had returned to the family business to help out.

"You size him up, and we'll decide how much he should be told. At some point, if he's going to be here, he'll have to know that he's not in Washington anymore, but back in the real world."

"I think Hank may work out," Damien said. "He's a gutsier guy than Jack was, and he's always been a realist. He didn't bat an eye last year when I told him that we were going to use our new computer installation to steal the money for his presidential campaign."

"A man after my own heart," Henry said, chuckling. "Are we going to rebuild the computer setup?"

"I don't think so," Damien said. "After the *Times*'s investigative campaign against us, the banking people will have completely gutted their security procedures and started over. It would be much, much harder to pull off another digital heist."

"I want Hank to become the public face of the company now," Henry said. "We've got four years to rebuild him as a serious presidential candidate, and you . . . Well, you know."

Damien nodded. He knew he was no longer a pretty face—and he'd make Barrington pay for that.

5

By mid-afternoon, people were arriving. First came Vanessa Pym, a svelte beauty with a mane of honey-blond hair, whose hired Rolls-Royce disgorged ten pieces of matched luggage. Craig made the introductions, and then Stone called Major Bugg and specified the former master suite for Craig and Vanessa, which contained a large dressing room. "And you'd better assign a maid to Ms. Pym, too. I think she's going to demand one, anyway. Move Mick down the hall a bit, so the maid can use his room for ironing."

"And you'll be five for dinner?"

"Yes, unless Mick also produces a female companion."

"And Dame Felicity?"

"She's in London. And if we hear from her, don't mention the presence of our guests."

In the late afternoon, two Mercedes Sprinters arrived and set down a team of eight men with bulges under their jackets and extra-long luggage. They were housed in a large cottage that had been used for the same purpose before—Stone had already ordered for a cook and a maid to be assigned to them. The tall-est among them reintroduced himself to Stone as Derek Forrest. "Same as last time, Mr. Barrington?" he asked.

"Pretty much," Stone said. "Whoever's out there has already missed me and wounded a guest, then left in a gray Ford van."

"I'll have a man on the front gate and another on the dock," Derek said.

"Very good," Stone said, handing him a card with his cell number on it. "Call me directly if there's an emergency. Other-wise, call Major Bugg, whom you've met."

"Yes, sir, I already have his cell number." Then the man went about his business.

Stone sent word to Craig that dress for dinner was lounge suits, not dinner jackets. When they turned up for drinks in the li-brary, Vanessa had apparently not received the message, since she was dressed in a floor-length yellow gown billowing around her breasts from cleavage nearly to her navel.

"Why didn't you tell me we were dressing up?" Jamie hissed in Stone's ear.

"Because we're not. Vanessa apparently dresses to a different standard."

"Did you see her luggage?" Jamie asked.

"I did. We're fortunate that it's a large house."

"I'll bet she has a ball gown and two fur coats packed."

"I've assigned her a maid."

"You didn't assign *me* a maid," Jamie said, pouting.

"That's because you are so wonderfully self-sufficient," Stone said, kissing her on the forehead. "I didn't want to insult you."

"*Well,*" Jamie said, smoothing her skirt.

Stone knew that to be a complete sentence.

Stone saw to it that everyone had been well lubricated and Craig anesthetized before they sat down for dinner, so they were all in a jolly mood. He observed that Craig knew exactly the level of attention that Vanessa required, and he admired the way the man managed it.

"I don't expect you have a projection room," Craig commented as they settled in with after-dinner drinks.

"No," Stone responded.

"How about a very large TV?"

"In your bedroom," Stone said.

"A pity. I brought a copy of my latest film—hasn't been released yet."

"We are desolated," Stone said. "I suppose we'll have to fall back on conversation."

"Are you sure you're not English?" Craig asked.

"On both sides, all the way back, but not by birth."

"I had rather thought you might be Eton and Oxford, but for the accent. I'm Harrow and Cambridge, myself."

"I'm PS Six and NYU," Stone replied.

"Not the Ivy League?"

"We used to call it the Poison Ivy League."

"Do you have a London club?"

"Sadly, no."

"I could propose you for the Garrick, but it takes years to work your way up the list. A lot of fellows have to die before your name comes up."

"That's kind of you, Craig, but I don't think it's worth bothering. I might not improve with age."

"Felicity tells me you belong to the Royal Yacht Squadron. How'd you manage that, not being English?"

"By not being English," Stone replied. "No members knew me well enough to vote against me."

"Very good," Craig said, chuckling, "very good."

"Another brandy?"

"Thank you, but Ms. Pym expects to be serviced, if that dress says anything. And I'd better be up for the task, so to speak. I warn you, she's noisy when in full flight."

"You're far enough down the hall, so don't worry," Stone replied. "She can cut loose."

"Believe me, she will." Craig got gingerly to his feet and, after good nights were exchanged, escorted her from the room, limping slightly.

Jamie was ready for bed, too. Mick O'Leary was in a chair before the fire with a book in his lap and glasses perched on his nose. "I think I'll have another brandy and give Craig and Vanessa a head start," Mick said. "I'm a light sleeper."

Stone left him the decanter and walked Jamie upstairs.

Upstairs, Stone drew the curtains before unzipping Jamie.

"Stone," she said. "Just how much danger are we in here?"

"Less than in New York, I expect," Stone replied. "There are eight armed men patrolling the grounds in shifts. All are ex-SAS or Royal Marines, and they don't mess about, as the Brits would put it."

"How far down the hall are Craig and Vanessa?" she asked, slipping out of her underwear.

"Far enough that we shouldn't hear Craig's pitiful cries." He got into bed with her. "I'm a little worried about them hearing you, though."

"Am I that noisy?"

"Only in extremis," he replied. "And I like it that way." He nibbled lightly on a nipple.

"You're going to have to do better than that, if you want noise," she said.

"I'll do the best I can," he said, turning to his appointed task.

Sometime later, from outside, he woke to the crack of a rifle.

6

Jamie sat up in bed. "Stone, what was that noise?"

Stone pretended that she had awakened him. "Did you say noise? What noise?"

"You didn't hear that?"

"All I heard was my name. Now I have to get back to sleep."

"I'm sure it was a gunshot," she said.

"What kind of gunshot?"

"A machine gun."

Stone tried not to laugh. "Jamie, everything is all right. Please go back to sleep."

"How can everything be all right, if there's a machine gun outside?"

"Do you hear anyone returning gunfire?"

"Not yet."

"That means everything is all right."

"Go see."

"Jamie . . ."

"Go see, or I won't be able to sleep."

Stone groaned, then got out of bed and into a dressing gown and slippers. "I'll be right back," he said.

"All right."

He left the room, went downstairs, and made sure the front door's exterior light was off before he unbolted the door and stuck his head outside. A man with some sort of weapon came out of some nearby trees and walked toward the house, his shoes crunching on the gravel beside the driveway.

Stone closed the door nearly all the way, but through a slit kept the man in sight. He didn't look familiar. Stone closed the door.

A moment later there was a soft rap on the door. "Mr. Barrington?"

Stone opened the door six inches but kept a foot jammed against it. "What's going on?" he asked. Somehow he felt he should not identify himself.

"You heard the gunshot?"

"Yes, a rifle?"

"An assault weapon. One of our men flushed a man out from some bushes near the front gate, and he went over the wall. Our man got off a round and thinks he hit the intruder, probably in the ass."

"Poetic justice," Stone said.

"Pardon?"

"They shot my guest in the ass."

"Oh, yes. Well . . ."

"Are you satisfied he won't be back?"

"I expect he's back in his van with his trousers down, being attended to. It's unlikely they'll come back tonight."

"Good, then I'll go back to bed." Stone thanked the man, went back upstairs, threw his robe on a chair, and got into bed.

"Well?" Jamie asked.

"A passing car backfired."

"Oh."

"Sleep."

"Yes, sir."

Stone slept peacefully in the knowledge that neither of the two men shot in the ass was himself.

The following morning Stone and Jamie were out horseback riding, followed by two men in a Range Rover. Stone's phone rang. "Yes?"

"Mr. Barrington, this is Derek Forrest."

"Good morning."

"I wanted you to know that we got a blood sample from the wall this morning, and we've sent it back to London for DNA testing."

"Oh, good," Stone replied.

"We'll run it against criminal databases in the U.K. and the States. I'll call you with the report later today."

"That's fine, Derek. Thank you." He hung up.

Jamie pulled up next to him. "What was that?"

"Just Derek, calling to say that all is well."

"Is that a euphemism for 'we're all in terrible danger'?"

"It is not. His words mean what they say."

"I never know when to believe you."

"Life would be simpler for both of us if you would try to believe me all the time."

"I don't believe *anybody* all the time," she said.

"You have a distrustful nature."

"It comes from being a journalist. When people speak to me, they are usually lying."

"How do you decide who to believe?"

"Instinct."

"How reliable is that?"

"Better than ninety percent, I think."

"I read somewhere there's a course you can take that teaches you how to identify liars."

"How do they do that?"

"Liars have what poker players call a *tell*."

"I know what a tell is. I play poker sometimes. What is a liar's tell?"

"It varies with the liar," Stone said. "Some blink rapidly when they're lying. Some don't blink at all. Some can't look you in the eye. Others can't or won't look away. Some distort their mouths when they're telling really big lies that they know aren't credible. These people often laugh when they're lying, too."

"Is that it?"

"Oh, no, there are dozens of other tells. This method was apparently developed by the Mossad, the Israeli intelligence service. It's taught to all their interrogators and to their security people at airports."

"Maybe I should take the course," Jamie replied thoughtfully.

"Well, you'd have to spend six weeks in Israel—and it costs twenty-five thousand dollars if you're not a Mossad agent."

"Maybe I could get the *Times* to pay for it."

Stone was making all this up, and he thought it was time he put an end to it before Jamie headed off to Israel. "They won't accept journalists in the course. That's the first question they ask you when you show up for training. If you lie to them, they take you out and shoot you."

"*Shoot* you?"

"The Mossad is tough. They don't fuck around." Stone spurred his horse into a gallop before he had to answer any more questions.

When they got back to the stables, another pair of horses had just been brought out for Craig and Vanessa.

Stone motioned Craig over.

"What is it, Stone?"

Stone leaned in and whispered, "Are you absolutely certain that you want to get on that horse?"

Craig made a disgusted noise and slapped his own forehead.

"What?" Vanessa cried when she was told they couldn't go riding.

"I'm sorry. I've been advised against it."

"Why not?"

"It's a security precaution," he replied with a straight face.

Stone and Jamie walked back to the house. "Could you tell Craig was lying?" he asked her.

"No," she replied.

"So much for instinct."

7

While Stone and his guests were having drinks in the library early that evening, Derek Forrest appeared at the door and motioned for Stone to come into the hall.

"What is it?" Stone asked.

"We got the DNA results back," Derek said, then read from a sheet of paper. "The man's name is Antonio Fenzi," he said. "Also, Anthony Farmer." He showed Stone a sheet of paper with a mug shot. "Also Albert Fender. It's the first time I've ever run a DNA check that came back with three names." He handed Stone two more sheets of paper.

"But all with the same face," Stone said. "And all three have arrests for assault, battery, and disturbing the peace, but on different dates. I wonder which name is on his passport?"

"Good question," Derek said.

"Can Strategic Services let immigration officials know that they've admitted this man to the country, and find out which name he used?"

"We can do that."

"You might let them know, too, that he's a part of an assassination team, heavily armed."

"We can do that, too."

"For what it's worth," Stone said, "I'd bet he's traveling as Anthony Farmer."

"Why do you think that?" Derek asked.

"The Italian name is probably in some files that the New York district attorney has, but it would have been changed legally at some point. I suspect that Albert Fender was an afterthought when he got busted later."

"I'll mention that."

"And you should tell them that, for an identifying mark, he might have a bullet wound in the ass."

Derek laughed. "I'll get right on it."

Stone went back to the library.

"What's happening?" Jamie asked.

"The best possible thing," Stone replied. "Nothing."

"Then what did that man want?" Jamie asked.

"Derek was just giving me a periodic report."

Craig Calvert, who seemed taller than usual because he was sitting on a loose cushion, said, "Nothing works for me."

Vanessa spoke up. "I'm not even going to ask," she said, "because I'm certain the answer would bore me to death."

"Good call," Stone replied.

The following morning, Dino called from somewhere south of Ireland. "Wheels down in an hour," he said.

"Great, I'll have customs waiting to arrest you." Stone asked Major Bugg to summon customs. Then, when some time had passed, Stone drove a golf cart down to the airstrip, arriving in time to watch the big Gulfstream touch down and taxi over to the hangar, where the customs van awaited. Stone stood off until his friends had been cleared, then collected them and their luggage.

"Is Craig Calvert still here?" Viv asked immediately.

"Oh, stop it," Dino said.

"He's working out with his trainer in the gym," Stone replied. "He works out for four hours a day, but he'll probably make an appearance at lunch."

"I hope he's still sweaty," Viv said. "Did our team arrive on schedule?"

"They did, and they've already wounded a would-be assassin." Stone handed Dino the three sheets.

"Have you had him arrested?"

"Derek has notified immigration, and we'll let them handle it. I don't want a lot of cops crawling all over the place. I'm told somebody will alert the media when they find out Craig Calvert is here, and you'll have to spend your little holiday indoors, hiding from the paparazzi."

Stone's phone rang. "Yes?"

"It's Felicity. Have Dino and Viv arrived yet?"

"How could you possibly know that?" Stone said. "Have you got a satellite trained on me?"

"Heavens, no," she replied. "Dino and Viv always arrive shortly after you do."

"I've been here for a month," Stone pointed out.

"Well, I do have my sources. In fact, I understand Craig is your houseguest. May I invite myself over for dinner? I should be down from London in time."

"Let me give you some fresh intelligence, then you decide. Vanessa Pym is Craig's houseguest."

"Oh, shit!" Felicity said.

"That was very unladylike."

"Perhaps, but it was heartfelt. If I go anywhere near that little bitch, she'll make the most awful noises."

"I'm told she does that anyway, but not at dinner."

"Well, it's beans on toast at home for me, then," Felicity said. "Goodbye." She hung up.

"Felicity says hello," Stone said to the Bacchettis.

"Is she coming to dinner?" Viv asked.

"Craig already has a date, and Felicity can't be in the same house with her."

"Anyone we might have heard of?"

"Vanessa Pym."

"Oh, my God! Two movie stars!"

Dino spoke up. "Put me next to Vanessa Pym at dinner," he said.

"Dino," Viv said, "you're too short to see down her dress."

"I'll sit on a phone book," Dino replied.

At the front door there was a line of six security officers to greet their boss from New York. Viv flattered them by asking each questions about what they were doing.

"I winged one of 'em," one officer said.

"Oh, good," Viv said, "is his hide nailed to the barn door?"

"Next time," the man replied.

. . .

Craig Calvert did appear at lunch, to the delight of Viv, but Vanessa Pym wasn't up yet, disappointing Dino. They were just finishing lunch when Major Bugg entered the kitchen and whispered to Stone, "Detective Chief Inspector Holmes to see you. I put him in the library."

Stone excused himself and walked down the hall, wondering how he should handle this. He decided to let Holmes, whom he knew, tell him.

"Good afternoon, Chief Inspector," Stone said as Holmes rose to greet him. "Can I get you something?"

"Well, I know it's five o'clock somewhere, but not in the South of England, old fellow." Holmes sat down again.

"To what do I owe the pleasure?"

"I've just had a call from immigrations warning me of an assassination team on my patch. Is someone after you again, Stone?"

"Possibly," Stone said.

"I'm sorry you didn't think to call me."

"Strategic Services in London handled it. I left it to them to call you, but apparently they didn't. I'm sorry."

"No, they didn't. I shall speak to them about that. Would you like to bring me up to date?"

"The short version or the long version?"

"The long version. I've plenty of time."

Stone started at the beginning and gave him every detail. When he was finished, it was nearly the cocktail hour, and the chief inspector succumbed to a scotch.

8

Rance Damien put down the phone and went looking for Henry Thomas, who didn't like to wait for news. Henry's grandson, Hank, was with him. It was the first time Damien had seen Hank since the fire.

"Come in, Rance," Henry said.

Hank turned in his chair to look at him. "Good God, man," he said, when he saw his cousin's face.

"It will get better," Damien replied, taking the indicated chair.

"You have news from England?" Henry asked.

"What's in England?" Hank wanted to know.

"Stone Barrington," Henry replied. "Damien sent a party to greet him."

"I just had a call," Damien said, trying hard to meet Henry's gaze.

"Let's have it."

"First of all, Tony Farmer has been shot."

"Was the body disposed of?" Henry asked.

"He's not dead. He took a bullet to his backside, but he received the proper medical attention. Problem is, the immigration people have discovered that he's in their country. We paid his way through Heathrow, but now immigration is putting all three of them on a plane to New York."

"That's better than being in a British jail," Hank said.

"The Brits put them in coach. There's going to be a lot of bitching and moaning about that, and they'll also be met by the NYPD at the gate."

"There are no charges against them here, are there?" Henry inquired.

"No. Anthony has an arrest record, but no convictions, and he has a good passport."

"Then they'll just get a ride home, won't they?"

"Problem is: I'm not going to be able to speak to them before the police pick them up at the airport. They're going to have to wing it, until a lawyer can see them. He'll be waiting for them, but I think the boys in blue are going to take the opportunity to question them. I got word that Dino Bacchetti and his wife are at Barrington's place in England, and I'm sure he's made a call or two."

"Is there a plan? Will they know what to say?" Hank asked.

"I'm afraid not. I hadn't anticipated this turn of events. However, they know enough to shut up until the lawyer finds them."

"Who do we know who can pave the way for them downtown?"

"I think we're better off relying on their natural-born aversion to talking to the police. If we start making it easier for them, suspicions will be unnecessarily aroused."

"I don't like being unprepared," Henry said.

"Neither do I," Damien replied, "but our names will never come up."

"Did they take weapons into the U.K.?" Hank asked.

"No, they were supplied over there, but immigration confiscated them when they were arrested."

"If you haven't spoken to Anthony, how did we hear about this?" Henry asked.

"The guy who supplied them with weapons and housing phoned me, but he hadn't been able to talk to them, either. He's staying away from the house and the weapons. There will be nothing to connect him to the guns."

"Okay, then," Hank said. "Once the three have been sprung, we're back to square one, are we not?"

"That's where we'll be."

"Then the good news is: We're no worse off than we were a week ago."

"No worse, no better."

"We'll have to settle for that," Hank said, "until you have a new plan ready to go."

"I'm already working on that," Damien said. "We've had word from a friend at the newspaper that the Cox woman has finished her book. So they'll likely be returning to New York soon, and they'll be more easily reached here."

"What about this copying-machine fellow, who planted the bomb?" Hank asked.

"One Robert Cantor, we think, but we can't prove it. Nobody here can make him from photographs. We visited his home and workshop and left something of a mess. He managed to clean that up, rearm his security system, and disappear again."

"Have you got word out on the street about him?"

"Yes, indeed, but he's clearly holed up somewhere. He has a big van that will be hard to conceal, though."

"No," Hank said, "he could put it in any parking garage in the city, and we wouldn't know."

"We own or control nearly a hundred parking garages in the city, and we've circulated a description and the license plate numbers," Damien said, "but no hits yet."

"Why are these people always a step ahead of us?" Henry asked. "Do we have a leak in our organization?"

"We're taking a hard look at that as we speak," Damien replied. "I had thought that one of the receptionists, the one who let him into the building, might be a leak, but we've scared her witless, and she swears she doesn't know the man."

"What do we hear from the D.A.'s office?" Henry asked.

"Our sources there tell us that Burrows is dragging his feet, so things are going very slowly. We've had time to patch up our machinery here and there, and the D.A. can't charge us for what our ancestors did."

"Well," Henry said, "we cleaned up H. Thomas & Son before Hank announced for the presidency, so they're not going to get anything out of our people."

"What have you done with the money from our contributors?" Damien asked Hank.

"We've completed all the paperwork for returning it to them, so they won't have any tax problems."

"What did that escapade cost us?" Henry asked.

"As best as I can figure it, about fifteen million dollars, but we're in negotiations with our insurance company about the replacement value of the equipment we lost, so that figure is likely to drop below ten million."

"Has the family of that boy who died in the fire been taken

care of? And the boy who's still in the hospital? I don't want any lawsuits."

"Yes, that's all included in the fifteen million."

"How will Barrington and the Cox girl travel back to New York?" Hank asked.

"He has an airplane that's hangared at his place in England, and it's being guarded."

"Where does it live when it gets back here?"

"In the Strategic Services hangar at Teterboro," Damien replied. "We don't want to tangle with those people, I think you'll agree."

"Agreed. How long is Barrington going to be bulletproof?"

"For a while," Damien replied, "but you know what they say: revenge is a dish best served cold."

9

Bob Cantor carefully applied a Van Dyke–style mustache and goatee to his face, and pasted on eyebrows heavier than his own, then he left his bedroom in Stone Barrington's house and took the elevator down to the garage and got into the car he had rented under another name. He drove up to P. J. Clarke's and parked on the side street, then went inside to the bar. The girl and three of her friends were having their usual TGIF date after work. He had trailed her there the week before.

He found a spot next to them at the bar and injected himself into their conversation, while ordering them another round on him. He introduced himself as Van.

Sherry, the receptionist stationed outside the computer room at Thomas, looked happier than she had the week before.

Two of the girls left for home and husbands, and a third began gathering herself to go also. Bob pounced. "Sherry, as long as we're here, would you join me for dinner? I have a table booked."

She hesitated until her friend nodded. "Sure, Van, I'd like that."

Bob showed her to the back room, where a table awaited.

"Would you like another drink, or just some wine with dinner?" he asked.

"I think wine with dinner is the better idea," she said. "Weren't you here last week?"

"I was. I saw you here, too. You're the reason I came back."

"Well, that's flattering," she said.

"It seemed to me that you look happier tonight than last week, or is that my imagination?"

"You're very perceptive," she replied. "I had a bad couple of days the week before. My employer seemed to think I had done something disloyal. But finally, after a lot of questions, they believed me. They transferred me to another department, though."

"You don't seem like a disloyal person to me, Sherry."

"Thank you for that."

They ordered dinner and wine, and got along swimmingly. When the check came, Bob paid it. "I've got my car. Can I give you a lift home?"

"Which way are you going?" she asked.

"Whichever way you're going."

"Thanks, Van, but I think I'll just get a cab."

"May I have your number?"

She wrote it in a notebook and tore out the page. "Sure, call me sometime."

Bob gave her a number, too, then he walked her outside and hailed a cab for her. He drove back to Stone's house, put the car away, and then went upstairs and called Sherry.

"Hello?"

"It's Van," he said. "There was something I forgot to tell you."

"What's that?"

"I bear some of the responsibility for the hard time they gave you at work. I want to make it up to you."

"I don't understand."

"Look in your handbag," he said. "There's a gift for you there, wrapped in a napkin."

"Well, that was sneaky," she said.

"Go ahead, take a look."

There was silence when she did, then a little gasp. "What is this?" she asked.

"It's ten thousand dollars in hundreds," Bob replied.

"Van, can I ask you a question and get an honest answer?"

"Certainly."

"Are you the copying-machine guy?"

"I was," Bob replied, "but I won't be paying any calls in the future."

"They think you planted a bomb in the office."

"They can think what they like," Bob said. "I'm just sorry they tried to blame you. I hope the money will make up for that."

"This is all so mysterious," she said.

"And it will have to remain so. Listen, don't put the money in your bank account. If you ever had a tax audit they would want you to pay taxes on it. Just hide it somewhere and use it whenever you need it. Don't be seen paying with hundreds, though. Pop into a bank—not your own—now and then and break them for smaller bills. Also, it's not impossible that your employer might take a look at your account, understand?"

"I don't entirely understand, but I'll do as you say, and thank you."

"You're very welcome."

"Will I see you again, Van?"

"Maybe after some time has passed we can meet again, but not for a while. The people you work for are unforgiving. Tell me: Is your new job as good as your old one?"

"No, it's not."

"Then, after a while, you might look for something better. You have my number. Call me, and perhaps I can help find you something."

"All right, I will."

"No one will answer, so just leave a message, as detailed as you like. No one but me will ever hear it, and I'll get back to you."

"Oh, Van, there's a telephone with the money."

"It's a throwaway," Bob said. "You can use that to contact me; never call on your office phone or from your apartment. Both lines are almost certainly tapped."

"I'm not surprised," Sherry said. "My employers can be creepy at times, especially Rance Damien. He was burned in the fire, and he looks creepier than ever."

"Your instincts are very good, Sherry. I've got to run. Call me, if you should need me." He hung up.

10

At dinner on Sunday night, Craig Calvert stood and raised his glass. "To Stone Barrington," he said, "and all of you." They drank. "Stone, you've been a marvelous host. Vanessa, Mick, and I thank you for all you've done. A car is coming for us tomorrow morning at five AM, since we have to be at Pinewood at seven. Our parting gift to you is not to wake you." He sat down, and they enjoyed a good dinner.

The following morning just after five, Stone woke to the sound of car doors slamming and an engine starting. A moment later, all was silence again. But now he was awake and sleep did not seem to want to return. He looked at the sleeping woman next to him, one arm thrown out in his direction, and decided it was too early to suggest sex. Instead, he got up, showered, dressed in riding clothes, then called down to the stables for a horse.

Fifteen minutes later he was galloping through a cloud of ground mist, turned a beautiful color by the rising sun. He reviewed the past few weeks in his mind and decided it was time to get back to reality.

. . .

They had breakfast in the kitchen. "Well," Stone said, "all the glamour has left the house. We may as well go home."

"I need to get back anyway," Viv said, "and so does Dino, even if he won't admit it."

"And I have corrections to make to my manuscript," Jamie said.

"Then it's unanimous. Breakfast at eight tomorrow, wheels up at nine. Given the time difference and the fuel stop and light headwinds, we should be at Teterboro by mid-afternoon, just in time to avoid rush hour going into the city."

Back at Turtle Bay, Stone had Fred take his and Jamie's bags upstairs, then he went to his office to see Joan and check his mail and messages. Bob Cantor was waiting for him. They shook hands and sat down.

"How's it going, Bob?" Stone asked.

"Not as well as I would have liked. The Thomases trashed my house and workshop, so I took you up on your invitation to stay upstairs, and I've been driving a rented car. I had begun to think things were cooling off, so I hatched a plan to find out for sure. I followed the receptionist I used to pass on my copy machine visits to P.J. Clarke's, and made her acquaintance, suitably disguised. We had dinner, and I slipped a throwaway phone in her handbag, along with some cash, by way of an apology for casting suspicion on her, and we talked later.

"I gave her my throwaway number, and yesterday she called

and wanted to meet for dinner at Clarke's. I parked my rent-a-car at the corner of Fifty-fourth and Third, half an hour early, and waited for her to show up. I watched three men take up stations within half a block of P. J.'s. Then, when she showed up, she got out of a black SUV with heavily tinted windows and went inside.

"I phoned her and asked how she had traveled uptown. She said she had taken the subway. I canceled dinner and hung up. Suddenly, I had three guys closing in on me. I started the car, drove it a couple of blocks, then got a cab, so I'm still in one piece."

"Apparently, your generosity was inadequate," Stone said.

"That, or they started putting pressure on her again. They had already done that after the fire. I guess she was more fragile than I thought, and she caved."

"Good moves covering yourself," Stone said. "I wouldn't go back for the car. Call the rental company and report it stolen. It'll find its way home. I take it you used another name."

"Sure. I'm disappointed about the girl, though. She was nice. Under other circumstances, who knows?"

"They'll do that, but don't stop trying. They're worth it."

"Can you put up with me for a few more days?"

"As long as you like."

"I'll be invisible." Bob left, and Stone went back to his mail.

Stone had a sandwich at his desk, and around five, Jamie walked in with a fat manuscript under her arm. "I finished it," she said. "The corrections were almost entirely technical."

"Lucky you."

"I'll get Joan to messenger it to Scott, if that's all right."

"Sure."

She went into Joan's office, but she was back a minute later, and they went up to his study for a drink.

"What happens now?" Stone asked.

"Scott and Jeremy will read it, then it will go through rigorous fact-checking. When that's done, it will go to my publisher, and I'll get a nice check."

"What are your plans while you're waiting?"

"Whatever you'd like them to be," she replied.

"I'm happiest when you're around."

"I'll stop by my place tomorrow and check out the mail, though all I ever get is bills and trash."

"Why don't you get someone to do that for you?" Stone asked.

"Do you think there's still a problem?"

"They're still looking for Bob Cantor. They could be looking for you, too."

"I'll get my secretary to pick it up and bring it here."

"No, have her take it to your office and go through it. She can messenger over here what you need to see. Or if you want to go to the office, Fred will drive you there and bring you back."

"I think I'll do that," she said. "I was hoping this would be over."

"So was I, but I don't think it is. Have you got a pub date for your book?"

"They're going to rush it, so four weeks after they get the final manuscript."

"Good. You can work on your autobiography, and when the book comes out, it will be over. That's my best guess, anyway. They'll have nothing to gain once the book is in print."

"Jeremy thinks the Thomases will try for an injunction to stop publication."

"They won't get it. In Britain, they probably would because they have stricter libel laws there. Anyway, their attempt to stop publication would be good publicity for the book."

"We'll play it for all it's worth."

"How are you feeling? Any jet lag?"

"Just a little tired."

"The trick, flying west, is to stay up as long as you can, then get a good night's sleep."

"Then you'll have to think of something to keep me awake," she said.

"I'll think about nothing else, until bedtime," he replied.

11

Sherry sat at her new desk, staring at the computer screen, at a letter Rance Damien had dictated. She was shaken. She had been caught twice, once by Damien and then by Van, or whatever his name was. It crossed her mind that she had enjoyed being around Van more than Damien. Someone put a hand on her shoulder, and she jumped. She looked up to find Damien standing there, staring at her with that gaze his facial scarring had given him.

"What's wrong, Sherry?"

"Nothing, Mr. Damien. I guess I was just daydreaming."

"You're still rattled by what happened on Monday night, aren't you?"

"I guess I am."

"Why don't you take some time off, recharge the batteries?"

"Well," she replied, "I've got some vacation time coming. Would you mind if I take a week, starting tomorrow?"

"Where would you like to go?" Damien asked.

"I don't know. I haven't given it any thought yet."

"Do you want to be with a lot of people or just alone?"

"Just alone, I think."

"We have a place up on the coast of Maine, near Rockland.

It's a comfortable house with some staff, with a beautiful beach and views of Penobscot Bay. Why don't you be our guest there, for as long as you like, then let me know when you're ready to come back to work?"

"That sounds lovely, Mr. Damien. It's very kind of you to offer it. Are you sure I won't be interfering with someone else's vacation?"

"You'll be the only person there, except for the housekeeper and the handyman—and the housekeeper is a good cook. You won't even have to buy groceries."

"All right, I'd love to. How should I travel? Plane or car?"

"Do you have a car?"

"No, I'd have to rent one."

"I'll have a company plane fly you to Rockland, and someone will meet you there. My secretary will have a car pick you up tomorrow and take you to Teterboro."

"What's the weather like in Maine this time of year?"

"Sunny, in the seventies right now. You'll need a sweater or jacket for the evenings, which turn cool."

"Thank you, Mr. Damien. This is very kind of you."

The following morning, at Teterboro, she was escorted to a small jet. An hour later, they were setting down at Rockland. As they taxied to the ramp, she saw a large man standing next to a green van with something painted on the side that turned out to be: GREEN HILL COTTAGE.

The man took her luggage and stowed it in the van, then helped her inside.

"My name is Hurd Parker," the man said to her. "You're Miss Spector?"

"Sherry will do."

The man nodded and drove her through Camden, then Rockland, and out the other side before turning toward the water. The cottage was larger than she had expected, and when she was inside she was surprised at how large the rooms were.

Hurd introduced her to Heather, his wife, who was the housekeeper, and she was shown to a comfortable bedroom on the second floor, with a deck and a view of the bay.

Sherry unpacked, then took a book down to a library off the living room and found a comfortable chair near the window. As the sun set, Hurd lit a fire for her, and Heather brought her dinner to the library and set it up on a small table.

Two days later Sherry was getting cabin fever. She asked Hurd if she could borrow a car to see some of the area.

"I'm afraid not," he said. "Guests aren't allowed to drive our vehicles. It's an insurance thing. I can give you a golf cart that will take you to the beach."

"Thank you, I'd like that."

Heather packed her a lunch, and she tossed that and her beach bag into the golf cart and followed Hurd's directions to the sea. Once there, she was surprised by how deserted the area was, so she spread a blanket and removed her bathing suit top to get some sun without tan lines. She stretched out and soon dozed off.

She was awakened by a noise she couldn't identify, exactly. She turned over on her stomach and had a look into the trees behind her. She saw movement and realized she was being watched, probably by Hurd. She put her top back on and tried to read for a while, then gave up and went back to the house.

In her room she began to review her situation. She was alone hundreds of miles from New York, and she hadn't even seen a telephone in the house. She got out her iPhone, but couldn't get a signal. Rummaging in her bag, she found the throwaway cell phone that Van had given her, but she couldn't get a signal on that, either. She got up and walked out onto her deck. She found that she could get a weak signal if she stood in a corner on the seaward side.

She sat in a lounge chair for a while, then she walked back to the corner, took out the throwaway, and pressed the button that called Van's number. No one answered, but she had been told to expect that. Instead, she heard only a beep.

"Van," she said hesitantly, "this is Sherry. I'm sorry about the other night. I was under a lot of pressure. I was sure they were after you, so I'm glad you didn't show. I'm at a house in Maine, near Rockland, owned by the Thomases. It's deserted, except for a handyman and a housekeeper, who seem to be watching me closely. I don't have a car, and I'm starting to worry about what could happen to me here. I'm getting a very weak signal from one spot on a deck outside my room. Will you call me on this phone tomorrow morning at ten o'clock sharp? I'll stand in this spot and wait for your call."

Bob Cantor got the message in the late afternoon and tried to call Sherry immediately, but the call wouldn't go through. He made a mental note to try her at ten the following morning, then he went down to Stone's office.

"What's up, Bob?"

"I've heard from Sherry, the girl from H. Thomas. She left a message saying they've got her stashed at a house in Maine, near Rockland, and she's nervous." He explained about the cell signal.

"Could this be another attempt to smoke you out?"

"Smoke me out in Maine?"

"Do you think she's in trouble?"

"I think *she* thinks she's in trouble, and she doesn't have a car."

"All right," Stone said. "Here's what you tell her." He gave Bob detailed instructions for the girl.

"I'll tell her tomorrow morning at ten," Bob said.

"If, after talking to her, you think she's in imminent danger, we'll fly up to Rockland immediately and find her."

"I've got a bad feeling about this," Bob said.

12

The following morning Sherry had breakfast in her room. Then, when Heather returned for the tray, she said that she wasn't feeling well and needed to sleep some more. Approaching ten o'clock, she got up and took the throwaway to the deck.

She had been waiting for a couple of minutes when the phone vibrated. "Van?" she asked.

"Yes," Bob replied. "Do you want to get out of there?"

"Yes, I do."

"But you have no transportation?"

"I have a golf cart available."

"Electric, or does it have an engine?"

"Electric."

"All right, here's what you do: you take the golf cart to somewhere out of sight of the house, where you can get a signal. Then you google a cab service and have yourself driven up the coast to Lincolnville, which is just a wide place in the road, but it has a ferry service that runs every hour or so to an island called Islesboro. When you get aboard the ferry, call a cab in the village of Dark Harbor, and have them meet the ferry. Tell the driver you want to go to the house next door to the yacht club. And when you get there, go to your left around the house, and you'll find the caretaker's cabin. His name is Seth Hotchkiss. He will let you into the house and give you a guest room. When you're settled, call me. Have you got all that?"

She repeated the instructions without error.

"All right, now I'll give you a plan B. If, for any reason, you can't get to Lincolnville go to Camden—to Wayfarer Marina, on the north shore of the harbor. Look for a large motor yacht called *Breeze*, and ask for Captain Todd. He'll know what to do. Have you got that?"

"Yes, both plans A and B."

"Call me when you're safe."

"Thank you, Van."

He hung up.

Sherry got into her bathing suit, then packed her single rolling bag. She opened the door of her room and looked up and down the hallway, then walked quickly down the hall and found a door leading to the back stairs. She knew the golf cart was kept behind the house in a shed.

She went back for her case and let herself out onto the stairway, then stopped and listened. She heard a sound like a lid being put on a pot, and she froze. Then she heard Hurd's voice.

"Where is she?"

"Still in bed, said she wanted to sleep some more."

Hurd seemed to leave the kitchen because they stopped talking. Sherry picked up her bag, slung her pocketbook over her shoulder, and walked carefully down the stairs, staying near the wall to avoid squeaking steps. At the bottom, she opened the rear door and looked around. She thought she heard the van start up at the front of the house.

She trotted to the shed, put her bag on the rear seat, then got into the golf cart. There was no key in the ignition. She took a couple of deep breaths to calm herself, then got out of the cart and began looking for the key. She heard the van drive away from the house.

She made a complete circuit of the shed's interior and found the key hanging on a nail behind the door. A moment later she switched on the cart, put it in gear, and eased out of the shed. She was at the corner of the house before she figured out that she was going toward the beach, not the road. She stopped, realizing that to get to the road she would have to drive past the kitchen windows.

She wasn't sure which way the van had gone, but she made a U-turn and drove slowly around the house, stopping at a corner to take a look out front. The van was nowhere in sight.

She got back into the cart and drove, not too fast, toward the road to the main highway. Halfway there, she came to a hard stop. Ahead of her perhaps fifty yards, the van was parked at one side of the road. She heard the sound of a chain saw, then she saw Hurd come out of the woods and load some cut wood in the back of the van, then return to the woods.

She started to move again, but then she saw something she needed beside the road. She got out, picked it up, and placed it on the seat beside her. The chain saw started again; this was her opportunity. Hurd was wearing ear protection, so he wouldn't hear her. She floored the golf cart and was disappointed when the speedometer registered only fifteen miles an hour, apparently the cart's top speed. She thought for a few seconds about stealing the van, then thought better of it. As she drew close to the other vehicle, she could still hear the chain saw. She couldn't see Hurd, but as she passed the van he stepped into the roadway, holding an armload of wood.

"Hey!" he yelled as she passed him, then he started to run after the cart. To her consternation, the cart began to slow down. She looked at the dashboard and saw the low-battery warning light flashing, then remembered that the cart had not been plugged into a charger in the shed.

She looked into the rearview mirror and saw Hurd running and gaining on her. She stopped the cart and grabbed the rock she had picked up from the road. It was the size of a softball but heavier. She got out of the cart, drew back, and threw it at his head. She hoped it would connect because she didn't have another one.

The rock struck Hurd on the left side of his forehead, and he went down like a sack of beans, then lay still, blood trickling from his forehead. She picked up the rock and threw it into the woods, then moved her bag from the cart to the van, got it started, and drove on toward the highway.

She wanted to separate herself from the van as soon as possible, so when a service station with a Subway sandwich shop attached came into sight, she pulled off the road, drove behind the building, and got her bag out. She googled *taxi services*, found one, and asked to be picked up at the Subway, destination Lincolnville.

The taxi took fifteen minutes to arrive, and in her imagination she could see Hurd awakening, getting to his feet, and going back to the house to call the police. She got into the taxi. "Lincolnville Ferry, please," she told the woman driving.

As they were driving through Rockland, a police car passed them going the other way, followed by an ambulance. Sherry made a quick decision. "Take me to the harbor in Camden," she said. "I forgot I have to pick up something there."

The driver drove into Camden, deposited her outside a row of shops, took her money, and pointed down an alley. "The harbor's right down there," she said.

Sherry trotted down the alley, pulling her case behind her, then came to a dock. She stood, staring at a sign that read: WAYFARER MARINA. It was on the other side of the harbor. It began to rain.

13

Sherry stood there. She was afraid to retrace her steps and walk to the north side of the harbor, so she looked around for a boat. As if in answer to a prayer, a small boat with an awning came out of the mist and stopped. "Taxi?" the driver asked.

She climbed aboard. "The Wayfarer Marina," she said, pointing. "Over there."

"Five bucks," the man said.

Sherry took shelter as best she could, and raked the coming shore with her eyes. There were a number of motor yachts, but none named *Breeze*."

The water taxi pulled up to the dock, and the driver set her bag ashore for her. She paid him, then looked around for a dockmaster. What she saw instead was a police car pulling into the parking area fifty yards away and a cop getting out of one side and Hurd out the other, sporting a bandage on his forehead and looking angry.

She spotted a shed at one end of the marina and ran for that. A young man had taken shelter inside and was reading a *Playboy*. "Yes, ma'am?"

"I'm looking for a yacht named *Breeze*," she said.

"Right over there," he said, pointing at a huge shed, the bow of a yacht sticking out.

"And where would I find Captain Todd?" she asked.

"Aboard *Breeze*," he replied.

Sherry looked out the window and saw Hurd making his way toward the dock, followed by the policeman. She got out her cell phone and dialed 9-1-1.

"Nine-one-one, what's your emergency?" a woman said.

"There's an abandoned green van behind a filling station and Subway south of here. I thought you should know." She watched through the rain-spattered window and saw the cop reach to his belt for a radio and say something, then he shouted something at Hurd, who turned and followed him back to the car. They turned the car around and drove away.

"Thanks for your help," Sherry said to the young man, then grabbed her bag and headed for the huge shed, which had a pair of rails out front that ran toward the docks. Near the stern, a half dozen men had taken shelter. "Captain Todd?" she asked. One of them turned around.

"That would be me," he said.

"I'm Sherry."

"I was told to watch out for you." He led her to a platform, then up the ship's stairs to the deck, then down below to a cabin.

"Right now," he said, "we have no electricity, but when the rain eases up we're going to launch her. And when the engines are started, all the systems will be working, and you can take a shower. Towels and a robe in the locker there." He pointed and left her to it.

Sherry stripped off her sodden clothes and put them in the

head, in the shower stall, then toweled her hair as dry as she could get it. Then she got under the bedcovers to get warm.

Not much later she was awakened by the yacht moving. Shortly after that they were afloat, and the engines were starting. Lights came on in her cabin, and she got into a hot shower, then used the hair dryer. The yacht was moving, but she didn't know where to. She got into some dry clothing, then called Van and left a message that she was aboard the yacht.

She went up a deck, through a large saloon, then through a dining room, forward, until she found the bridge. Captain Todd was at the helm, and two young women were with him.

"Hi, there," Todd said. "You get a nap and a shower?"

"Both," she said.

"I've let Bob know you're aboard."

"Where are we headed?"

"To Islesboro. We're going to put you ashore at Barrington's dock, where you'll be met." He switched off the windscreen wipers. "We'll have some sunshine shortly," he said.

"Was something wrong with the yacht?" she asked.

"Just the annual inspection and bottom painting. Your timing was good."

One of the girls spoke up. "We're Jean and Jennifer. We'll be taking care of you. I take it you have some wet clothes somewhere?"

"In my shower."

"We'll launder and dry them for you," Jean said, and they both went aft.

Sherry's throwaway buzzed, and she answered it. "Van?"

"Call me Bob," he said. "I take it you're safe."

"Yes. They were looking for me, but I'm safe aboard *Breeze* now."

"They'll give you some lunch, then drop you off at Stone's house in Dark Harbor. We're on the way to the airport now, and we'll be at the house almost as soon as you will. See you then." He hung up before she could ask who "we" was.

"Have you had any lunch?" Todd asked.

"No, I haven't."

He picked up a phone and gave some instructions. "Be ready shortly."

Soon, Jennifer appeared with a mug of hot clam chowder and a ham and cheese panini, and Sherry settled into a seat and watched their progress as she ate. The sun came out, and Penobscot Bay became more beautiful.

"This is a spectacular yacht," she said to Todd.

"She certainly is. Built just a few years ago. Stone and his partners bought it from the estate of the owner. They got a bargain. It would cost twice what they paid to build her now."

An hour later the yacht dropped anchor, and she was taken ashore in a tender to a dock. There a man introduced himself as Seth Hotchkiss and took her into the house. He answered his phone, said a few words, and hung up. "Stone and Bob are taking off from Rockland now. I'm going to meet them at our little airstrip."

"May I come along for the ride?" she asked.

"Sure." He led her downstairs and outside to a very old but very well-restored Ford station wagon. "She was built in 1938," he said. They drove to the airstrip where a Cessna 182 was setting down. It taxied to the car and cut its engines. Two men got out.

"Hello, Sherry," the taller of the two said. "I'm Stone Barrington and this is Bob Cantor. I believe you know him as Van."

They all shook hands and got into the car. Ten minutes later, Stone was pouring drinks in the living room of his house.

"I've heard both your names," Sherry said, "taken in vain."

They laughed.

"I'm not surprised," Stone said.

"And, Bob, you look better without the beard."

"Thank you," he said, smiling.

"Now," she said, "can you tell me what the hell is going on?"

"Well," Stone said, "the first thing I can tell you is that if you hadn't been smart enough to get out of that house when you did, you'd probably be dead by now."

"I had that feeling," Sherry replied.

14

They dined that evening on Lobster Newburg, prepared by Mary, Seth's wife, and a fine French white Burgundy. When Mary had served the food and left them, Stone began to talk.

"Now we have to decide what to do next," he said. "Sherry, would you feel more secure here or back in New York?"

"Here," she said immediately, "if I can have a gun."

"Do you have any experience handling guns?" he asked.

"Yes, my father owned guns, and when I was a teenager he often took me to the range with him."

"So you know how to load a gun, fire it, and reload?"

"Yes, and I pretty much hit what I aim at."

"I will supply you with a gun."

"Thank you."

"Bob is going to stay here, too, since he faces pretty much the same threat that you do."

Sherry turned to Bob. "Did you engineer the explosion at H. Thomas?" she asked.

Bob drew a breath, but Stone held up a hand. "We won't ask that question," he said, "because we don't want to hear the answer, whatever it is. We could be asked about it later, and we don't want to have to lie."

"I understand. Excuse me, Bob."

"Quite all right," Bob replied.

"Bob is going to be armed, too, and so is Seth. Let me tell you something about this house. It was built by a first cousin of mine, Richard Stone, who, at the time, was the London station chief of the CIA. He was promoted to be head of covert operations, and on his way back from London to Langley, he stopped here with his family for a couple of weeks. During that time Dick, his wife, and daughter were murdered."

"In this house?" Sherry asked.

"Yes. Are you superstitious?"

"No. Why were they murdered?"

"Because of a family disagreement—nothing to do with his work for the CIA, which nobody here knew about, anyway. His older brother died as a result, and the man's two sons are in prison for life without parole."

"I'm glad to hear it," she said.

"But, as a result of Dick's rank in the Agency, this house was built to their high security standards. Underneath the shingled siding and roof is half an inch of steel plating. And the windows can stop a high-velocity round. The fire and security systems are the best available. My point is: with the doors locked and the windows closed, this house is a fortress."

"Sounds like where I want to be," Sherry replied.

They finished dinner, then Stone led them across the living room and around a corner, where he moved a small picture aside to expose a keypad. He gave Sherry the combination and asked her to enter it. A door, part of a bookcase, opened, and the lights inside came on automatically. They went inside. "This room was where Dick did Agency business. His computer was, and probably still is, connected directly to the Company mainframe."

The room was about nine by twelve, and the wall at the short end was covered with mounted weapons. "Take your pick," Stone said.

Sherry looked around and picked up a smaller-than-usual Model 1911 .45 Colt.

"That's an officer's Colt," Stone said.

"I know. My father preferred a .45 to a 9mm, mostly because he considered the .45 beautiful. He disliked Glocks because they weren't. I like this one because it's smaller and lighter than the original."

Stone opened a cabinet to reveal stacks of loaded magazines. "Take as many as you want."

She took a half dozen magazines, and he put them into a small case and handed it to her.

"I brought my own pistols," Bob said, "but I'd like a rifle." He took down an AR-15 and a half dozen magazines.

"Then you're ready for war," Stone said. "Let's go have an after-dinner drink. I'm expecting company."

They went into the living room, and Stone poured them each a cognac. "Our guest is Ed Rawls, who should be here shortly— and who has an interesting background. You've never met Ed, have you, Bob?"

"No, but I've heard about him."

"Ed was a CIA lifer until, while serving as station chief in Stockholm, he was caught in a honey trap and compromised by the KGB. He never gave them anything of importance, but he got arrested and sent to federal prison. The officer who nailed him was one he had mentored, Kate Rule, now Katharine Lee, President of the United States.

"Later, Ed, even in prison, was able to dismantle a plot against the reputation of Kate's husband, Will Lee, a Georgia senator who was running for president. As a result, after he was elected, Will gave Ed a presidential pardon, which was sealed. Ed returned here, where he owned a house and has lived here and in a couple of other places, pretty much happily ever after." Stone paused. "And that, I think, is the cue for the doorbell to ring." He turned and looked at the door, waiting. The bell rang, and Sherry and Bob laughed.

"I could do that," Stone said, "because Ed always arrives precisely on time, and it's eight-thirty." He went to the door and admitted a beefy, heavily mustachioed man of indeterminate age.

Stone made the introductions and brought Ed a cognac, then he threw another log on the fire.

"Sorry I couldn't join you for dinner," Rawls said. "I had a date at the yacht club for dinner with an attractive widow. Lots of them hereabouts."

Stone gave Rawls a rundown on what Sherry and Bob were doing in Dark Harbor.

"Sounds like you two lead exciting lives," Rawls said. "Not much excitement around here, but that seems to change when Stone is on the island."

"Well," Stone said, "I'll stick around a few days and see if I can drum up some."

"Who knows you two are here?" Rawls asked.

"Nobody," Sherry said.

"Nobody," Bob echoed.

"That's the first rule of personal security," Rawls said. "Invisibility. Is either of you traceable?"

"In my experience," Bob said, "everybody is traceable these days."

"You have a point," Rawls said. "Sherry, how did you get to this house?"

"I was staying at another house down the coast, one owned by my employer, who is suspicious of me. I felt uncomfortable with the circumstances there, so Bob and Stone arranged for me to come here."

"How did you travel?"

"I left Teterboro in a private plane, was met at Rockland Airport and taken to the house. This morning, I hit the man guarding me with a rock and stole his van. I abandoned that outside Rockland and got a taxi to Camden, where I met Stone's yacht, *Breeze*, which brought me here."

"Have the police taken an interest in you?"

"They have, but I avoided them."

"I think we have to assume that you're traceable," Rawls said, "if your employer is willing to make the required effort to locate you. Is he?"

"Maybe, but I doubt it. I'm a small fry to him."

"Bob, how about you?"

"I abandoned my residence and workshop a few weeks ago.

I lived in Brooklyn for a while, then at Stone's house in Manhattan. We flew to Rockland in Stone's airplane, then flew a small Cessna to Islesboro."

"Then you are traceable," Rawls said. "There's no cutout."

"What's a cutout?" Sherry asked.

"That's a point where you disappear before you continue to your destination. You both have traceable paths. Sherry, a taxi driver and, no doubt, a person or two at the Camden marina saw you. Bob, Stone's airplane is traceable to Rockland, and you were no doubt seen leaving Rockland in the Cessna, which is known around here. A good private detective could find you both in a couple of days."

"That's depressing," Sherry said.

"Maybe not," Rawls replied. "Now all we need to know is how badly your pursuer wants you. I expect we'll find out before long."

15

They were just saying good night to Ed Rawls and one another when Stone's phone rang. "Hello?"

"It's Jamie. Where are you?"

"I'm sorry I didn't call you earlier, but I've been traveling. I'm at my house in Maine."

"You've abandoned me?"

"Only for a few days. Would you like to join me here?"

"Is it a business or pleasure trip?"

"You could turn it into a pleasure."

"Well, that's enticing. How do I get there?"

"I'll arrange a flight for you from Teterboro. It'll take an hour, a little more, if I can find a single-engine plane. It's a short runway, too short for a jet."

"What do I do?"

"Ask Fred to drive you to Jet Aviation, at Teterboro tomorrow morning at nine. You'll take off at about ten and land on Islesboro an hour or so later."

"What clothes will I need?"

"I like you in as little as possible."

"On the occasions when I'm not naked?"

"Casual stuff. A sweater for the evenings. I'll see you for lunch, then."

"I'll look forward to it," she replied, then hung up.

Stone called the Strategic Services hangar and learned that an old airplane of his that he had sold to them was available, and so was a pilot. He scheduled it, then went upstairs to bed.

Stone drove to the airport, arriving a little after eleven and waited. A few minutes later his old JetProp, a single-engine turboprop, set down and disgorged Jamie and a couple of bags. He got her into the station wagon and headed for the house.

"Have we got time for a tour of the island?" she asked.

Stone glanced at his watch. "Sure, lunch isn't until one."

"Are there other guests?"

"Bob Cantor and a woman who's on the run from the Thomases."

"Why?"

"She worked there, near where the bomb went off, and she was suspected of being involved. She was not, but they shipped her up to a Thomas house near Rockland. I think she might have disappeared if she hadn't escaped and called Bob."

"Did Bob set the bomb?"

"We don't ask that question. When you know the answer to an awkward question, sooner or later somebody you don't want to lie to will ask you about it."

"Got it," she said.

Stone drove her around the periphery of the island, showed

her the lighthouse and where a couple of movie stars lived, then took her home and installed her in the master suite. "Lunch in half an hour," he said, leaving her to unpack.

Stone settled into a chair in the living room and answered his cell phone.

"It's Joan."

"Hi, any calls of importance?"

"Maybe. I've followed instructions and said you were unavailable. You might want to call Dino back."

"Dino has my cell number. Anybody else?"

"Somebody who said he was a stockbroker—sounded like a cold call. He called twice."

"Give me the number," he said, and wrote it down. "Talk to you later."

Jamie came down, then Bob appeared with Sherry from the direction of the hidden office. He introduced Sherry to Jamie.

"That's some computer setup in there," Bob said. "There was a password next to the machine, so I wandered around in there for a while. It's like a cross between the Library of Congress and FBI headquarters. You can find out just about anything."

The landline rang, and Stone picked it up. "Yes?"

"Who's speaking, please?"

"You, first."

"This is the communications center at Langley. I'm Evan Tilley, the duty officer. We've seen some activity on your computer station. Are you Stone Barrington?"

"Yes. I'll be in the house for a few days, and I might use it again."

"I'll make a note of that for the next shift," the man said.

Stone thanked him and hung up. Then Mary called them to lunch.

Halfway through their mussels, Stone said, "Bob, Sherry, I'd appreciate it if you would stay inside the house for the next couple of days, until I get a sense of who's on the island."

"This seems like a pretty out-of-the-way place," Sherry said.

"It is, but it has a rich assortment of summer residents and visitors, and you never know who you might run into. You should especially avoid the yacht club and the village shops, and even the back porch, until I've had a report."

"A report from who?" Jamie asked.

"A friend, Ed Rawls, who lives on the island. Bob and Sherry met him last night for a drink. He's old-school CIA, and although he's been retired for some years, he still likes to think of himself as on the job. He makes the rounds, and if there's anybody on the island he doesn't know or who doesn't fit, we'll hear about it."

"That's handy," Bob said.

"It can be," Stone replied. "Sherry, what's the name of the caretaker at the Thomas house?"

"Hurd, and his wife is Heather."

"Last name?"

Sherry stared at the ceiling for a moment. "Parker," she said finally. "He introduced himself when he met me at the Rockland Airport."

"Was there anything about him to make you think he was something other than a caretaker?"

"No, not really. They both did the chores around the house, and Heather cooked."

"Well . . ."

"Wait a minute," Sherry said. "Hurd wore a wide, thick belt, the kind that you see around shooting ranges, and there was kind of an indentation on the left side, where a holster might go."

"Did you ever see a gun?"

"No."

"Was he right- or left-handed?"

She thought again. "Right-handed, I think. He wrote my name down when I got there, and he used his right."

"So, if it's a gun belt, he uses a cross-draw."

"Yes, if I'm right."

"What about Heather? Anything unusual?"

"She was a fairly husky woman. She didn't seem fat, just strong. I wouldn't want to tangle with her."

"You know," Stone said, "I think the rock was a good idea. Do you have a lot of throwing experience?"

"High-school softball," Sherry replied. "I played on a Thomas team in Central Park, too."

"You seem to have a lot of relevant skills," Stone said. "I hope you won't need them again."

16

Everybody scattered around the house after lunch. Bob and Sherry said they needed naps and disappeared upstairs. Stone suspected they were napping together.

"What should I do with myself?" Jamie asked, settling on the sofa beside him.

"Work on your autobiography," Stone suggested.

"Too much like work."

"What are you in the mood for?"

She placed a hand on the inside of his thigh.

"Listen, you nearly crippled me last time," Stone said. "Give me another day to restore my health."

The doorbell rang.

"Saved," she said. He went to the door, came back with Ed Rawls, and introduced him to Jamie.

"I saw your piece on the Thomases in the *Times*," Rawls said to her. "Good job."

"Thank you," Jamie replied. "Stone, I think I'm going to like him."

"Don't worry, the Pulitzer's yours," Rawls said. "Stone, there are a couple of people on the island I don't like the look of."

"Where did you see them?" Stone asked.

"At the village store, eating ice cream."

"That sounds pretty innocuous," Jamie said.

"They're not innocuous," Rawls replied. "The man is six-three, two-forty, mostly muscle. The woman is a little smaller, but she looks like she knows how to handle herself."

"Did the man have a bandage on his forehead?"

"Yes, he did."

"Sherry threw a rock at him yesterday, knocked him out cold."

"Good girl."

"She took a cab yesterday," Stone said, "and gave the Lincolnville Ferry as her destination. She got off in Camden instead, but the police would have talked to the driver."

"Looks like Sherry's boss thinks she's worth the trouble of killing," Rawls said.

"*Killing?*" Jamie asked, appalled.

"They didn't hunt her down to spank her," Rawls replied.

"Maybe if we leave them alone, they'll get the next ferry back," Stone said.

"Dream on," Rawls came back. "That Cessna of yours is at the airfield. They could know it from Rockland. They know you're on the island, and pretty soon they'll know where."

"What's your advice?" Stone asked.

"I'd kill 'em and put 'em at the bottom of the bay," Rawls said, "but I know you're not going to do that."

"They'd just send somebody else," Stone pointed out.

"Good point."

Jamie spoke up. "I can't believe you two are standing around talking about killing people."

Rawls sat down. "There, is that better?"

Stone sat down, too. "Are the state police on the island today?"

"Nope, not until the weekend. If you had a good enough reason, you could call them, and they'd chopper in."

"Were the two people packing?"

"The man was. I don't know about the woman. Women hide things."

"He's probably got a Maine carry license," Stone said.

"Probably. You could wait until they take a shot at you, then kill 'em," Rawls said. "Trouble is, they might kill you first."

"I wouldn't like that," Stone said.

"Neither would I," Jamie echoed. "Why don't we just get the hell out of here?"

"And go where?" Stone asked. "Back to New York? The Thomases have people thick on the ground there. If we have to fight them, I think I'd rather do it here."

"Shoot first," Rawls said. "Think later."

"Good advice," Stone replied.

"Call the state police," Jamie said.

"If I did that, they'd arrest Sherry. The Parkers have reported the van stolen, and after all, she assaulted Hurd with a rock."

"She was in fear of her life on both counts," Jamie said.

"She'd still spend a couple of days in jail before we could get her released," Stone pointed out. "She'd be vulnerable inside—there are no rocks."

"I can try to scare 'em off," Rawls said.

"If you did, they'd come back with reinforcements," Stone said.

"Why don't you just get your ass aboard *Breeze* and get your party the hell out of here?" Rawls asked. "I'll cover you while you're getting aboard."

"I like that idea," Stone said. "They may not know about *Breeze*."

Bob and Sherry came down the stairs, looking rested. "Did I hear we're decamping?" he asked.

"Sherry," Rawls said, "who at the Camden marina could connect you with *Breeze*?"

"There was a kid in the dockmaster's shed who told me where to find her, and there were three or four guys who helped launch her. They were in the big shed, getting out of the rain, when I went looking for Todd."

Stone got out his phone. "Let me make a call. I'm a pretty good customer over there." He dialed the boatyard and asked for the manager, Jim Hughes.

"Yes, sir?"

"Jim, this is Stone Barrington. How are you?"

"Not bad," Jim replied.

"Yesterday, a young lady boarded *Breeze* in the yard."

"I heard," Hughes replied.

"Who else knows?"

"Half a dozen people, I guess."

"Has anybody inquired about her?"

"No. My people are tight-lipped about who does what on our yachts. And if somebody was asking questions, I'd hear about it pronto."

"Good," Stone said. "I'd like to keep it quiet."

"I'll speak to the lads."

"Get a case of beer out of my storage shed, ice it down, and spread it around at the end of the day."

"I'll do that. They'll be appreciative."

"Thank you, Jim." Stone hung up. "Okay, that possible leak is sealed."

"Are we sailing away?" Bob asked.

"After dark. We'll have dinner here, then go before the moon rises. Ed, you want to join us? A few days at sea would do you good."

"You could be right," Rawls said.

"Throw something in a bag and join us for dinner," Stone said.

"How are you fixed for arms aboard?" Rawls asked.

"Bring your personal weapon. We've got a small armory."

"See you for dinner," Rawls said, then left.

Stone brought Bob and Sherry up to date, then called Captain Todd and gave him his orders.

17

The moon was just rising as they left Stone's dock in the yacht's big tender, purring along at five knots, so as not to disturb anyone sleeping in the moored boats. They heard a loon emit its haunting song from somewhere. Stone looked around; he had heard many loons in Maine but had rarely ever seen one.

They clambered aboard the darkened yacht, using a crew member's flashlight to show them the way. The engines were already idling. They went to their assigned cabins as the anchor came up, and by the time they had reassembled in the saloon for coffee and brandy, they were motoring slowly south. Five miles out of Dark Harbor, Captain Todd turned on the lights.

"That was well done," Rawls said. "The only way they could have seen us depart is if they had been standing on the yacht club dock, watching for us, and it was deserted. There was some drinking going on inside, but nobody outside."

"Then we can breathe easier," Stone said.

"We can't breathe easier until we're ready for an assault."

"'An assault'?" Jamie asked, alarmed.

"Relax, that's unlikely to happen, but that doesn't mean we shouldn't be ready for it." Rawls and Stone went to a locked cabinet and took down weapons, which they placed strategically around the saloon and deck, one for everybody except Jamie.

"I'd just shoot myself in the foot," she said, sitting in a corner of the saloon with Stone. "Where are we headed?"

"Nantucket," Stone replied. "We'll be there before sunrise, so we won't be making an entrance that might attract attention, and there's an airport, should we wish to decamp."

"Where would we decamp to?" she asked.

"Anywhere but New York. I've got houses in L.A. and Key West."

"How about Santa Fe?" Jamie asked. "I love Santa Fe."

"I sold my Santa Fe house a couple of years ago—or, rather, traded it with Will and Kate Lee for a house in Georgetown, which I lease for a dollar a year to the government as a residence for the secretary of state."

"Oh, that's right. You're tight with Holly Barker."

"We're very good friends, and the government didn't supply her with a suitable residence, so I helped."

"And I suppose you're supporting her campaign for president?"

"You suppose correctly."

"I think I'm a little jealous," Jamie said.

"When you run for president, I'll support you," Stone replied. "Does that help?"

"Oh, loads, thanks. Tell me: What is it like to have that much money?"

"It's the most fun you can have with your clothes on," he said. "Or off."

"But money can't buy happiness, can it?"

"Scarlett O'Hara once asked that question of Rhett Butler, who replied, 'Scarlett, generally it can. And when it can't, it can buy some of the most remarkable substitutes.'"

She laughed. "Such as?"

"Such as the yacht we're currently cruising on," he replied.

"Is being very rich much different from being a little rich?"

"Being a little rich means not having to worry about making the mortgage payment every month; being very rich means not having a mortgage."

"So, if you want something big, like a yacht or an airplane or a house, you just write a check?"

"No, Joan writes a check."

"Someone once said that behind every great fortune is a great crime."

"Every penny of my fortune was honestly earned by hard work and wise investment. *I* didn't earn it, but somebody did."

"Who?"

"Thereby hangs a tale," Stone said.

"I've got all night."

"All right, many years ago I met a girl named Arrington Johnston. We saw each other for a time, lived together for a time, and I bought her a ring. We planned a trip to the island of St. Marks, where I intended to propose. But she was a writer, and at the last moment, the *New Yorker* asked her to write a profile of a movie star who was in town for a few days. I was waiting at the airport for her, it had begun to snow, and when I got her call, I decided to go on to St. Marks and have her join me in a few days."

"And did she?"

"She did not. She fell in love with the movie star and married him."

"That was Vance Calder?"

"It was."

"Who was murdered some years later, wasn't he?"

"He was."

"And wasn't Arrington a suspect?"

"Briefly. Oh, and I forgot to mention that the night before I left for St. Marks I impregnated her. I didn't know it at the time, but I could count. It was a boy and, of course, Vance thought it was his.

"After Vance's death, Arrington moved back east, to a house she had built in Virginia, and she was looking for an apartment in New York. We reconnected, so to speak, and were eventually married.

"A few months later we—Arrington, our son, Peter, and his girlfriend—were at the house in Virginia. The kids and I went riding one morning. While we were out, a former lover of hers— the architect of the house—went into the house and, in a burst of extreme jealousy, killed her with a shotgun."

"I remember all this. I just didn't make the connections. But what did that have to do with your wealth?"

"Arrington inherited Vance's wealth at his death, and he had become very wealthy after a fifty-year career and some spectacular successes in L.A. real estate. He left her everything. And when Arrington died, she left most of it to Peter, in a trust, and the rest to me. Voilà."

"And today, the boy is the film director, Peter Barrington?"

"He is, and I'm very proud of him."

Captain Todd came into the saloon. "We're well out, so I'm increasing our speed to twenty knots," he said. "Okay with you?"

"That's fine," Stone replied.

"We'll be in Nantucket before dawn, and our usual berth will be waiting for us."

"Very good, Todd. Also, will you disable our locator beacon?"

"Already done, while we were still at Dark Harbor. Nobody can track us, except in daylight."

"Good," Stone said. Todd went back to the bridge.

"I'm getting sleepy," Jamie said, yawning and stretching for effect. "Have you managed to restore your health?"

"I'll just lie back and allow you to ravage me."

"I can handle that," she said, and they went below.

18

Stone awoke to the calls of gulls in the harbor. He got out of bed without waking Jamie, showered, shaved, and went up to the saloon. Ed Rawls was there alone, dining on a buffet breakfast. Stone joined him and snagged a passing crew member. "You may as well wake everybody and announce breakfast before it gets cold."

"We'll keep it freshly supplied," she said, "if you want to let them sleep."

"It's already nine o'clock," Stone said. "Roust them out." He helped himself to scrambled eggs, sausages, and a Wolferman's English muffin, then joined Rawls.

"What are your plans for the day?" Ed asked.

"I thought I might catch up on my reading," Stone said, "or we could take the tender out and do some touring."

"Don't do that until I've had a look around the village," Rawls said.

"Okay, we'll save it for after lunch. Is that enough time for you?"

"Should be."

"Maybe I'll come with you," Stone said. "If you can wait until I've finished breakfast."

"I don't want to be seen with you," Rawls said.

"What? Am I such bad company?"

"If they're here, they're looking for you—and they probably have a photograph. They don't know me."

"As always, Ed, you have a point."

Rawls stood up and put on a sweatshirt, his sunglasses, and a floppy hat. "There," he said, "I'm disguised."

"See you for lunch at one," Stone said, and Rawls trotted down the gangplank and walked up the pontoon toward the village.

Sleepy people began appearing in the saloon—Sherry and Bob, a few minutes later, Jamie. By the time they had each finished their first cup of coffee, they were fully awake and eating with both hands.

When they had finished, Jamie said, "I think I'll walk into town and do some window-shopping. Will you join me, Stone?"

"I'd better stay here with Bob and Sherry," Stone replied. "Ed has pointed out to me that if anybody's looking for us, they might have a photo of me."

"But not me?"

"Not yet." He gave her a credit card. "Get yourself some things. If anybody gives you any grief about the card, have Amex call me."

"How nice of you," Jamie said, "but I have my own credit cards." She handed his back.

"Please yourself," Stone said. "Call, if you have any problems at all. Ed is around, and I can be there in five minutes."

Jamie kissed him and went ashore.

. . .

Ed Rawls had attended The Farm, as the Agency's training school was known, more than forty years ago, but he still retained the tradecraft he had learned there. On every block of Main Street, he looked at every face and figure. Before he went into a shop, he stood at the window and checked out the customers—and the reflection in the window of those behind him. He was doing just that at an appealing art gallery when, reflected in the store window, he saw a large SUV stop on the street behind him and two familiar figures get out. He continued to watch them as they began moving downhill, toward the harbor.

Stone was reading when his phone rang. "Hello?"

"It's Ed. The people I saw in Dark Harbor yesterday are in town, and the bad news is, they were in a car with two other people, so there are at least four to worry about. I'd get your guests below before they turn up there."

"I'll do that. Ed, Jamie is in the village. I'll call her and tell her not to come back to the yacht until we're clear."

"Good, I'll mosey on down there and keep an eye out."

He hung up.

Stone rang up Jamie.

"Yes?"

"Where are you?"

"In the changing room of the cutest little shop," she said.

"That's a good place to be. Stay in the shop until I call you back." He hung up before she could ask questions, then herded Bob and Sherry below.

Captain Todd came into the saloon. "Where's everybody?" he asked.

"Jamie and Ed are in town. The others are below, where I'm going, too."

"Anything wrong?"

"There are some wrong people in town, and they may turn up here."

"What do they look like?"

"A man and a woman, both hefty in build. The man may have a bandage on his forehead. If they try to come aboard, stop them. If they ask questions, lie to them."

"Gotcha," Todd replied. Stone took his book and went below. He stood at one of the ports in his cabin and peered past the curtains at the dock. Sure enough, here came Hurd and Heather.

Captain Todd winched up the gangplank and then stood outside the deckhouse, sipping his second cup of coffee of the day and watching the dock. He spotted the two people as they came down the dock. They stopped, looking admiringly at the yacht.

"Good morning," the man said.

"Good morning," Todd replied.

"She's a beauty, isn't she?"

"Yes, she is."

"Is the owner aboard?"

"No, he and his party are not due until tomorrow afternoon."

"If it's not too much of an imposition, could we have your permission to come aboard and have a look around? I'm a fan of boats of this period."

"I'm sorry, but the crew is in the middle of preparing the yacht for guests, and the owners have a policy of not allowing visitors aboard, unless they are present to receive them."

"Well, thanks anyway," the man said, then he made a show of walking the length of the yacht, taking in everything.

Stone saw him from below and stepped back from the curtains. After a couple of minutes of looking, Hurd and Heather turned and walked slowly up the dock toward the village, stopping to look at other yachts along the way. Finally, they were out of sight.

Stone called Jamie and Rawls and told them to return slowly to the yacht, then he went to get a report from Todd.

"I told them the owners weren't due until tomorrow afternoon," Todd said.

"Perfect," Stone said. He got his cell phone out and called Faith, his chief pilot, who was back in New York.

"Having fun?" she asked.

"Not enough fun," Stone replied. "I'd like you to fly the airplane to Nantucket, land after dark, refuel, find a room for the night, and be ready for wheels up at six AM tomorrow."

"Certainly. Destination?"

"Key West. I'll put you and your copilot up while we're there."

"Wonderful. I can use some sun."

"And I want our tail number off the FlightAware program. I don't want anyone tracking us."

Stone looked around. Jamie and Rawls were approaching the yacht from different directions. He went to lower the gangplank.

19

They gathered for lunch at one. Captain Todd came and stood by the table. "We'll be moving early tomorrow," Stone told the group, "to Key West for a few days." There was a murmur of approval.

"Why are we moving?" Sherry asked.

"Because Hurd and Heather and at least two others are in town. I'd appreciate it if you'd all stay aboard with the curtains and blinds drawn for the rest of the day. Todd, can you leave the marina tonight, anchor offshore near the airport, and take us ashore in the tender?"

Todd shook his head. "We're going to have twenty-five-, thirty-knot winds from the south by morning. We'd best take you in a van. I'll rent one."

"All right. I'd like to leave the yacht at five AM; wheels up will be at six. You can all sleep some more on the flight."

That night, as Stone and Jamie were preparing for bed, Stone's phone rang. "Hello?"

"Stone, it's Faith. We landed in Nantucket fifteen minutes ago, and there were some people hanging around the terminal, as if they were expecting us."

"Describe them."

"Three men, all large and tough-looking, and one large woman."

"Did one of the men have a bandage on his forehead?"

"Yes. They left the terminal as we were coming in, but there didn't appear to be any reason for them to be there, except to see us and our airplane."

"Thank you, Faith. We'll see you tomorrow morning about five-thirty."

"Okay." She hung up.

Stone stretched out on the bed. Jamie was already asleep. He thought about it for a while, and it occurred to him that they were not being followed; they were being preceded. He was too sleepy at the moment to try to figure out how that worked.

The following morning they met at five, and Stone addressed the group. "Last night I got a call from my chief pilot telling me that when they landed, they were met by three men and a woman. One of the men wore a bandage on his forehead, and they left as soon as my pilots entered the terminal."

Rawls practically choked on his coffee. "How the hell would they know your airplane was coming? For that matter, how would they even know we're on the island?"

"Because somebody in our group is telling them," Stone said.

Everyone looked at one another.

"I've known everybody here for some time," Stone said. "Except for one person." He turned to face Sherry. "You're new to this circle," he said to her.

Sherry looked panicked. "I haven't spoken to *anyone* about my whereabouts."

"What about your cell phone?" Stone asked. "Have you been using that?"

"Only the throwaway that Bob gave me," she said.

"Just a minute, Stone," Bob said. He got up and walked over to where Sherry sat. "Gentlemen, please avert your eyes." They did so. "Sherry, please stand up and put your hands on top of your head."

"It's not me," Sherry said vehemently, but she did as Bob asked.

Bob began with her feet. He took off her shoes, inspected them carefully, then set them down. He reached around her, unfastened her jeans, and inspected them, inside and out. Then he pulled her panties down to her knees and inspected them. That done, he pulled her clothing up and refastened her jeans, then he went over her upper body from navel to armpits, feeling her bra and inside it. Finally, he took off the light leather jacket she was wearing and inspected her shirt, then the jacket. "Sherry," Bob said, "you're the spy."

"I am not!" she shouted.

"Gentlemen, you may look again." Bob held up her jacket, turned up the collar, and removed a small, flat disk, about the size of a dime. "You just didn't know you were the spy," he said. He sat back down, took a tool from his pocket, and opened the disk. "This is not mass-produced stuff. It's handmade to a clever design. Do you want me to destroy it, Stone?"

"Not yet," Stone replied.

"But Sherry hasn't been to the airport," Rawls said. "How'd they know to go there?"

"Probably just making the rounds of likely places," Bob said. "They got lucky at the airport. But, Sherry, when did they attach it?"

"I don't know," she said. "Wait a minute. Shortly after I arrived at the house I found a button loose, and Heather offered to sew it on for me."

"There you go," Bob said.

"Then why didn't they find you at the boatyard when you were looking for *Breeze*?" Stone asked.

"Because I saw Hurd drive up with a policeman. I called nine-one-one and told them where to find the van I'd stolen. Shortly after, the cop got a radio call, listened for a moment, then he and Hurd got back into his car."

"That was a smart move," Stone said.

"Smarter than I knew," she said. "By the time they checked out the van and returned, *Breeze* had sailed."

"What sort of range would that thing have?" Stone asked Bob.

"Hard to say. Maybe a mile or two. But it could be better than I know. I'd need to disassemble it, put it back together, and test it, and I don't have what I need for that here."

"Then take it outside and leave it on the deck when we leave. They'll think we're still here. Once we're at the airport and take off, they won't be able to track us on FlightAware. And if I know Faith, she'll have filed for someplace like Teterboro, and after we're out of sight she'll ask the ATC for a destination change and head for Key West."

"Do these people know about your Key West house?" Bob asked.

"I don't see how they could. It's not like it's been featured in *Architectural Digest*."

"Then after we take off we'll have shaken them," Bob said.

"I hope you're right," Stone said. "I'm getting tired of them. Ed, maybe I should have taken your original advice on how to handle them."

"Yeah," Rawls replied. "And now there are more of them, we don't know how many."

"At least four," Stone said. "If I start seeing them in Key West, I'm going to take more than evasive action."

"I'll be glad to help with that," Rawls said.

Captain Todd came into the saloon. "Your van is here."

They got their luggage together, put it on a cart, and went to the van. Rawls looked behind them all the way to the airport.

Once there, Stone got out and looked around. "They must think we're still aboard the yacht," he said.

"More likely, they're just not up yet," Rawls replied, looking at his watch.

They took off at six o'clock sharp.

20

S tone flew left seat. He took off and flew the clearance he had been given for Teterboro, while Faith worked the radios. "Boston Center," she said, "this is N123TF, climbing through 210 for flight level 450. Request a destination change." She waited for the response, then: "Request jet routes along the coast to final destination Echo Yankee Whiskey. She stood by while the controller worked it out, then gave her the clearance. "Okay," she said to Stone. She entered the new route into the flight computer and pressed DIRECT to the first waypoint, then pressed the autopilot button. The autopilot was flying the airplane now.

Stone gave up the left seat, Faith moved over to replace him, and her copilot took the right seat.

Stone went back to speak with his group, but they were all fully reclined under blankets and dead to the world. He found a blanket and a pillow and, satisfied that his pursuers had no idea where they were going, fell asleep himself.

He was awakened by a reduction in power and the beginning of a descent. His watch said a little after nine; he turned on the small screen next to his seat and selected the moving map: eighteen minutes to destination. "Okay, everybody, we're landing in fifteen minutes."

The dead bodies began to move and sit up, blinking. Window shades went up and sunlight streamed in. "My housekeeper and property manager will meet us with an SUV and a convertible. Luggage goes into the SUV until it's full, then into the convertible's trunk. It's a ten-minute drive to the house."

The airplane set down gently and taxied to the ramp outside Stone's hangar, where the two vehicles waited. He told Faith to hangar the airplane, then rent a car and drive to the house he leased for visiting staff. She had been there before.

Once at the house, they garaged the vehicles, unloaded the luggage, and then Stone gave them a tour. "The house is pretty much built out to the property lines and the street, except for the driveway, so you can swim and sunbathe without being seen by unwanted eyes. There are two courtyards: one large, with a pool, spa, and outdoor seating and dining. And there's a smaller one with just seating. Lunch will be served at one, indoors, where it's cool, and we'll meet out here at six for drinks— and dinner—when it's cooler. Whether we dine indoors or out is up to the weather." He assigned them to rooms, with Rawls on the ground floor in the middle of the house, then he showed Jamie to the master suite, which occupied a small house of its own.

"I'm going to go outside and read for a while," Jamie said.

"It's going to get hot, so if you start to feel uncomfortable use my study." He hung up his clothes, then went to his study and called Joan.

"I've left you a couple of messages," she said.

"I'm sorry. I haven't had time to look at them."

"Dino called again. He's worried that he hasn't heard from you. And somebody who smelled like a process server came to the door. I told him you were out of the state."

"Any idea what that was about?"

"Yeah, somebody is suing you—or Jamie. He asked for her, too."

"That sounds like the Thomases," Stone said.

"I told him there was no use coming back for a couple of weeks."

"Good."

"Do I get to know where you are?"

"We're at the Key West house."

"You and Jamie?"

"And three other people. Faith is staying in the staff house."

"I envy you all."

"Don't, it's hot in Key West."

"Okay, I'm here." They both hung up.

Jamie was standing in the doorway, holding the *New York Times* and a book. "Knock, knock," she said. "It's hot out there."

"Take a seat."

"I just talked to my office," she said. "My assistant says the Thomases are suing both the paper and me, personally."

"For what?"

"Telling the truth, I guess, but they're calling it defamation."

"They tried to serve us both at my house. You'll need an attorney. I'll take care of that."

"You won't represent me yourself?"

"No, we're both defendants, and you know what they say about a lawyer who represents himself."

"He's an idiot?"

"Something like that. I've got the perfect guy, at Woodman & Weld, to defend both of us. His name is Herbert Fisher."

"Is he the scary one I've heard about?"

"Yes, but only in court. You'll like him."

"When am I going to meet him?"

"When we get back, but I don't know when that will be, yet. I'll brief Herbie and tell him to accept service. He'll want to speak to you, too."

"Can I afford him?"

"I'll make Jeremy Green pay him for you."

"It's not the first time I've been sued," she said. "I've already got all my notes together at the office; he can read those."

"Good. I can pretty much guarantee you that Herbie is going to publicize this suit to the max, and that should include a front-page piece in the *Times* about it."

"I'll talk to Scott and Jeremy and ask them, but my guess is, they're already working on it."

"Pick up any phone," he said.

She chose the one on the coffee table, while Stone switched on his computer and read his e-mail.

Ed Rawls came to the door and picked up a military-looking rifle that was leaning against the wall. "What's this for?"

"It's an air gun, for shooting iguanas," Stone said. "They infest the island. Raul, the property manager, has already killed eighty-odd."

"I can use some target practice," Rawls said.

"Try not to bombard the neighbors' roofs or shoot out their windows," Stone said. "Other than that, you're in charge of the iguana squad. Sack 'em up two at a time, the bigger the better, and put them in the garbage cans on the street."

Rawls picked up a box of pellets and wandered toward the main courtyard.

"Are iguanas not nice?" Jamie asked.

"Don't ask," Stone replied. "The good thing is, they're ugly, not cute—and they shit all over everything, so they don't get any sympathy."

"Not even from the animal activists?"

"They've all got pellet guns," Stone said. "You know the old saying in the army that there are no atheists in foxholes? Well, there are no animal activists with iguana shit on their shoes."

21

S tone called Dino.

"Bacchetti."

"It's Stone."

"Where the fuck have you been?"

"I've been in Maine and Nantucket, and now I'm in Key West."

"And why aren't you answering your phone?"

"I'm only answering a throwaway." He gave Dino the number.

"Is somebody after you?"

"Everybody, everywhere," Stone replied. "If you'll shut up for a couple of minutes, I'll tell you the whole story."

"Shoot."

Stone told him everything.

"So you've got a house full of people?"

"I do."

"What is Ed Rawls doing there?"

"Shooting iguanas. It keeps him from shooting people."

"Well, that's a good trade-off. When are you coming back to New York?"

"I'm not sure."

"Is there any reason why you shouldn't?"

"The idea is, I'm harder to find here."

"They'll find you wherever you are. You'd be safer in New York."

Stone thought about that. "You may have a point."

"Come on back. I'll put a couple of men on your house."

"That's a generous offer. Let me talk with Jamie about it."

"Give me as much notice as you can, and I'll pull a couple of people off whatever they're doing and send them to your house."

"I'll get back to you on that."

"Bye." Dino hung up.

Jamie was on the other line; a moment later she hung up. "They want me to come back to New York," she said.

"Who?"

"Everybody. The *New Yorker* wants to take photographs, and my editor wants to talk about trimming the book by a hundred pages. The *Times* wants me to talk to their lawyers, and I guess we both need to talk to Herbert Fisher. And I have a shopping itch that I can't scratch in Key West."

"Is tomorrow soon enough?"

"You betcha."

Stone called Faith and asked for wheels up at nine, then he called Fred about meeting them at Teterboro. "Done," he said. "Dino is putting a couple of cops on the house, so we'll feel more secure."

"I can't quarrel with that," Jamie said.

"Sara's making dinner for us, and she advises indoors. We're due for some rain tonight."

"By the way," she said, "this is a wonderful house. I love the interior gardens and the koi pond and all that."

"It's nicer in winter, when the temperature is more suited to human beings."

"And it's less suited to them in New York."

"Exactly. There's a lot to be said for a warm place in winter."

"I've got a title for the book," Jamie said. *"Excelsior: The Tommassini Files.* That's if my publisher can photograph your safe."

"Sure, and it's a great title."

"Maybe Dino shouldn't put those cops on your house. It's better publicity if somebody takes a couple of shots at us."

"The only trouble with your idea is that one or more of those shots might connect with your ass or, worse, mine."

"There is that."

"I don't think it's necessary to spill blood to publicize your book."

"But . . ."

"Put it out of your mind."

"Oh, all right. We'll play it safe."

The rain arrived in the late afternoon, so they met in the indoor living room for drinks.

"Jamie and I are flying back to New York tomorrow. You're all welcome to come or stay here and fly back commercial when you can't take the heat anymore."

Rawls spoke up. "I bagged fourteen iguanas this afternoon, and that's enough for me. I'll go to New York with you and spend a few days catching up with friends."

"You're welcome to stay with me," Stone said.

"Is there room for Sherry and me, too?" Bob asked.

"Of course. Sherry, my Turtle Bay house is built a lot like the Maine house: it's a fortress, with Joan and her .45 guarding the moat."

"Sounds great," Sherry said. "Do you think I can sneak over to my apartment and get some clothes?"

"Bob's good at sneaking," Stone said. "He'll take you."

"I want to check on my place, too," Bob said.

"Okay. We're leaving for the airport at eight AM," Stone said.

Sara called them for dinner, and they settled into the dining room.

At midday the following day, they touched down at Teterboro. Stone kept everybody aboard until the airplane had been towed into the Strategic Services hangar, then with Fred in the Bentley and another hired car, they all drove into the city and into Stone's garage before they got out of the cars. Joan met them and handed out room assignments.

She took Stone aside. "The process server showed up again today," she said.

"Ask Herbie to come over. We can brief him, and he can accept service."

"When?"

"After lunch, if he's free."

Herbie arrived around three and shook hands with Jamie.

"I've already accepted service, and I've spoken with the *Times* attorneys and with the opposition, as well. I think I put the fear of God into those guys about their client having you tracked all over the eastern seaboard. I think they also understand that they don't have a case, but they're not turning down the Thomas money, so they're stringing them along."

"Well deserved," Stone said. "I hope their lawyers bleed them dry."

Herbie took out a legal pad and ran over a dozen points with Jamie. "I don't have any points for you, Stone."

"That's okay, I'm just an innocent bystander."

"They'll call you the instigator of the whole thing, if we ever get as far as a courtroom."

Jamie spoke up. "I'll bet the *Times* will make more from the increased circulation and advertising revenue than the lawyers cost them."

"That would be poetic justice," Herbie said. He snapped his briefcase shut and stood up. "Now, let's see if I can get out of here without somebody shooting me."

22

Bob drove his rental car around Sherry's block a couple of times and saw nothing amiss. He parked the car, and they went up to her apartment. Bob cleared every room before he let her inside, then he whispered in her ear, "Don't say anything while we're here. The place is probably bugged, and I don't have time to sweep it."

She nodded, then went into her bedroom, got a large suitcase from her closet, and began filling it with her things. While she was doing that, Bob had a look around the place but couldn't find any cameras. A half hour later they let themselves out and went back to Bob's car.

They drove downtown to Bob's place, and he performed the same security check he had at Sherry's. As they pulled into the garage, he said to her, "Same deal here as at your house. Say nothing."

She nodded and followed him past the double locks into his workshop. She smiled and gave him a thumbs-up. *Nice*, she mouthed.

Bob filled a toolbox with electronics gear and a suitcase with extra clothes, then they locked up and went back to the car. Before opening the garage door, Bob had a look at the street through a peephole. A gray van was parked across the street that hadn't been there when they arrived. He went back to the car. "We've got company outside," he said. "A van. I'm going to have to check it out, so you stay here."

"My gun is in my bag," she said.

"For God's sake, don't shoot anybody. There'll be hell to pay, no matter how right we are."

"I'll try not to," she said.

"Don't even consider firing unless someone who's not me opens the car door." He let himself back into his workshop and opened a vault the size of a bathroom. There were all sorts of weapons—legal and illegal—on the walls, and he picked up a rifle with a nightscope that fired darts. He loaded the magazine, then let himself out a basement door at the rear of the house, locking it behind him.

He moved around the house, staying between the shrubbery and the outer wall, until he had a clear view of the van. He switched on the nightscope and peered through it at the vehicle. As he did a bright light flared in the front seat, and he squinted as the man behind the wheel lit a cigarette. Two men sat there; the one in the passenger seat had nodded off.

Bob lowered his aim to target a front tire and pumped a dart into the chamber. He squeezed off a round and saw the dart strike the tire, then he quickly aimed at a rear tire and fired at it. Neither shot had made much noise, but he thought the men inside might've heard the darts strike the rubber.

He watched them through the scope; the driver was starting to nod off, too. Nothing had startled them. He retraced his steps and let himself into the house, double-locking the door behind him. He returned the rifle to the vault, spun the wheel to lock it, and went back to the garage.

"Now," he said, "I want you to lie down and put your head in my lap."

"What's the matter?" she asked. "Can't you wait until we get home?"

"Just put your head there and don't move until I tell you to."

"Oh, all right." She made herself comfortable.

Bob started the car, then clicked the remote control. The garage door slid silently up; he put the car in reverse, and it rolled backward and onto the street without revving the engine. He closed the garage door and drove down the street, past the van, with his lights off. As he passed the vehicle, the driver looked up and saw his car, then started the van.

Bob drove slowly down the street and didn't turn on his lights until he reached the corner and turned uptown. He looked back and saw the van stopped in the street, as the two men checked out the tires. "They won't be giving chase," he said.

"Listen," Sherry said, "as long as I'm in your lap . . ."

Bob had expected that the two men would have made a call for help, but he appeared to be clean when they arrived at Turtle Bay. "They weren't ready for that," he said.

Sherry sat up and looked around. "Are we home?"

"We are."

"Then let's go to bed."

"First, the luggage," he replied.

. . .

They passed Stone's study and found their three companions having a nightcap.

"Have you been out?" Stone asked.

"We picked up some things at Sherry's apartment and my house."

"Was the trip uneventful?"

"Not entirely," Bob replied, then told him about his encounter with the van.

"We had something like that rifle at the Agency," Rawls said. "This guy named Teddy Fay worked in operations, and he invented things like that."

"I didn't invent this one," Bob said, "but I modified it a little, and I make my own darts—some that will penetrate a tire and some that are small and light enough to penetrate a neck to deliver a dose of a drug. As it was, we left them in the street with two flat tires, and we got back here before they could raise the alarm."

"No one saw you enter the garage?" Stone asked.

"No one."

"Would they have seen the license plate?"

"I disabled the plate light as soon as I rented the car. We're clean."

"That's good," Stone said, "but it bothers me that they're still looking for us."

"Not us, me," Bob replied. "They blame me for the bomb and for, ah, changing Rance Damien's appearance."

"He's suing the rest of us," Stone said, "and until you get a subpoena, assume that they still have other plans for you."

"At some point," Bob said, "I'm going to have to . . ." He stopped, deciding that it was better not to go on.

Stone nodded but said nothing.

"Well," Rawls said, "I don't think anybody is looking for me. Is there anything I can do for anybody in the outside world?"

"I think you're okay on the street, Ed," Stone said, "but don't assume they don't know you. They've had a look at you a couple of times."

"I guess you're right about that," Rawls replied. "I'll just assume I'm being tailed and take pleasure in losing them."

23

Rance Damien checked out of the clinic late in the afternoon, went home, and got drunk on pain pills and scotch. The following morning he went into the office for a scheduled meeting with Henry and Hank Thomas. He found Hank alone in Henry's office.

"You're looking better, Rance," Hank said. "The old man is not feeling well today. He couldn't make our meeting."

Damien took this as a possible transition. From here on, he'd have to suck up a bit more to Hank, who, lately, had seemed a little inflated from his flirtation with the presidency. Damien had the feeling that Hank would be trying again in four or eight years, and that he might do some house cleaning with that in mind. He was going to have to become more essential than ever around here, he thought.

"Rance," Hank said, "I've been reassessing the organization, and I've come to the same conclusion that Dad and Granddad did: you're the most capable man on the premises."

Damien had not been expecting flattery, and he tried to put it out of his mind. "Thank you, Hank."

"How many more operations?"

"Two or three. My doctor is very pleased with my progress."

"Well, you won't be appearing at any board meetings until your, ah, condition has cleared up. It's been my observation that rich, powerful men are suspicious of people with physical disabilities or even scars. Just shows you how stupid they can be. Still, the next time they see you, I want it to be when you're fully recovered."

"I understand, Hank," Damien said, though it infuriated him. After all, he had received his injuries in the service of those men.

"What are our chances of rebuilding the software we lost in the fire?"

"Nil," Damien said, "and it would be pointless to try. We were able to succeed before only because we had bribed a man in their management for the information we needed. Now, as a result of our first attempt, they are rewriting all their code."

"Can't we bribe someone else there?"

"The best thing is to wait until they've perfected the new code, then buy a copy of it from someone there."

"How long?"

"Perhaps two years." Damien didn't know that, but he didn't want Hank on his back all the time about trying their scam again.

"What about this fellow who posed as the copying-machine technician? Have you identified him?"

"His name is Bob Cantor, from what we've picked up while surveilling the girl, Sherry. But he called himself something else when he was in our offices."

"Haven't you found his residence?"

"Yes, but it's owned by a Delaware corporation, and a lawyer's name is the only one on the deed. It's possible even he might not know Bob Cantor. There's no mortgage on the house. His neighbors don't know him. He seems to live in a kind of bubble he's made for himself."

"I'd like him in the East River," Hank said.

"Believe me, so would I. We actually caught him visiting the house last night, but he disabled our vehicle, and our people couldn't give chase."

"What about the girl, Sherry?"

"She's dropped off the planet. None of the girls here have heard from her. We had our chance, but Hurd and Heather blew it."

"Didn't they have a bug on her person?"

"It came off in Nantucket, our last sighting of her. She left in a private jet."

"This girl can't possibly have that kind of support at her beck and call."

"That's coming from Barrington."

"Well, we can't touch him at the moment, since we're suing him, along with the *Times* and some of their people. That's too good a motive."

"I understand that. Our best bet is to concentrate on Van and Sherry, but we've been shorthanded. I'm considering pulling in Hurd and Heather from Maine, but their faces are known to Sherry."

"I understand that Heather is adept at extracting information from women," Hank said.

"She has gifts in that area."

"Then let's find Sherry and give Heather an opportunity to display her skills. Nobody will notice if Sherry disappears."

"I agree, but she has already disappeared," Damien pointed out.

"Surely she must have some family."

"All dead. She didn't even list a next of kin on her employment application. She's apparently alone in the world."

"From everyone except this Van character," Hank said. "Find him, you find her. They're a loose end, and I don't like loose ends."

Neither did Damien. He excused himself at the first opportunity and went back to his own office.

24

Stone was beginning his workday when his phone rang. Joan was running some errand or other, so he picked it up.

"Stone Barrington."

"Stoney, how are you?" a booming, vaguely familiar voice said.

"Who is this?" Stone asked.

"An old friend."

"If you were an old friend, you would know that no one has ever called me 'Stoney' and gotten a civil response." He hung up.

A moment later, the phone rang again.

"Yes?"

"Mr. Barrington, I apologize for the unfamiliar familiarity," the same voice said. "This is Senator Joseph Box, of Florida."

"I might have known," Stone replied, straining to be civil. "What can I do for you, Senator?"

"Well, I'm calling to share some secret news with you."

"'Secret news' is an oxymoron," Stone replied. "Kindly state your business."

"My business is running for President of the United States," Box replied. "And you, my friend, are the first to know."

Stone refrained from pointing out that they were not friends.

Box anticipated him. "He who is not my enemy is my friend," he said, "or, at least, potential friend."

"What's on your mind, Joe?" He immediately regretted the familiarity.

"Stone, I'm calling to ask for your support," Box replied.

"Support for what?"

"I'm running in the New Hampshire Republican primary. In fact, I'm in New Hampshire as we speak."

"Senator, I'm not a Republican, and I don't vote in New Hampshire, so you should skip to the next name on your list."

"Fortunately," Box said, "the denizens of New Hampshire still accept American dollars for TV time and newspaper space, and you can vote with your dollars in any amount up to twelve hundred dollars."

"Senator," Stone said wearily, "may I give you some advice?"

"Why, that's the thing I would value most from you, Stone, right after your dollars."

"If you're going to run in New Hampshire, or anywhere else for that matter, you should either take the time to read the rules, or hire a campaign manager who either already knows them or can read them to you. The maximum personal campaign contribution, under law, is sixteen hundred dollars."

"Well, thank you for that correction, Stone. That's going to increase my campaign income by twenty-five percent."

"That would be by one-third, Senator. Let's hope your campaign manager is proficient in arithmetic, as well as campaign law."

"Thank you for your opinion," Box said.

"It is not my opinion but that of Miss Helen Troutman, who taught me in the first grade at PS Six, and no one has yet questioned her contention that four hundred dollars is one-third of twelve hundred dollars."

"Don't confuse me with logic," Box said. "Now, can I put you down for sixteen hundred dollars?"

"You may not."

"We take checks."

"You may not have from me a check, cash, or even postage stamps."

"That's all right. I've already leased a postage meter for our campaign quarters."

"I won't give it to you in quarters, either. May I ask, Joe, what on earth made you think that I would contribute to the cause of electing you president?"

"Why not?" Box asked, sounding wounded.

"Let me count the ways," Stone said. "One, I am not a Republican, as I have already mentioned. Two, I am a good friend of your likely opponent, Holly Barker, who, I believe, introduced us. And three, I regard you as unqualified, by experience, intellect, and moral character, to hold *any* public office."

"Now wait a minute, Stone. Let's not bring morals into this. The media will root out that stuff soon enough."

"I expect so," Stone replied, "and I can't wait. Are we done here, Joe?"

"How about a thousand dollars?"

"Same answer." Jamie walked into his office. "Now, if you'll excuse me, I have to report this conversation to the *New York Times*."

"Tell 'em to spell my name right. That's B-O-X."

Stone hung up.

"What was that about?" Jamie asked.

"The junior senator from Florida would like you to know that his name is spelled B-O-X."

"I'll make a note of that," she replied. "Why were you talking to that buffoon?"

"Because Joan is out and therefore was unable to lie to him about my availability."

"Why would he call you?"

"You're not going to believe this," Stone said. "Joe Box is running for the Republican nomination for president."

Jamie burst out laughing.

"And he wanted a campaign contribution, though he was uncertain about what the maximum legal contribution is."

"That's not all he's uncertain about," Jamie said, "though he speaks with certainty about everything."

"Well put!"

"Well, I'm going to phone this in," Jamie said, reaching for the phone on Stone's desk and dialing a number. "Andy, this is Jamie Cox. I have a story for you. The junior senator from Florida, the dishonorable Joseph Box, is running for president." She held the phone away from her ear while he roared with laughter. "I kid you not," she said, finally. She covered the phone. "Where is Box now?"

"In New Hampshire," Stone said, "probably in the presidential suite at Motel Six."

"He's already in New Hampshire, signing up," Jamie said into the phone. "He's a Republican, though they might wish to deny it." She covered the phone again. "Anything else?" she asked Stone.

"He has trouble with arithmetic," Stone replied.

"That's all I've got right now, Andy. See ya." She hung up. "That should make page sixteen of the front section," she said. "How do you know that clown?"

"I was introduced to him in the bar of the Key West Yacht Club last fall, then he turned up a couple of evenings later at my front door, as a hurricane was rising, and begged to be let in. He was in a state of near-drowning and required half a bottle of distilled spirits to revive him. A few weeks later, he turned up in London at a dinner arranged by the CIA for the purpose of . . . Well, I shouldn't talk about the purpose. Suffice it to say that when shots were fired, he dove under the table and was not seen again by me."

He picked up the phone. "Excuse me, I should tell Holly Barker about this."

25

Stone dialed Holly Barker's secret cell number, and to his surprise, she picked up immediately. "Hey!"

"Hey, yourself. Got a minute?"

"I have the luxury of two minutes before I have to receive the ambassador from France."

"I just got a call from the redoubtable United States Senator Joseph Box, informing me—before anyone else, he claimed—that he is now a candidate for the Republican nomination for president. He's in New Hampshire, filling out papers, no doubt with serious help, and he wanted a campaign contribution."

"I hope you gave it to him," Holly replied.

"What did you say?"

"I would like nothing better than to have Joe Box muddying the Republican waters for the next few months. He'll drive them crazy and entertain the members of the media. I may contribute to his campaign myself."

"I admit I had not thought far enough ahead to consider that. It's difficult to plan when you're laughing so hard."

"I have the feeling that, at some point, he's going to get a lot less funny," she said. "We're going to have an opportunity to find out how large a slice of the Republican electorate shares his incomprehensible views."

"You have a better political mind than I," Stone said.

"I certainly hope so," she said. "Tell me: Are you the ambassador from France?"

"Not since I last checked."

"Then I can't talk to you anymore because that gentleman is about to replace you in my affections."

"Come to New York, and we'll re-replace me in your affections."

"I'm not going anywhere near you, until well after I've taken the oath of office. Love ya, though!" She hung up.

Nearer the southern tip of Manhattan, Hank Thomas was taking his regular, early-morning meeting with his grandfather, who now exhibited only a small cough. Rance Damien joined them.

"Gentlemen, I have news," Hank said. "I've just had a phone call informing me that Senator Joe Box of Florida is announcing his candidacy for the Republican nomination for president, starting in New Hampshire. This is very good news."

The two men stared at him. "You're pleased about this?" his grandfather asked.

"I am positively delighted," Hank said.

"Please tell us why," Henry said.

"Certainly, Poppa. One of my objectives in running was to do what I could to destroy the Republican Party, so I could start a new one. I no longer have that opportunity, but Joe Box, whether he realizes it or not, does. He's going to drive them nuts, and he's going to win some primaries, too, in the South and in the Rust Belt."

"Surely not enough to win the nomination," Henry said.

"Of course not, but he's going to get a lot of votes and thereby weaken the party's chosen candidate. They're much more certain to lose the presidency now, and after eight years of Holly Barker, the party will crumble to dust. When and if I get back into it, it will be as the head of a new conservative party, one that shuns the yahoos, one that can draw support from independents, women, and educated whites. I'm going to have a better shot at it then than I would have had now."

"Actually, that makes a lot of sense," Henry said, bestowing a warm smile on his grandson.

"I think so, too," Damien said.

"Rance, we have a PAC kicking around somewhere, don't we?"

"We do."

"A fairly anonymous one?"

"Yes."

"How much is in it?"

"Something like sixty million," Damien replied.

"Then let's get twenty million into Senator Box's campaign war chest, anonymously. The new campaign law we got past the Democrats will allow us to do that."

"I'll get it done today," Damien replied.

"That will cheer Joe Box no end, and he won't care that he doesn't know where the money is coming from. Before the week is out he'll be driving his party crazy."

Henry Thomas rubbed his hands together. "This is going to be fun," he said, with a little giggle.

Hank had never heard his grandfather giggle before.

Stone tuned in to the evening news to find Holly Barker and the French ambassador answering questions from the press about tariffs on French cheeses. At the end of it a bold reporter stood up and said, "Madam Secretary, you've always been very guarded about your privacy. When are you going to loosen up and tell us something about your social life?"

"Eh?" Holly asked, cupping a hand behind her ear. "I don't believe I'm familiar with that term." A good laugh.

"You know, going out to dinner with friends, perhaps even a man?"

"Well," Holly said, "I hope one day to have such a life, and when I do, I promise that you in this room will be the very last to hear about it." More laughter.

"What about this fellow from New York, Stone Barrington? We used to hear about him, from time to time."

"That name is vaguely familiar to me," Holly said, eliciting more laughter. "Unfortunately, he and I reside in different municipalities and are only infrequently colocated. Nice fellow, though."

"Didn't you see quite a lot of him once?"

"I saw quite a lot of quite a lot of people once, until I got this job. I don't knit or play solitaire, and a girl's got to get somebody to buy her a steak now and then, but not now or for the foreseeable future. Now, I'm getting out of here before you try to marry me off to somebody or other." She picked up her papers and left the room.

The reporter handed off to the anchorperson in New York. "Thank you, Gracie," she said. "It's worth remembering that although she has never married, Holly Barker is known to enjoy the company of men. In fact, she was very nearly married quite some time ago, when she was serving as chief of police in the small Florida town of Orchid Beach. But on the day before the wedding, her fiancé, a local attorney, went to his bank to buy traveler's checks for their honeymoon and, while he was waiting in line for a teller, four men wearing masks and carrying shotguns came into the bank to rob it.

"When her fiancé objected to the way they were treating a teller, one of the men turned and fired his shotgun into his chest. He died on the way to the hospital.

"Oddly enough, the man Ms. Barker used to see now and then, Stone Barrington of New York, was in the bank on other business and witnessed the killing. He and Ms. Barker first met when she was investigating her fiancé's murder, and reportedly, they remain friends. Although they see each other infrequently, he is a major contributor to her campaign."

Stone switched off the TV, feeling crowded somehow. Holly was right. They shouldn't meet again until after the election.

26

Stone and Dino were having lunch at their club with no name when the junior senator from New York entered the dining room. He was Peter Rule, the son of the president, Katharine Lee, by her first marriage to one Simon Rule, deceased, who had once been a major figure at the CIA. The senator waved at them, then went to his table.

"That kid has turned out well, hasn't he?" Dino asked over his lobster bisque.

"He has indeed," Stone agreed. "He got good committee assignments as a freshman senator, and he dug in, did the hard work, and got commended for it on both sides of the aisle."

"He's good-looking, has an even better-looking wife, and a couple of cute kids, right?"

"When you're right, you're right, Dino." Stone had never been able to entirely cure Dino of his habit of ending sentences with an interrogatory.

"Then what's standing in his way of running for president?"

"Youth, I think, and the fact that both his mother and father have already committed themselves to Holly Barker's candidacy. He'll be a major factor when Holly leaves the post."

Dino nodded and went back to his bisque.

. . .

They had just finished their dessert, when Senator Rule wandered over to their table. "Stone, Dino," he said.

"Peter," Stone and Dino said simultaneously.

"Pull up a chair," Stone said.

Peter borrowed a chair from a nearby table and sat down.

"I hope you're as well as you look," Stone said.

"At least that well," Peter replied. "I have a couple of questions for both of you."

"We're just full of answers," Stone said.

"In complete confidence, of course," Peter said. "I'm interested in becoming the next vice president of the United States. What are your opinions of that notion?"

"Peter," Stone said, "I'd say you'd make an excellent vice president, but that would be insulting, given how little a vice president has to do in order to be excellent at his job."

"That's almost a very nice compliment, Stone," Peter said, displaying a mouth full of teeth, all of them his own and each one perfect.

"Stone," Dino said, "I think what Peter wants to know is if we think he should run now or wait four or eight years for a better opportunity."

"Dino," Peter said, "now I know why you have such a great reputation for interrogating suspects."

"Go for it," Stone said. "Anything could happen while you were waiting. Joe Box could get elected, for God's sake." Everybody laughed. "Nail down the job, make it your own, and be unwaveringly loyal to your president, except when you think she's wrong."

"What should I do in that case?"

"Tell her so. If she doesn't see the light, tell everybody, as diplomatically as possible. That will earn you a quick reputation for being an independent mind. However, avoid being a pain in the ass."

"I think that's good advice," Peter said, "and I think I'll take it."

"Hear! Hear!" Dino interjected.

"What was your second question?" Stone asked.

"Will you tell Holly I'm interested?"

"Wouldn't you rather tell her yourself?"

"No, I don't want to embarrass her, if she has to say no."

"All right, I'll mention it to her."

"When you do, tell her I haven't talked with either of my parents about this—and I don't intend to, unless they bring it up. In which case, I'll ask their advice, then tell them I'll think about it and get back to them."

"I'll mention that to Holly, too."

"Good. Now I'll reward you two with a little gossip," Peter said.

"I love gossip," Dino replied. He jerked a thumb in Stone's direction. "So does he. Lay it on us."

"Ready? Hank Thomas has donated twenty million dollars to Joe Box's campaign, through a PAC that keeps it anonymous."

Stone and Dino sat silently, contemplating this information. Finally, Stone spoke. "Of course he has. He's sticking a thumb in the eye of the Republican Party."

"We are of one mind on that," Peter said.

"When I speak to Holly, how shall I put it to her? As a feeler?"

"You can be as direct as you like," Peter said. "And I hope she gives you a direct answer."

Stone nodded. "I think it's a little early in the campaign for her to give you an answer right away."

"Tell her that if a better political option comes her way, I will stand down. I mean that. And I understand that she would not wish to announce her decision any time soon. She can pick her moment, and I'll be there."

"It make take a day or two to reach her. I don't know what her schedule is like."

"She's at the State Department for the rest of the week," Peter said, standing up and offering his hand. "Then she hits the campaign trail. Thank you both for your attention and your good advice." He walked away.

"What do you think of that?" Dino said.

"He's either a very smart politician or absolutely nuts. I can't figure out which."

Back at his desk, Stone called Holly's secret cell number and got only a beep. "Call me when you can," he said, then hung up.

Jamie Cox bustled in and threw herself into a chair, looking excited.

"You look excited," Stone said. "What's up?"

"They're publishing my book next Tuesday," she said.

"Jesus, that's short notice, isn't it?"

"I told you they were rushing it, and they have. They're

sending me on the road for two weeks—a month, if initial sales are good. They're putting together an appearance schedule as we speak."

"I guess that means no sex for a while," he said.

"Not unless you're into phone sex."

"I'm more partial to the real thing," Stone replied.

"Who isn't? In this life, we have to take what comes to us."

"I have the feeling that if we did, the Thomases would be listening to us panting—and in real time."

"Well, I guess we have to make the most of the time we have left until Tuesday." She stood up, took his hand, and pulled him to his feet. "Not on that grungy sofa," she said. "Let's go upstairs. We can start in the elevator."

Stone did as he was told.

27

Hank Thomas called in Rance Damien and sat him down. "I've changed my mind about contributions to Joe Box's campaign," he said.

"You're pulling out? I haven't sent the twenty mil yet."

"No, I'm doubling down and tripling. I want you to set up a campaign that parallels his own—not in every state, but in places where he can do well with more money—a shadow campaign, if you like. And I want you to find the senator a first-rate speechwriter, who can blend his work with Box's style of speaking."

"People with those skills are already aligning themselves with more important candidates."

"People like that are always late on their mortgage and car payments. Figure out how much it would take to turn a writer's head, and tell him or her that no one will ever know what he did, unless he wants to reveal it in his post-campaign book. Get Box some first-rate TelePrompTer instruction, too, and get him trained to not go off the reservation and sound stupid. Tell him that if he sticks to the scripts, he could actually be elected."

"Right, I'm perfectly willing to lie to the guy."

"You need to spend an hour in a room with him and scare

him shitless. Make yourself out to be his only path upward, and let him know that if he strays from the plan, he'll be humiliated and destroyed. Tell him you have no policy demands, but his speechwriter may suggest some likely ones. Remember, this is a guy with a net worth of less than half a million dollars. He can be bought, and in a hurry."

"All right," Rance said, "I'm on it."

"And remember not to be seen with him anywhere, especially anywhere near a reporter; your face is too memorable at the moment. Of course, that will change with time."

"What's my total budget for this project?"

"Sixty million dollars," Hank replied. "Now get your ass in gear."

Holly Barker saw Stone's message on her cell phone but waited until she had some free time before returning it.

"Hello, there," she said.

"And to you. How fast do I have to talk?"

"I've got a few minutes."

"I've got some interesting gossip, and I've got a campaign offer for you. Which do you want to hear first?"

"The gossip, but I warn you, I've probably already heard it."

"Hank Thomas is putting twenty million dollars into Joe Box's campaign through a PAC."

Silence.

"You need to apply a squirt of oil to your brain, Holly. I can hear the wheels turning from here."

"All right, I'll buy that, and it's pretty obvious why. Hank wants to wreck the Republican Party so he can have a clean shot as an independent in four years—maybe as the leader of a new party."

"Consider yourself lubricated," Stone said.

"What's the campaign thing?"

"I had a conversation with Peter Rule yesterday, and he asked me to tell you that he'd like very much to be your running mate."

"That's surprising this early in the campaign," she said.

"He also told me to tell you that if politics dictate a different choice, he'll step aside and help."

"I've always been very impressed with Peter," Holly said. "Tell me, has Kate weighed in on this?"

"He told me that he has not discussed this with either of his parents and does not intend to, unless they bring it up, in which case he'll tell them he'll get back to them."

"Do you believe that?"

"Peter is a young man who has never had to lie to get what he wants."

"I think that's an accurate assessment. I hope it lasts. You can tell Peter I'm interested—no, I'll tell him myself. I need a few people—surrogates, I guess you'd call them—who can speak on my behalf when I can't make a venue. I'll invite him to join that group, then assess him as we move along."

"That's a good move," Stone said. "If you want him, I think you'll need to get him in front of the electorate often enough and with enough good material that, by convention time, a large pack of them will be clamoring for you to select him."

"Make him the obvious choice?"

"If you want him. Don't string him along, if you're not interested."

"I'm interested, and I'll tell him so."

"Then my work is done," Stone said. "Try not to get us into
any wars before November." They both hung up.

Rance Damien sat across the table from a middle-aged woman
in a diner. "What do you have for me, Florence?"

Florence Heath was a New York–based member of the re-
cruiting committee for Harvard and had seen the résumés of
thousands of applicants over the years. She passed Damien a
large envelope. "Before you sit down and read this, let me give
you the CliffsNotes version."

"All right."

"He has just finished his doctorate work in political science,
and his dissertation knocked it out of the park. I've had my eye
on him since he applied as a junior in high school. It was heavy
lifting to get him accepted at that age, but I did it."

"Why is he the right guy for me?"

"There isn't a better brain in the country for what you want,
but he comes up short in the personality area. In fact, he may be
somewhere on the spectrum. For example, the board loved his
dissertation but not his orals; they thought him excessively
blunt with his elders and betters, though they gave him high
marks. Where he excels in communication is through his writing, both for publication and for speaking. He gave an address
at his graduation ceremony that is still remembered, but he read

every word of it from a script. He also wrote some witty columns for the *Crimson,* under a pseudonym."

"What are his current circumstances?"

"In spite of his achievements, because of his personality, he has been unable to find a university teaching position. And since he comes from a modest background, he has a quarter of a million in student loans. He's working as a teaching assistant, but only for the summer program, so he's about to be homeless and broke.

"His name is Ari Kramer. His contact information is in his file."

"Florence," Damien said, pushing an envelope across the table. "You've done well. I may call upon you again."

She took a peek in the envelope. "Please do," she said. "Anytime."

Damien went back to his office and read every word of the file. He thought Ari Kramer was just what he was looking for.

28

Holly Barker was at home in Georgetown, in the beautiful house that once belonged to Will Lee, but for which Stone had traded his Santa Fe property, and then made available to the State Department for her residence. She buzzed her secretary who worked with some others, including campaign workers, in storerooms adjacent to the commodious downstairs garage.

"Yes, ma'am?"

"Please call Senator Peter Rule's Washington office, and tell him or his secretary that there is a package being delivered to him as we speak. Ask her when he has a free moment, and to ask him to unwrap it and wait for a call."

"Right away, ma'am." She called back. "The senator is waiting."

Holly took her throwaway phone and pressed a button.

"This is Peter, Holly," he answered.

"Good. Stone Barrington has relayed to me your expression of interest in running for higher office. I was very interested to hear it."

"Thank you, I'm pleased to hear of your interest."

"Stone has also told me that, should a political necessity arise, you're willing to step aside."

"That is correct. I'm not running for reelection to the Senate for another two years."

"Peter, I've asked a small number of prominent Democrats to act as surrogates and give speeches and talks on my behalf at times when I have a scheduling conflict, or the event doesn't quite rise to the level of a major campaign appearance. I'd like you to join that group."

"I'd be delighted for the opportunity," Peter said, realizing immediately that, even if he wasn't selected as her running mate, he would be speaking to the same people whose support he would need at a later date.

"Do you have personal transportation available?"

"I have an enormous SUV and a smaller airplane that will hold nearly as many on fairly short flights."

"Very good. You can bill the campaign for your fuel costs, but we can't cover damage, maintenance, insurance, garaging, or hangaring."

"Understood. I'll set up a bank account separate from my own to handle campaign expenditures and receipts and keep accurate records."

"Fine. I'm messengering over to you a packet of position papers, which you should commit to memory, if possible. Before each appearance you'll get a briefing paper that includes specific talking points and a list of important people you'll be meeting at the speaking locations. The campaign will handle hotel arrangements and, if necessary, airline tickets for you and an aide or two. A campaign advance man or woman will be assigned to each venue to select auditoria and other speaking places, such as the rear of a flatbed truck, and to see that an audio and video system are up and running. We'll keep recordings of each event for the DNC and posterity, which will help keep us from being misquoted. We'll have four Dixieland bands on the road, and one of them will usually play what we might call preludes and recessionals for each event. Do you have any questions?"

"To whom do I report?"

"To Senator Sam Meriwether, the campaign chairman, and anyone else he may designate. If something really important comes up that I need to know about immediately, you may call me, but only on the phone I sent you. My private number is on the contacts list. There is also a custom-made holster for the phone, which you will wear on your belt, and you must never lose the phone or loan it to anyone else, even for a single call. If, God forbid, you should lose the phone, call Sam or his designee, and it will be wiped clean remotely and made unusable by any-one who should steal it or find it."

"What about scheduling conflicts for myself?"

"Have an assistant keep your schedule on our website, and we'll endeavor not to interfere with important committee meet-ings or votes. We will accept your judgment on what you can't miss. Anything else?"

"Nothing, Holly. I'll await your instructions. One comment, though: I expect there will be venues where a country band might be more attractive to the audience than Dixieland. I'll leave it to the campaign to decide which bands and which venues."

"I'll pass that along. Welcome aboard, Peter. I hope we'll be together for a long time."

"So do I." They both hung up. Peter took a deep breath to calm himself. This was his second step; the first had been his conversation with Stone Barrington. He would note this in his diary, which he kept secret from everyone but his wife.

Moments later Peter's secretary, Anna Lopez, came into his office, followed by a man pushing a hand truck containing two large cardboard boxes. "This came from Holly Barker," she said.

"Have a seat, Anna," he said, then waved goodbye to the porter. "We need to talk." He noticed a look of concern flicker over her face, and he held up a hand. "Nothing like that, poorly chosen words. It's just that you have a decision to make, and I stress that whatever you decide will be gratefully accepted by me. There is no wrong answer."

"What is the question, Senator?"

"You have to choose between two jobs: one is what you're doing now, but with increased authority over the staff. Your title will be administrative officer, and you will move up one civil service grade. The other may be less attractive to you."

"And what is that?" she asked.

"You will take a leave of absence from my Senate office and work directly for me, paid by me, with an increase in salary, at an office in my home."

She looked concerned again. She was an attractive woman with a lot of experience working in the Capitol, and she was adept at fending off passes gracefully. "Yes?"

"Secretary of State Holly Barker has asked me to join her campaign as one of a few surrogates who will speak for her when she is unavailable, or when an event may not be important enough to her election to require her attendance. I would like for you to manage my time, keep my speaking schedule, with attention to conflicts with Senate votes and committee hearings, and essentially hold it all together. The hours may be odd and long."

"May I assume that your participation has a long-range purpose, beyond getting the secretary elected?"

"You may assume anything you like," Peter replied with a small, conspiratorial smile. "Let's say that I hope you won't be working in my basement for too very long."

"What will you do, if Ms. Barker is not elected?"

"You and I will both return to this work and wait for another day."

"Then my decision is to accept your second offer," she said.

"Good. You may choose your successor in this office, and you may hire another person to assist you, at a salary you designate. I hardly need tell you what a high level of intelligence, hard work, and integrity I will expect from such a person, because you have, yourself, long maintained that standard."

"Thank you, Senator. Now, what should I do with these boxes?"

"Have them delivered to my house, along with yourself. There is parking in my basement, and you will find a couple of usable rooms there. Start outfitting them for your use and that of your assistant.

"Thank you for your service to the United States Senate. You are now relieved from your duties for an undetermined length of absence."

Anna Lopez turned to her new work.

29

Ari Kramer sat in his obsessively neat dormitory room—
his residence for the summer term in Cambridge—
selecting, shredding, and discarding any materials
that he would not be needing or archiving at his faculty storage
unit, which he was being allowed to keep until he had a more
permanent address. It was early on his last day at the TA job.

His laptop computer made a noise that indicated he was re-
ceiving a Skype call, a program he favored as he preferred it to
actual face-to-face meetings with strangers. He swung around
in his chair and faced the machine, then answered the call. A
man wearing a business suit and facial bandages appeared before him.

"Good morning, Mr. Kramer," the man said. "My name is
William Smith. We have not met. I apologize for my appearance, but I am recovering from an accident, pending further
surgeries."

"What is the purpose of this call?" Ari asked in his typically
blunt manner.

"It is in the nature of a job interview," Smith replied.

"What sort of a job?"

"A political job, one as chief speechwriter and advisor to a candidate for office. There may be other duties attached as well."

"Who is the candidate?"

"If we can agree to terms I will tell you that at the end of this conversation."

"When does the job start?"

"Today. I believe this is your last week as a TA."

"Correct. Describe my duties in more detail."

"The candidate is one who presents well to the public, but needs to be coached in certain skills, such as the natural use of a teleprompter. He must also be trained never to speak extemporaneously, as he is prone to gaffes. You must be in constant contact with him, through Skype, which he currently uses to keep in touch with a number of women in his home state and in Washington."

"Is he married?"

"Divorced, twice. He will have handlers who will discourage him from being alone with women."

"I don't have to 'handle' him?"

"Only his speeches and, perhaps, political strategies and his intellect, which is superficial. He appears to know a great deal about a great many subjects, but his facts are often wrong, and you must guard against that."

"Why are you considering me for this post?"

"I have read much of what you have written while at Harvard, which is considerable, and I've spent time with a member of the Harvard recruitment board, who has taken an interest in you. I have liked what I have heard."

"Do you understand that I have certain limitations where communication with others is required?"

"I do, just as I understand my own current limitations in that regard. And I believe yours are surmountable. I understand, for instance, that you communicate orally better through Skype than through actual contact."

"That is correct, at least with strangers. I have no problem with face-to-face contact with people I know and have experience with. What does the job pay?"

"One hundred thousand dollars."

"For the whole campaign?"

"Per month."

Ari sucked in a quick breath. "That is acceptable," he said. "Who is the candidate?"

"Joseph Box, the junior senator from Florida."

"I can see how you might think he needs my help," Ari said.

"One of the things I have noted in your writings, Ari, if I may call you that, is that you seem able to assume any political stance—whether or not you are in agreement with it—and defend your position. A happy skill in a debater or a political operative. One of the things you will need to do is to help select policy positions for Box to use in his campaign. Some of these positions brush against the far right, but most would be described as right-center, though not far enough right to put off college-educated white men and women and independents."

"I can handle that."

"Good. A package will be delivered to you shortly containing a complete biography of Joseph Box, including the legislative record of his votes and many of his speeches."

"How will I be paid?"

"An LLC account is being opened as we speak, with you listed as president, at New England Trust in Harvard Square."

"I know the bank. I keep my personal account there."

"You may also hire a full-time assistant and pay that person from the account at a salary you consider attractive for the job.

"You will use the new account only for your personal campaign expenses, and you will submit monthly reports of your expenditures, with receipts. Your salary will be deposited into your personal account, and you must file quarterly tax returns and remain current on your payments."

"Of course. I do my own accounting and use TurboTax for filing."

"Good. The new LLC account will have a balance of two hundred thousand dollars. You are to rent an apartment immediately—today, if possible—and pay the rent from this account, a maximum of ten thousand dollars per month, and the attendant deposits. You may choose a property suitable for your office, as well as residence, and that of your assistant. Install a landline, if you wish, but all of your campaign conversations will take place on two telephones, one for your assistant, being sent to you. Keep it on your person at all times. Do you possess a driver's license?"

"Yes, and I am quite a good driver."

"As soon as possible, buy a new car. It should be a large American-made SUV, with a secure trunk area. Arrange for garaging in or near your apartment building. You may not have a firearm in the vehicle at any time, and if you possess one, throw it into the Charles River today."

"I do not possess a firearm. They disgust me. When will I meet Senator Box?"

"You will phone him on Skype about seventy-two hours from now and transmit his first speech to him. A teleprompter instructor will be working with him in the meantime, and you may rehearse him. The location and subject of the speech is in the packet being delivered to you. At a time of your own choosing, visit some of his campaign events for the purpose of assessing the candidate's progress. You will be known to his advance and security people and will be issued campaign staff credentials, as will your assistant. But avoid mixing with Box's staff socially. As few people as possible should know who you are and what you are doing."

"I understand. How may I contact you, Mr. Smith?"

"I am listed among your contacts on the phone in your package."

"Whom do you represent?"

"An entirely legal political action committee. That is all you need to know. If anyone should inquire about your employment, tell them that you are a self-employed, freelance campaign operative. As I mentioned, an LLC corporation is being established and you will receive stationery and business cards at your new address, which you should e-mail to me as soon as you have signed a lease. When that is accomplished, credit cards will be issued in your name and that of your assistant, to be used strictly for campaign expenses and no other."

"Thank you, Mr. Smith."

"You may call me William."

"Thank you, William. I won't disappoint you."

"Oh, Ari, one more thing: At the conclusion of the campaign, if your work has been exemplary, your student loans will be paid in full."

He hung up, which was a good thing, since Ari was speechless.

There was a knock at his door, but when he answered it, no one was there. A large box was on the floor. Ari sat back down and gathered his thoughts for a moment. In that time he had decided whom to hire, where to look for an apartment, and what car he would buy.

He opened the just-delivered box and spread its contents on his bed, in order of importance, then he used his new cell phone to call Annie Lee, a colleague during his summer term.

"Hello?"

"Hello, Annie, it's Ari Kramer."

"You're not calling on Skype. Is anything wrong?"

"Nothing. Have you found employment yet after the term?" Annie had completed her master's degree in political science, and had been accepted for doctorate study.

"No," she replied.

"I believe I can solve the problem for you," Ari said. "Please come to my room directly."

"Of course."

Ari hung up without further ado.

30

Stone and Jamie dined in his study and drank a very good wine.

"So, it will be some time before I see you again?" he asked.

"I'm afraid so," Jamie replied. "They've got me scheduled for twenty-nine cities—that's so far."

"What about network interviews?"

"I'll do them from local stations. What are you going to do for sex while I'm gone?"

"Why are you concerned about that?"

"I know what your appetites are, and I can't expect you to be chaste for all that time—maybe not even as long as a day or two."

Stone had no comment about that. "I should ask you the same question," he replied.

"Masturbation works for me."

"It works for everybody," he said. "But not all by itself, or for very long."

She laughed. "I forgot that you know my appetites as well as I yours."

"You'll need to be more careful than I," Stone said.

"What do you mean?"

"You're about to become a public figure, and you'll have to conduct yourself as such. Be careful to whom you bestow your gifts."

"That's good advice," she said. "How about you?"

"I am the essence of a private person," he replied. "Nobody cares about what I do."

"But you're a close friend of a candidate for the presidency. I can't believe that's a sexless relationship."

"We have agreed to take pains to be in separate cities at all times," Stone replied. "I've never figured out how to include a sex life in that."

"That's a good plan, if it works."

"It has worked for some time."

"Did you see Joe Box's announcement speech from New Hampshire?"

"I avoided it," Stone said. "He annoys me."

"He wasn't bad. I was impressed with the way he used the teleprompter. Somebody is tutoring him, I think."

"I hope not well enough to make him a serious candidate."

"He exuded seriousness. He's a good actor."

"In spurts, I suppose, but not good enough to keep my skin from crawling." He poured them an after-dinner cognac. "What are they doing about security for you?"

"Two women with guns," she replied.

Stone laughed. "Perhaps they know you well enough not to give you male companionship."

"They said it was so they could accompany me to the ladies' rooms along the way. Apparently, that's not a good place to be alone."

"I don't think the Thomases are after you right now."

"How can I be sure of that?"

"They can't harm you in the middle of a book tour—not when the book is about them."

"You have a point. How about you?"

"When I go out, I have Fred, who is very competent and well-armed."

"How did a Brit on American soil get a New York City carry license?"

"He has a friend high up in the police department."

"Ah, yes, Dino. I'll miss Dino and Viv."

"I'll tell them you said so."

"Please do." She refilled her own glass and stood up. "Now," she said, "come with me. This one has to be great because it has to last a long time." She held out her hand.

Stone took it and followed her upstairs.

There was a knock at Ari's door, and he opened it to find Annie Lee standing there: Eurasian, petite, and very fetching to him. He showed her in and pointed to a chair.

She didn't take it immediately. "What's all that on the bed?" she asked.

"You can read it after our conversation," Ari replied. "Your speed-reading skills will be very useful for the next few months."

"What will we be doing?"

"We will be making Senator Joseph Box into a credible candidate for president," he said.

"I love a challenge," she replied wryly.

"Those things are his bio, his speeches, and pretty much everything ever written about him. The articles will point out areas of his persona that we'll have to pay particular attention to."

She picked up a stack of papers and sat down at his desk. "Let me read a few," she said. She started with the bio, then continued through a two-inch stack of paper. "I've got the gist," she said shortly. "Does this job pay money?"

"Ten thousand dollars a month plus room, board, and travel expenses."

Her mouth dropped open. "That's more than sixty dollars an hour."

"Then you must try to be worth it. Come on, we have to go find an apartment." He took his new checkbook and tucked it into a coat pocket. "And buy some clothes and a car."

"Good God! Who's paying for this?"

"A perfectly legal political action committee."

"Which is committed to making Box president?"

"Nearly president, I think."

"Why 'nearly'?"

"Who in their right mind would actually want Box to be president? I think they have other motives."

"Such as?"

"Scaring the shit out of the Republican Party. Let's go." Ari led her from the room and double-locked the door behind him.

"What kind of apartment are we looking for?" she asked.

"One with two bedrooms and baths, with workspace, too. I saw a sign off the Square the other day that I'd like to know more about." They walked over to the Square, then to a side street. "There," Ari said, nodding toward a tall, new condo building.

"Nothing cozy, huh?"

"Nope." They went into the building to where a woman sat at a desk. "We'd like to see that," he said, pointing to a sign that read: MODEL APARTMENT ON VIEW.

The woman looked him up and down. "Certainly, sir," she said. She took some keys from a desk drawer and led him to the elevator. They rose to the top floor, where she opened a door and ushered them through.

There was a large living room with a dining area, an excellent kitchen, and three bedrooms. It was furnished as if it was a department store. Even kitchen utensils and tableware were in place.

Ari walked quickly from room to room. "How much to rent?" he asked.

"Seventy-five hundred, per month. Unfurnished, of course, minimum one-year lease."

"How much for the furniture?"

"You'd have to speak with the decorator about that."

"I'll take the apartment if you'll speak to the decorator and get me a favorable price for the furniture."

The woman took out her cell phone, dialed a number, and then wandered into the kitchen to talk. Then she came back. "The retail price of everything here is thirty-eight thousand dollars, but you can buy it all for twenty-five thousand."

"Done," Ari said, producing a checkbook.

"There's a security deposit of a month's rent, and you pay the first and last months now." She told him whom to make the checks out to, and she produced a lease and began filling in the blanks.

"Oh," Ari said, "does that include parking in the building?"

"Yes, for one car."

He turned to Annie. "Do you own a car?"

"No," she replied.

"That is satisfactory." He wrote a check for the rent and another for the furniture.

"When would you like to move in?" the agent asked, handing him the lease and a pen.

"Now," Ari replied.

"I'll need half an hour to clear the checks," she said.

"That's all right. We have some shopping to do."

She handed him two sets of keys, he gave one to Annie and they went downstairs.

"What kind of shopping?" Annie asked.

"I'm going over to J. Press and buy some suitable clothes. Why don't you do the same? I don't think Harvard Graduate Student is a good look for a political operative of either gender. We need to look more prosperous."

"J. Crew is good for me," she said.

He signed a blank check and gave it to her. "I'll need receipts. I'll meet you back here in a couple of hours."

He shopped for an hour, chose some suits, jackets, shirts, and shoes, then got his clothes marked up for alterations to the cuffs and sleeves and ordered everything delivered to the apartment. Then he got into a cab.

"Take me to a Chevrolet car dealer," he said to the driver.

Three-quarters of an hour later, he drove a new Tahoe off the lot and to his new building. He went upstairs and smelled cooking as he got off the elevator and let himself into the apartment.

The living room was crowded with shopping bags from J. Crew and J. Press, and Annie was in the kitchen. "Hi," she said, "I did some grocery shopping."

31

Bob Cantor knocked, then walked into Stone's office and sat down. "I think you've had enough of Sherry and me," he said.

"Nonsense. You can stay as long as you like."

"What I'd like is to go back to my hideout in Brooklyn and take Sherry with me."

"Do you think that will be safe?"

"It'll be safe because they don't know about it," he replied. "I've swept the neighborhood here for the past couple of days, and it's been squeaky clean. I think Brooklyn will be, too. I've also taken a couple of trips to my house downtown, and there's no human surveillance on it. No electronic surveillance, either, if I'm any good at what I do."

Sherry joined them and thanked Stone profusely.

"Our stuff is all packed and in the car," Bob said.

"You okay for money?" Stone asked.

"Oh, yeah. I've always got cash on hand." He stood up and offered his hand. "Call me, if there are any developments."

"I don't think there will be," Stone said, "now that Jamie's book is coming out. Since we've already done our worst, we're not a threat to them anymore."

"I hope you're right," Bob said. "Just remember, revenge runs deep in the Italian character."

"That's what Dino keeps telling me," Stone replied.

They said goodbye and left.

Ari sat in front of his laptop and made a Skype call. Senator Joseph Box answered. "Ari?" he asked.

"Yes, Senator."

"Welcome aboard."

"I've been following your campaign on the Internet, and I have a couple of observations."

"I'd be happy to hear them."

"Senator, I get the impression that you have a good memory."

"An outstandingly excellent memory," Box replied. "I can recite whole chapters from books that I read in high school."

"Can you memorize a fifteen-minute speech?"

"Certainly. I've pretty much been ignoring the teleprompter."

"So I have noticed," Ari said. "I don't want you to confuse reciting a speech from memory and improvising one. They're two different skills, and somehow, when you improvise, too many things come out wrong."

"I'm hurt," Box replied.

"Don't be. Your memory will carry you through. It's important, too, not to exceed the fifteen-minute limit. You run the risk of boring your audience, and it's better to leave them wanting more than offering them too much."

"I take your point."

"I want you to have your clothes pressed more often, too," Ari said.

"Oh?" Box looked hurt again. "I've been told you're sometimes excessively blunt."

"I try to say what needs to be said as quickly as possible. You have a tendency to look rumpled at the best of times, and keeping your clothes pressed lessens that. Assign a campaign volunteer to that task. Also, I'd like you to wear more solid-color ties or ones with very small figures, like pin dots."

"Am I choosing my ties badly?"

"Yes."

Box winced. "All right, I'll do as you say. By the way, your speeches have been excellent."

"Yes, they have been," Ari agreed, "and they will continue being so. The press is picking up the lines I have intended them to."

"Am I ever going to see you live?" Box asked.

"I'll catch an occasional appearance on the trail, and I'll introduce myself."

"I'm told you don't like shaking hands."

"The custom of shaking hands arose from a desire to show others that one is unarmed. I am always unarmed."

"I'm glad to hear that."

"Goodbye, Senator." Ari hung up.

Senator Box turned to his bodyguard. "That kid is weird," he said.

. . .

Annie appeared, reflected in his computer screen. "I know you don't like being touched," she said.

"It's good that you know."

"I'm going to put my hands on your shoulders, and I want you to relax." She reached out to him and detected an immediate stiffness.

"I had a massage once," Ari said. "I disliked it intensely."

"If you want a full and happy life," she said, "you're going to have to do some relearning." She squeezed his shoulders slightly.

He took a quick breath.

"Now I want you to make a concerted effort to relax your shoulders, even though I'm touching them."

"I don't know if I can do that," he said.

It took her ten minutes to feel a little relaxation in his body, and another ten minutes before he seemed to like it. "There," she said. "Was that awful?"

"It became less awful as you went along," he said.

"We're going to do that for a few minutes every day. You'll have more energy, and you'll sleep better."

"If you say so."

"That's what I like to hear," she said, kissing him lightly on the beginnings of his bald spot.

Ari jumped. "Too much, too soon," he said.

32

After a fervent goodbye, Jamie was picked up in Stone's garage by a black SUV with a driver and two women in the rear seat. The women got out and greeted her.

"Hi," said the slightly taller of the two. "I'm Lane, and this is Ida."

"Hi, Lane and Ida," Jamie said. "It's good to have you aboard for this tour."

"A few words of explanation," Lane said. "We're both armed." She patted her large handbag. "And in some circumstances we're trained to shoot first and think later. If you see either of us pull a gun, drop to the floor on your belly immediately. Is that clear?"

"Clear," Jamie said.

"It doesn't matter where we are when it happens, do it at once."

"Very clear," Jamie said.

"When we go into a ladies' room, all three of us go. One stands outside your stall, or in the next one, if she needs to go; the other washes her hands or freshens her makeup. You must never, ever go into a ladies' room alone in a public place. In the back room of a bookstore or an auditorium, we'll wait outside until you're done."

"Got it."

"All your hotel accommodations have two large beds in the bedroom. One of us will sleep on one of them, the other on the living room couch, in sight of the door."

"Tell me something," Jamie said. "Do you have some special information that warrants this?"

"It's routine," Lane said. "All you have to do is learn to trust us."

"I'm feeling very trusting," Jamie replied.

They opened a door, and Lane got into the rear seat with Jamie, while Ida rode shotgun, and they headed for LaGuardia.

"We have all your airline tickets and copies of your ID," Lane said, "so we'll do all the checking in and, later, luggage retrieval. We've arranged it with the airlines that your bags will always be the last on board and the first off. Saves time."

They arrived at LaGuardia, where a waiting skycap with a cart took charge of the luggage and placed a red tag on each bag, and then they disappeared with him. The women started their journey to the gate. They were admitted to a side lane that took them past the security checkpoint, and when they arrived at the gate they were told that there would be a short delay.

"I've got to go to the ladies'," Jamie said.

"Right this way," Lane replied and led the way. They went into the room, and Ida put Jamie into the last stall, then stood outside while Lane washed her hands.

The door to the restroom opened. Lane looked in the mirror and saw two men in dark suits enter. One of them stood by the door and wedged his foot against it. Lane turned, smiling, and stuck her hand into a pocket in her large purse. "That's far enough, gentlemen," she said.

One of the men unbuttoned his jacket and let it fall open. Lane got her weapon out first. "That's far enough," she repeated. "Take your weapons out with two fingers and let them drop to the floor."

"You can't get us both," one of the men said.

"If you want to bet on that, then go for it," she said quietly. "We're close enough for head shots. You'll be dead before you hit the floor. Do it *now!*"

The two men glanced at each other, and the doorkeeper nodded. They removed two Glocks and set them on the floor.

"Kick them to me," Lane said, "and do it right, to avoid accidents."

They kicked their weapons across the tile floor.

Ida joined Lane, picked up the guns, and tossed them into the stainless-steel trash bin built into the wall beside the sink.

"Jamie?" Ida said. "Join us, please."

"Now," Lane said to the two men. "Open the door and run. *Sprint.*"

The two men disappeared out the door, and she followed them to be sure they were running down the corridor.

Ida guarded the outside of the door while Lane made a call. "Baggage? Four red tags to the sidewalk right now," she said, then dialed a second number. "Plan B," she said. "Half an hour."

"How would they know I'd be at LaGuardia?" Jamie asked. "My schedule hasn't been published."

"There's always somebody who can be bought," Lane said. "Or maybe they're just checking airports."

They hustled Jamie down a back hallway to where an electric cart waited, then rode back to the set-down entrance, where their bags were tossed into the waiting SUV.

"Where are we going?" Jamie asked, once the car was moving.

"Teterboro," Lane replied. "You've been upgraded."

"But there's no scheduled service from Teterboro, is there?"

"No, but there's unscheduled service," Ida replied.

A half hour later, at Teterboro, they drove into a rear door of a hangar marked STRATEGIC SERVICES and stopped next to a small jet. Moments later they were buckled in and being towed onto the ramp, and shortly afterward engines were started.

"This is very nice," Jamie said, looking around.

"It's a Citation CJ3-Plus," Lane said. "We'll beat the airline to Atlanta."

"You planned for all this?" Jamie asked.

"There's always a plan B," Ida said. "Sometimes a plan C, too. If you'd like some music, put on your headset."

In Atlanta they landed at Peachtree-DeKalb Airport, where another SUV awaited them. And soon, they were installed in a suite at the St. Regis.

"Surely these people will have my signing schedule, won't they?" Jamie asked.

"Your schedule is unpublished," Lane said. "All the promotion is being done at bookstores. I'm told we can expect a crowd tonight. Drink?"

"Oh, please," Jamie said, getting out her cell phone.

"Hello," Stone said.

"Well," Jamie said, "we've already dodged the first attempt on my person."

"What part of your person?"

"My neck, I guess. These women with guns are very, very good."

"Viv Bacchetti handpicked them."

"She has a good eye." She told Stone what had transpired.

"Did you get ruffled?"

"Only in my head. We went to Teterboro and got onto a smaller jet."

"That's my old CJ3," Stone replied. "I did a trade with Strategic Services."

"I wish you were here."

"I guess Strategic Services isn't supplying that service," he said.

"Not yet," Jamie replied, "but the women with guns are starting to look pretty good."

33

Stone sat and thought after Jamie had hung up. This wasn't supposed to happen. It was too risky for the Thomases to try such a bold move in a public place; the fact that they had worried him. He called Bob Cantor on his throwaway phone, but all he got was a beep.

"Bob," he said, "this is Stone. Please call me right away. The opposition made a move on Jamie." He hung up and waited. And waited. He checked his watch. They had had time to get to Brooklyn, even if they had stopped at Bob's house to pick up some things.

After a couple of turns around the block, Bob pulled into his garage and closed the door behind them. "I need to pick up some clean clothes," he said to Sherry. "You want to come in?"

"Sure," she replied.

They left the car and went inside. Bob went upstairs to pack a bag. Fifteen minutes after their arrival, they were back in the car while Bob checked the outside cameras on his iPhone. No threats.

Bob drove to Brooklyn, to the tree-shaded street where he had bought and renovated a house years before. He rented out apartments on the two lower floors, both to cops, and occupied the top two. He drove around the block twice and saw nothing of interest, then he went back to the house and parked in front. They each took two bags from the trunk and started up the front steps.

Bob heard a slight noise, then Sherry collapsed on the stoop while he dove into the doorway and freed a weapon. He reached out, got Sherry by an ankle, and pulled her into the shelter of the doorway. Her head left a bloody trail behind her, and she was unresponsive.

Bob got out his throwaway and saw a missed call on the screen.

"I was worried," Stone said.

"You had good reason," Bob replied. "Sherry has taken a bullet to the head. I can't tell how bad. She's alive, but unresponsive. I need an ambulance *now*. I also need two squad cars. I can't move her into the wagon while the threat is still out there." He gave Stone the address.

"I'm on it," Stone said. He hung up and called Dino.

"Bacchetti."

"It's Stone. We weren't careful enough. Bob's at his place in Brooklyn with Sherry, and she's taken a bullet to the head. He needs an ambulance and a couple of cars for protection while they load her."

"Address?"

Stone gave it to him.

"Three minutes, tops," Dino said, then hung up.

Stone thought he should go to Brooklyn, but then thought better of it. He called Bob back.

"Yeah?"

"Help is on the way. I don't know which hospital they'll take her to, so call me as soon as you find out, and I'll meet you there."

"Don't do that," Bob said firmly. "There won't be anything you can do, and if we start breaking cover they'll be all over us."

"Good point." Stone could hear an ambulance in the background. "How's Sherry doing?"

"She's moving a little, but still unconscious. Here's the ambulance and a squad car; I can hear another one on the way. I'll call you when I know something." He hung up.

Stone called Viv on her cell.

"I've already heard about Jamie," she said. "Precautions have been taken."

"You haven't heard about Sherry."

"What about Sherry?"

"Bullet to the head. Still alive, but it looks bad. Dino responded, and she's on the way to the hospital. I just wanted you to know that the Thomases are throwing caution to the wind. I expect I'll be next."

"I'll have some people at your house in twenty minutes," she said.

"Thank you." He hung up.

Bob was walking rapidly down a hospital hallway beside Sherry, who was on a gurney, holding her hand. Suddenly, she squeezed it. He bent over her.

"It's okay, babe, you're in the hospital."

Sherry whispered something and he put his ear to her lips. "Don't let them cut off my hair," she said.

Bob laughed. "You're gonna be fine."

The gurney was wheeled into the ER and into an examination area. A doctor pushed him out and pulled a curtain.

"She says don't cut off her hair!" he yelled at the opening in the curtain.

"Got it!" the young doctor yelled back.

Bob went out into the hall, where an NYPD sergeant walked up to him. "The commish got involved," he said. "She'll be moved to a protective custody area when they're done. For witnesses, and the like."

"Thank him for me," Bob said.

The cop nodded, and Bob took a seat and called Stone.

"It's Stone."

"We're at Bellevue. She squeezed my hand and told me not to let them cut her hair."

"That's sounding good," Stone said. "I'll speak to Dino about a round-the-clock guard."

"Not necessary. Dino has already arranged for her to be put in a room in the protective custody area."

"That'll be locked and guarded twenty-four-seven," Stone said. "Have you talked to a doctor yet?"

"It'll be a while, I think. They'll have to do X-rays and tests."

"Keep me posted."

"What are you doing about security?"

"Viv has people on the way."

"And Jamie?"

"They went after her at LaGuardia, but Viv's people got her out unharmed. She's in Atlanta."

"That's a better place to be than here," Bob said.

"Did you look over the neighborhood before you got out of the car?"

"Yeah. Nobody at my house and nobody here. I think somebody had built a nest across the street and was just waiting for us."

"I hope it was a small-caliber round," Stone said. "Were you hit at all?"

"No, I'm still in one piece, but that's more than anybody will be able to say about the Thomases when I'm done with them."

"Easy, Bob. Don't go off half-cocked."

"That's easy for you to say."

"Just put that out of your mind. We'll talk when you're done there. Come back here then. Don't go home."

"We'll see," Bob said.

34

Jamie was getting a manicure in her Atlanta hotel suite when the phone rang and one of her guards answered. "Got it," she said into the phone, then hung up.

"What was that?" Jamie asked.

"Nothing to worry about," Ida answered.

"If it was nothing to worry about, then it won't matter if you tell me what it was," Jamie said. "I insist."

"Sometimes it's better if you don't know everything," Lane said.

"Well, if it's something I don't know, I really need to hear it, and right now."

"Oh, all right. You know a woman called Sherry in New York?"

"Yes."

"Someone took a shot at her in Brooklyn this afternoon."

"And I shouldn't know that?"

"Does it make you feel better?"

"It makes me feel more knowledgeable," Jamie said. "Is she dead?"

"No, she's recovering in the hospital."

"Now I feel better. What were the circumstances of the shooting?"

"I don't know, just in Brooklyn."

Jamie called Stone with her free hand.

"Hello?"

"It's Jamie. Tell me about Sherry."

Stone told her. "I don't know any more than that. Bob will come here when he's willing to leave her."

"It looks as though your prediction about the Thomases not acting while they are suing us and the book is out was not accurate."

"I can't deny that," Stone said. "I thought they were more careful people."

"Reckless, sounds more like it."

"I can't disagree. Do you feel safe where you are?"

"I'm on a high floor of a very good hotel with two armed guards. I feel safe for now, but tonight I have to speak to a public audience at a bookstore."

"Viv tells me you will be speaking to an *invited* audience of press and public officials, plus whoever might be in the bookstore at the time. The location was not advertised."

"That's encouraging."

"Just do what your guards tell you to do, and don't argue with them. You'll be fine."

"If you say so, though your track record on this subject is less than perfect."

"If you want perfect, I'm sure Viv can find a nice steel room to lock you in."

Jamie laughed in spite of herself. "Oh, all right. I'm sure I'll be safe tonight." They both hung up.

Early in the evening Bob showed up at Stone's house.

"What's the latest?" Stone asked.

"She's stable and out of the ICU. They put her in a room. Her doctor showed me an X-ray. It was like shooting a bullet through the side of a football without hitting the air bladder inside, so there's no brain damage. I caught a nap in a reclining chair, then she woke up and talked a bit, but the doctor hustled me out and told me to go home. Sherry wanted it that way, too. I'll go back tomorrow."

"Consider yourself at home," Stone replied.

"What happened to Jamie at LaGuardia?" Bob asked.

Stone told him, then looked at his watch. "She'll be arriving at the bookstore about now. How about some dinner?"

"Sure."

They went upstairs to Stone's study and had a drink first.

"I want to go on the offensive," Bob said.

"I know you do, and I understand why. Do you understand why you shouldn't?"

"Because they'll be expecting me?"

"Exactly. You've already nearly burned down their building— or rather, some unknown person did. They're going to be ready. Wait until they're not."

Bob nodded but said nothing.

. . .

Rance Damien attended dinner with the two Thomases.

"I watched a few minutes of a Joe Box speech," Henry said. "He wasn't awful. I didn't cringe once."

"He is improving rapidly," Rance replied, "under the tutelage of Ari. It turns out that he has a remarkable memory, so the teleprompter instructor has been returned to the wild."

Henry laughed at that, something he didn't do often, unless there was a woman involved. "He even looks better," he said.

"That's because Ari instructed him to have his clothes pressed daily."

"Tell us about this Ari," Hank said. "Is he personable?"

"Not in the least," Rance replied. "He's blunt to the point of rudeness, and beyond. He has the uncomfortable faculty of always saying what he's thinking—unadorned."

"Is he trainable?"

"Not in that regard, I think, but he can learn anything. Mostly, he already has. He would be erudite, if he had any charm."

"I didn't know charm was a factor in erudition," Hank said.

"It is, if you want people to continue to listen to you. A recitation of facts gets pretty cold without charm."

Ari Kramer and Annie Lee stood offstage in a school auditorium and listened to Senator Joseph Box orate, except it was more like a chat among friends. Box at times gripped the podium with both hands; at others, he leaned on it with an elbow and emphasized with intensity in his voice but not volume.

"He's word perfect," Annie said.

"He certainly is. I don't think I could have recited my own speech as perfectly. The man should have been on the stage."

"He is on the stage," Annie said, "and will be until at least November."

"I was nervous about this being televised," Ari said, "but now I'm glad it is. Let's go and watch the rest on TV. I want to hear what the pundits have to say afterward."

They arrived in their hotel suite, sat on the edge of the bed, and switched on the TV in time to watch a standing ovation. The local anchorman came on and introduced a panel of New Hampshire newspaper editors.

"They loved him," Annie said. "Can I scratch your back?"

"It doesn't itch," Ari said.

"You shouldn't take everything I say literally."

"You mean, scratching my back is a euphemism?"

"As in, 'You scratch my back and I'll scratch yours.'"

"Does your back itch?"

"It's a different kind of itch," she said. "Why don't we start with rubbing your neck? You've grown to like that."

"Yes, please, do that."

She had just begun when Ari's computer rang and the person they knew as William Smith appeared on the screen. Ari sat down before the machine. "Did you watch?"

"I did, and frankly, I was amazed. So were my colleagues."

"He truly doesn't need the teleprompter. He has a prodigious memory."

"Who knew?"

"It isn't necessarily a sign of intellect, or even intelligence,"

Ari said. "It's more of a savant thing, like some mentally challenged people being able to do complicated math in their heads."

"We couldn't ask for more," Damien said. "In fact, we don't want more. You just keep him stocked with speeches and position papers."

"I will do that," Ari said.

"I got your new address. Are you settled in?"

"We are."

"I notice you're dressing better, too."

"Yes, I am. We both are."

"I'll say good night, then." Damien switched off.

Annie spoke up. "It sounds like they want more of a puppet than a candidate," she said.

"I think that's an accurate assessment," Ari replied. "Does that trouble you?"

"Not particularly, not at sixty dollars an hour, anyway. How long are we going to follow him around?"

"I think we'll watch him on TV after this. I don't want to stand around a lot of school halls, waiting for him to make a mistake."

"Good idea," she said.

"Weren't you rubbing my neck?"

35

An SUV pulled up to a Barnes & Noble in Buckhead, in north Atlanta, and Ida opened the door for Jamie.

"Aren't you going to check inside first?" Jamie asked.

"Already done by our local people. They've given us the go-ahead." She held up her cell phone. "These work."

Jamie got out of the vehicle and, braced by Ida and Lane, was marched into the bookstore.

An announcement came over a loudspeaker system. "Good evening, book lovers," a woman's voice said. "*New York Times* Pulitzer Prize–winning reporter Jamie Cox is about to speak about her new book, *Scandalous,* in our audience area. Please feel free to join us there now."

Jamie saw a few people emerge from the stacks and wander over to where she was being directed. They were getting subtle, but close inspection by the local security people. While she was being miked by her publicist, the bookstore manager gave a short introduction, then remarked that questions would be taken at the end of the talk. She turned the podium over to Jamie.

"Good evening," Jamie said to the crowd. "I thought you'd like to know that, earlier today, at LaGuardia Airport, two men entered the ladies' room I was using, pulled guns, and were disarmed by my security guards. They fled on foot and have not yet been found. I do hope that none of you are armed, but if you are, you should know that women with guns are watching you."

This got a laugh from the audience and seemed to relax them.

Jamie spoke for fifteen minutes about her book and the events recounted in it, then took questions for another fifteen minutes. She then sat at a table while the audience lined up to have their books signed.

Later, she asked the bookstore manager how they had done.

"Very well," the woman replied, "a hundred and twenty-two sales, much better than average."

Shortly afterward, she was hustled into the SUV and driven back to the St. Regis, where she had dinner in her suite with her publicist and a publisher's representative.

"Tomorrow night," Jamie said to Lane later, "do you think I could have dinner in the hotel restaurant? I'd feel less like a caged animal."

"Tomorrow night we're in Palm Beach, where you're speaking to an arts society, and you're staying at the Brazilian Court. If everything is quiet, you can dine in the restaurant, which is very good."

"Oh, thank you," Jamie replied, then got ready for bed.

Stone, Dino, and Viv had dinner at Patroon.

"What do you have on the two guys at LaGuardia?" Stone asked Dino.

"They had an escape route planned, so we didn't get them.

We got their weapons, though, from the trash receptacle in the ladies' room."

"Any prints?"

"Nothing. They had apparently handled the weapons only when wearing latex gloves. We found some talc residue that's used to make the gloves easier to pull on."

"Were they Italian?"

"Why do you ask?" Dino said.

"Because the Thomases are really the Tommassinis."

"The descriptions from witnesses were generic—nothing about ethnic appearance. One of the witnesses thought one of the shooters was a woman."

"So much for eyewitnesses," Stone said. "Anything unusual about the weapons?"

"Both were Glocks with homemade silencers, apparently never fired. They were originally sold at a gun shop in Virginia last year."

"How about the hit on Sherry?"

"We found a single shell casing behind the parapet on a house across the street. A .22 long rifle, chosen for a head shot."

"So everybody's a pro."

"People like the Thomases don't hire their assassins at the unemployment office. Like you say, everybody's a pro."

Viv spoke up. "All went smoothly for Jamie in Atlanta."

"I'm glad to hear it," Stone said. "The way you've arranged the signing audiences is very good."

"Thank you. I wish we'd started her out at Teterboro, instead of LaGuardia. That was my mistake; I didn't believe they would try it."

"How about other people at the *Times*? Any threats?"

"All the principals are under guard. The computer kid, Huey, vanished. Apparently he went underground."

"I'll bet he's in his new apartment, which is under construction."

Viv looked at him, surprised. "Nobody at the *Times* told us about that."

"Probably because he didn't tell anybody at the *Times* about it."

"Then we're guarding what must be his old apartment."

Stone wrote the new address down and gave it to her. "Be discreet," he said. "The kid would probably rather not know your people are there."

Annie Lee awoke, naked, in the king-sized bed in Ari's suite. He was sitting at his computer in his pajamas. She reflected on their night together. Having sex with someone who didn't like to be touched was a new experience for her. Still, if he had been awkward, he had also been enthusiastic, once they started. She was not all that experienced herself, having a strict father.

She got up, put on a robe, then went and stood behind him.

"William called," Ari said. "He had the results of some private, overnight polling: it wasn't a big sample, but it shows Box with a six-point lead over the incumbent Republican congressman, who won the seat last time by twenty-two points."

"Wow, that's progress!" Annie said.

He turned to face her and, to her surprise, put his hands on her hips. "What did you think about the sex last night?" he asked. "It was my first time, so I don't have anything to compare it to."

"I've only had sex twice before," she said, "so I'm not way ahead of you."

"What did you think, compared to the other two?"

"The other *one,*" she said. "Twice."

"Okay."

"I thought it was very, very good," she said. "It will only get better, as we become accustomed to each other. I warn you, you are now subject to being murdered by my father, should he ever suspect us of this."

He pushed her back and looked into her face. "Was that a joke?" he asked. "I'm never sure when you're joking."

"It wasn't entirely a joke," she replied.

"I don't understand. What does that mean?"

"It means that, should we ever find ourselves in the company of my father, you should not touch me or speak to me affectionately or do anything else that might allow him to think for a moment that we have had sex."

"I understand that," Ari said. "Maybe you should just keep me away from him."

"Good advice," she said.

36

Elise Grant went into Henry Thomas's office without knocking, as she had been instructed to do, and set his mail on his desk. He was meeting with his grandson, Hank, and Rance Damien. They immediately switched to a Sicilian dialect, which they did not know she understood—her mother being Sicilian. She had failed to note that language skill on her employment application and was not sorry. She had heard some pretty good stuff.

"Sit down for a moment, Elise," Henry said in English. "I want you to take a letter for me when we're done."

"Yes, sir," she replied, taking a chair against the wall.

They switched back to Sicilian. "I understand everything went wrong yesterday," Henry said. "Rance?"

Damien shifted in his chair. "Our people did not realize that Cox had security that would follow her into the ladies' room," he said. "They stuck to the plan and got away, but left their weapons, which were clean in every respect. We had more luck with the girl, Sherry."

Elise wanted to pee in her pants, but she held on.

"We had a man across the street who shot her in the head.

But she survived and is at Bellevue, in a protected ward, so we can't get at her."

"She survived a head shot?" Hank asked, incredulous.

"It was a small-caliber round, to keep the noise down—and I didn't want her head exploding like a watermelon. The angle wasn't right."

"Can we get at her?"

"No, her area is under twenty-four-hour police guard. There are a couple of murder witnesses in the ward, too."

Henry took a sip of water from a glass, then turned to Elise. "Please get me some ice for my water."

Elise rose, went to the door, then ran for the ladies' room, getting there just in time. Then she ran to the ice machine, filled an ice bucket, and went back to Henry's office, where they were still speaking Sicilian. She poured him a fresh glass, then resumed her seat.

"What about Barrington?"

"He's a tough nut to crack," Damien said. "I got the plans for his house from the city, and the house is armored."

"'Armored'?" Hank asked. "The whole house?"

"Believe it or not. He has some sort of government connection. One of our people got a good look at the Bentley, and that's armored, too."

"Keep at it," Henry said. "Now get out of here, both of you." He turned to Elise. "Now."

She took a seat next to his desk and got her pad ready. He began to speak, still in Sicilian.

"Excuse me, Mr. Thomas," she said. "You're speaking another language I can't understand."

"Sorry," Thomas said. He dictated the letter in English.

Elise went back to her desk, typed and printed the letter, got it signed, ran it through the postage meter, and put it in her out box.

She was trembling. She and Sherry had known each other fairly well at work, had had lunch a couple of times. She had been in a downstairs department at the time. Now, transferred to the executive offices, she was learning who she worked for, and she feared Sherry might be dead. She was afraid to quit her job.

After work, she bought some flowers at a Korean market and took a taxi to Bellevue. She couldn't find the ward on the hall-way directory, but she saw two policemen get onto an elevator and followed them. They emerged into a hallway, mostly blocked by a steel desk, manned by a uniformed officer. She approached and gave him Sherry's name and her own.

He consulted a list. "You're not approved," the officer said. "State your business."

"Sherry and I worked together. She's not expecting me, but she'll want to see me."

"Let me see your driver's license," he said. A nurse passed through, and he gave her the license. "See if the girl wants to see this lady."

A minute later, Elise was seated at Sherry's bedside.

"Hello, Elise. This is a surprise," Sherry said.

"How are you?"

"Better than I should be. I still have a headache, but at least they didn't cut my hair off. How did you find me?"

"I overheard a conversation among the bosses, and your name came up. Why are they trying to kill you?"

"Probably because they think I know more about them than I do."

"I know a *lot* about them," Elise said. "They speak all the time in Sicilian and my mother is Sicilian. I grew up speaking it at home with her and my grandmother."

"You should get out of there," Sherry said.

"I'm afraid to. They could come looking for me, like you."

"You have a point. Listen, Elise," Sherry said, lowering her voice. "Would you speak to someone I know and tell him about this?"

"Who? I don't want to get caught at it."

"He lives over in Turtle Bay, you know it?"

"Yes. Katharine Hepburn lived there, didn't she?"

"That's the one. He has ways of getting in and out of his house without being seen."

"Who is he?"

"A lawyer named Stone Barrington. My boyfriend is living there at the moment. His name is Bob Cantor."

"I've heard them mention both of those names, but I couldn't figure out who they were."

"Well," Sherry said, looking toward the door, "here's Bob now." She made the introduction.

Elise got out of a cab at a corner of Third Avenue, then she stood in front of a flower shop and waited, as she had been instructed. A moment later, Bob Cantor appeared and took her through a door, and after a walk down a tunnel, into a garage. They went up a floor and into a living room, where Bob took her coat.

"I can hear him on the phone," Bob said. "Have a seat, and I'll come get you when he's finished with the call."

Elise sat down and looked around her. It was a handsome room, she thought, with a lot of nice pictures. For just a moment, she had to fight off panic. What if, in spite of all the precautions, some of the Thomases' people had seen her come here? Maybe they had followed her from the hospital.

Bob came back. "This way," he said, and he showed her into a smaller room with a lot of books. Two men sat in chairs before the fireplace, and they stood up as she entered.

"Elise," Bob said, "this is Stone Barrington." He indicated the taller of the two men. "And this is Dino Bacchetti, who is the police commissioner of New York."

Elise heaved a sigh of relief. "May I use your bathroom, please?"

37

While Elise was in the bathroom, Stone called Jamie Cox.

"Hello?"

"Hi, do you have a few free minutes to listen to somebody?"

"Sure. Who is it?"

"I'll leave the phone on speaker, so you can hear our conversation. Later, you may want to ask her some questions. Take notes."

"All right."

Elise returned from the bathroom and sat down.

"Would you like something to drink, Elise?" Stone asked.

"Thank you, I'd like a bourbon and Diet Coke."

Stone winced, but made the drink and handed it to her. "A friend of mine, Jamie Cox, is on the phone. I'd like her to hear our conversation, if that's all right."

"The woman who wrote that big piece in the *Times*?"

"That's the one."

"It's fine." She took a swig of her bourbon and Diet Coke.

"Now," Stone said, "for Jamie's benefit, your name is Elise Grant, is that correct?"

"Yes." She spelled it for them.

"May I ask your age, Elise?"

"Twenty-four."

"And you work for H. Thomas & Son?"

"I do."

"How long have you worked there?"

"Almost two years. I started downstairs in accounting, then I got a promotion to legal, then I got moved upstairs to the executive offices about eight months ago."

"Who do you work for there?"

"There are five of us on the floor, and we all work for whoever needs us: Mr. Henry Thomas—he's the old one; his grandson, Hank Thomas, who used to be a congressman; and a relative—I'm not exactly sure how they're related, but he's family—Lawrance Damien. They call him Rance. Old Mr. Thomas's son, Jack, shot himself in the office, though I've always thought Rance had something to do with it."

"That's very interesting," Stone said. "We'll come back to that. Do you often overhear conversations among these three men?"

"All the time. You see, my grandparents came to this country when my mother was three years old. Grandpapa died when I was six, so I was raised by my mother and grandmother, and they always spoke Sicilian around the house. I didn't put the language on my employment application because I thought nobody spoke it, except in my family."

"Do the Thomases often speak in Sicilian?"

"Yes, whenever they don't want anyone to know what they're talking about, like earlier today."

"And you were there?"

"Yes. Old Mr. Thomas asked me to take a letter after they were done and to sit down and wait, so I heard their entire conversation."

"What did they talk about?" Stone asked.

"About killing you and Bob and Sherry. Oh, and about trying to kill Ms. Cox, in the ladies' room."

"Holy shit," Dino muttered, the first time he had spoken.

"Yes, that's pretty much what I thought, too," Elise said, "but I managed to keep a straight face. It was the first time I heard that Sherry was still alive. She took some time off, and they sent her someplace in Maine, and none of us heard from her again. I thought they had done her in."

"Is that how you learned that she was in the hospital?"

"That's exactly how."

Dino spoke up again, but in Sicilian. "Can you tell me what they said in Sicilian?"

Elise laid out their conversation.

"Thank you, that's good," Dino said. "She speaks very good Sicilian, so she won't have got it wrong. Elise, please repeat what you just said, in English, for the benefit of the uneducated present."

Elise laughed, then recounted the conversation in English.

"Holy shit," Jamie said over the phone.

For two hours, they questioned Elise, and she happily told them everything she knew. They broke for dinner, and Dino sat next to her.

"Elise," he said, "would you keep doing what you're doing? And report it back to us?"

"You mean, like a spy?" she asked.

"We call it a confidential informant, and you'll be paid for your efforts."

"Sure, I guess."

"Dino," Bob Cantor interjected, "I think it's better if Elise plants some bugs for us and we record everything. It's safer for her, and we'll have a record that she can confirm."

"I didn't hear that," Dino said, "and I don't hear things like that, unless I have a warrant in my hands." He stood up. "If you'll excuse me, I have to get home."

Stone stood also. "I'll see Dino out," he said, and they both left the room.

"I have some equipment that will work," Bob said, undeterred.

"Bob," Elise said, "they have some experts come in about once a week to sweep the place. Won't they find your equipment?"

"I'll set it up so that you can turn the bugs on and off with an app on your iPhone. That way, when you know the sweepers are coming, you can switch them off. They won't be detected because the equipment is not broadcasting."

"That sounds good," she said.

"Also, the bugs will have to be replaced every three days, since that's as long as the batteries last."

"Okay," she said.

"You'll want to be very sure that you aren't seen replacing them."

"I'll do it at lunch. Almost everybody goes out, but I usually have a sandwich at my desk."

"Good."

Stone came back. "I trust that part of the conversation is over," he said.

"Can I go to see Sherry again?" Elise asked.

"That's not a good idea," Stone said. "Every time you go into the hospital, it increases the risk that you'll be seen there. In a few days, Sherry will be discharged from the hospital, then you can come see her here, getting in the way you did today. That will also give us a chance to debrief you."

"I understand, and that's fine," Elise replied. "Tell me, will I have to testify in court against the Thomases?"

"Eventually," Stone said. "When that happens, though, they'll be in jail and won't be able to hurt you."

"I don't think you understand how much reach the Thomases have," Elise said. "They can get at anybody. I'll never be safe again."

"I understand your feelings, Elise, but I'll see that Dino makes it his personal mission to keep you safe. Where does your family live?"

"There's only my mother now, and she lives in Little Italy."

"Elise," Stone said, "it's important that you not visit her in Little Italy."

"But that's where she lives."

"You can invite her to lunch uptown as often as you like, but when you do that, don't either of you speak in Sicilian."

"I get your point," she said. "Can I tell my mother what I'm doing?"

"It's better that she doesn't know until this is all over."

"When will that be?" Elise asked.

"Maybe several months," Stone replied.

"I'll also give you a special cell phone, so you can contact us, if you need to," Bob said.

Elise nodded, and went back to her dessert.

38

After dinner, Bob took Elise downstairs and explained the bugging equipment to her. Then he took her out of the building, where she could get a cab home.

Stone went upstairs, undressed for bed, and called Jamie.

"Hello?"

"How'd your talk go?" Stone asked.

"Very well. I've discovered that they all usually ask the same questions, so I can polish my answers."

"What did you think of Elise?"

"I can't believe it. Is she for real?"

"She certainly is."

"I'll file a new story tomorrow."

"Wait a minute. You can't use anything she told us tonight."

"Why not?"

"Because you'll blow her and get her killed. You're going to have to be patient. Don't even tell anybody at the *Times* about this."

"I've already told Scott Berger," she said, "but I didn't tell him who she is."

"Then call him back right now, tell him you can't publish yet

191

and why, and swear him to secrecy. Stress that she's already a police informant, and you can't blow her."

"All right."

"Good night, then."

"What, no phone sex?" she asked.

"You've just frightened me and made me incapable."

"I'll try to be gentler next time."

They both hung up.

Shortly after eight AM the following morning, in Atlanta, a florist's delivery van pulled up to a trade entrance at the St. Regis Hotel, and the driver removed a box from the rear of the van and walked it inside to the front desk.

"May I help you?" a clerk asked.

The man set the box on the front desk. "Flower delivery for a Miss Jamie Cox," he said, giving the clerk a clipboard so that he could sign for the flowers.

"It will go up with her breakfast," the clerk said.

"What time will she have it in hand?" the driver asked.

The clerk checked a room service schedule. "She ordered breakfast for eight-thirty," he replied.

"Thank you." The driver returned to his van and made a phone call. "They're going up with her breakfast at eight-thirty," he said and then hung up.

Back at the front desk, the desk clerk supervisor came back from the men's room and found the flower box. "Who are these for?" he asked.

"Jamie Cox," the man replied. "Room service will pick them up and deliver them with her breakfast."

"Too late," the supervisor said. "Miss Cox checked out half an hour ago. She had a flight to make. Who delivered them?"

"I don't know which shop," the clerk said, "and I didn't recognize the driver. What should I do with them?"

"Put them with the other flowers that are collected every morning. They'll go to a hospital later today."

The clerk opened a closet door and placed the box on a shelf.

Jamie boarded the Citation at PDK Airport, buckled herself in, and opened a fresh copy of the *New York Times*. The pilot closed and locked the cabin door, then went to the cockpit and started the engines. Fifteen minutes later, the airplane took off for Palm Beach.

At the St. Regis the desk clerk left his post for a moment and went into a back room. As he closed the door behind him, he heard a loud noise from the front desk. He opened the door to find a cloud of smoke and a closet door lying atop the desk. He looked around and found no corpses, then he picked up a phone from the floor and called security.

Elise followed Bob's instructions: she turned up for work exactly when she did every day and did the things she always did.

She distributed the mail, newspapers, and magazines, then went back to her desk and waited to be called in. She was not called in.

At lunchtime she ate half her sandwich and watched the Thomases and Damien leave, then she went into each office, starting with Henry's. She peeled off the tape on the bottom of the bug and placed it under the center drawer of each desk, then followed suit in Hank's and Damien's offices.

She had one more device to plant: the master unit, which controlled the bugs, received their transmissions, and sent them to a secret website on the Internet. She placed it under a colleague's desk, two desks away; then she went back, switched on her iPhone, and opened the new app Bob had installed. It was disguised as a calorie counter. She switched on the master and the three devices, and the app ran a check on each, confirming that they were operational.

Then she finished her sandwich.

Just after three PM Elise was called into Rance Damien's office.

"Yes, sir?" she said.

"Why didn't I get a *Times* this morning?" he asked.

Before she could answer, there was a knock on the door.

"Come in!" Damien shouted.

A man in coveralls, carrying a toolbox, walked in. "May I sweep now, Mr. Damien?"

"Yes, go ahead."

"I'll get you a *Times*," Elise said and fled the office. She went to her desk, opened her handbag, found her iPhone and went to the calorie app. As quickly as possible, she switched off the base unit and all three bugs, then she grabbed a *Times* and hurried back into Damien's office. "Here you are, sir."

But he was already reading a *Times*. "That's all right, I found it on the floor."

"I'm very sorry, sir." As she closed the door she looked back to see the electronics man, wearing earphones and walking around the office, with some sort of wand in his hand.

"Any luck?" Damien asked the man.

"I got a single beep, but it didn't recur. Probably some trash from a passing car or truck down on the street," the man replied.

"Okay, wrap it up," Damien said.

"Yes, sir."

Elise went back to her desk and watched as the man went from office to office. No alarms were raised.

At her desk in New York, Viv Bacchetti took a call from Atlanta. "Yes?"

"We had a bomb delivered to Jamie Cox at the St. Regis this morning," a man said.

"Good God! Was she hurt?"

"Lane and Ida got her out early. She had a noon thing in Palm Beach. No one was injured at the hotel. The bomb went off in a closet near the front desk."

"Get hold of Lane," Viv said. "Tell her what happened and to shake up all of the day's plans. Go to plan B and, if necessary, plan C."

"Right."

Viv put down the phone and breathed deeply until her pulse returned to normal.

39

Stone said goodbye to Viv and put down the phone. He didn't need to think long before calling Dino.

"Bacchetti."

"It's Stone. Have you spoken to Viv?"

"Not yet. I got a message, but I haven't had time to return her call."

"When you do, she's going to tell you that somebody delivered a bomb in a box of flowers to Jamie in Atlanta."

"Was she hurt?"

"Fortunately, she had already left the hotel."

"I'm glad to hear it. I'll call the Atlanta cops."

"I'm sure Viv or the St. Regis has already done that," Stone said.

"Yeah, I guess."

"Dino, I know you'd like to take the time to sew this case up seven ways, but I think we're all out of time. The Thomases are just going to keep going until Jamie, Sherry, and Elise are all dead. Maybe me, too."

"You have a point."

"I think it's time to go to the D.A. with what you've got."

"Well, let's take a look at that," Dino said. "Sherry has a dark story to tell, but nothing that would get a conviction in court. Whatever Jamie knows, the world knows already, so there's no point in trying to kill her. So all we've got is Elise. If the D.A. will get us a warrant based on her story, we'll go with Bob Cantor's idea and use his new equipment to bug everything they say. Then maybe we can get a conviction on some attempted murder charges."

"Back up there a minute," Stone said. "They've already shot Sherry in the head and show no inclination to stop trying. A couple of hours ago they were still trying to kill Jamie, and sending a rank amateur like Elise in there to bug the place could get her killed, too."

"We could wire her up, so that what she overhears can be recorded."

"And if they search her, she'll never leave the building alive. What you've already got, though, is the conversation Elise heard about them trying to kill all of us, and that, combined with whatever she might have heard before, might be enough to get a conviction."

"Well, she'd be a damned fine witness," Dino said.

"Then go see Ken Burrows."

"All right," Dino said. "I'll try to get in there this afternoon."

"Good idea."

"Oh, I almost forgot. The hospital detail just called, and Sherry can be released today. They want to know where to send her on a stretcher."

"To my house," Stone said. "We can make her comfortable here, and I'll hire a nurse to administer her medications and to be here in the event of an emergency."

"Okay. You'd better get the place ready for her." Dino hung up.

Stone called in Joan. "We're going to have a visitor today, and she'll be staying with us for a week or two. She'll be arriving on a stretcher."

"This is Sherry, then?"

"Right. Ask the housekeepers to get Peter's old suite ready for her and to make room for a hospital bed. Then ask my doctor to recommend a private nursing service and a place to rent a hospital bed."

"Is she going to need a lot of monitoring devices?"

"If she does, we'll hear about it before she arrives."

"Okay, I'll get right on it," she said.

Rance Damien, out of an abundance of caution, was reviewing the personnel files of the five secretaries who worked on the executive floor. He stopped when he came to a name: D'Orio. That was the maiden name of Elise Grant's mother. He buzzed Elise, and she came in.

"Have a seat, Elise," he said pleasantly. She did so. "I was just reviewing everybody's files for vaccinations, and I see that your mother's maiden name is D'Orio."

"Yes, sir, that's right."

"Where was she born?"

"In Italy, but she came to this country when she was only three years old."

"Did she speak any Italian?"

"She once told me that her mother and father wanted the

family to be American, so they had a rule of speaking only English at home. Both my grandparents already spoke English, and they didn't want my mother to be at a disadvantage when she started school."

"Did your mother retain any of her Italian?"

"No, we only spoke English at home. My father was British, and I was sometimes accused by schoolmates of having an English accent."

"Did you ever study foreign languages?"

"I took French in high school, but I was never really conversant. When I went to Paris, I could ask questions in French, but I couldn't understand the answers."

"Have you ever visited Italy?"

"I spent a week in Rome on a tour when I was in college."

Damien suddenly switched to Sicilian. "If you're lying to me, I'll have your tongue cut out," he said, with a small smile.

"Sir?"

"Didn't you understand me?" he asked in English.

"No, sir."

"It's not important, Elise. Thanks for coming in."

"Any time, sir. When are we getting vaccinations?"

"That's in the planning stages. We'll let you know."

Elise returned to her desk and sat down. She made a point of going on with her work, as if nothing had happened, but she was having a hard time controlling her shaking. Something had happened. Damien was now suspicious of her. She hoped Bob had overheard her conversation with him through his bug.

. . .

When she got home she was about to call Bob Cantor when her new cell phone rang. "Hello?"

"Don't say anything," Bob said, "until I sweep your apartment. Say I got the wrong number, then hang up."

"I'm sorry, ma'am, but you've got the wrong number. That's all right, goodbye." She hung up and switched on the TV news. A few minutes later there was a soft rap on her door. When she opened it, Bob Cantor came in with a toolbox and a finger to his lips. He motioned for her to sit down and say nothing.

She watched the news but retained none of it. A few minutes later Bob came back and motioned her to follow him outside into the hall.

"What did you find?" she asked.

"Bugs in every room," he whispered. "I heard your conversation with Damien and thought something might be up."

"What do you want me to do?"

"Go back inside, fix yourself some dinner, watch TV for a while, then pack a couple of suitcases. We're going to get you out of here tonight."

Elise did as she was told.

40

The nurse arrived first, reminding Stone of Mrs. Doubt-fire, save the Scottish accent. She took charge and began issuing rapid instructions to Joan.

Joan came into Stone's office with a list. "This is what that woman wants me to get!" she nearly shouted.

"Joan," Stone said soothingly, "don't argue with her, just get what she wants. Do we need monitoring equipment?"

"No. And she doesn't want Bob Cantor sleeping in the same room."

"By the way, Bob called, and we're going to have to put up Elise Grant for a while, so please ask Helene to get a room ready for her right away."

"Who's next? The cast of *Cats*?"

"She'll be here any minute."

"There's always a room ready," Joan said. "We'll put her next to Sherry. They can keep each other company."

Dino turned up next, and Stone took him up to the study and gave him a stiff drink, which he seemed to need.

"Tell me," Stone said, suspecting bad news.

"Bad news," Dino said. "Ken Burrows is holding us back. He might as well have an anchor out."

"What's his problem?"

"He says that Elise's story is not enough to get a judge to issue a warrant for the executive offices of a major investment bank."

"Does that translate into a major campaign donation?"

"I wouldn't be shocked to learn that," Dino said. "The Thomases are in half of the hip pockets in the city."

"Bob Cantor is going to be here any minute with Elise, and we can't let her go back to work at H. Thomas."

"She seemed to be doing pretty well."

"She's not an undercover cop, Dino, or a CIA operative. She's a twenty-four-year-old woman—a brave one, I'll grant you—but with no tradecraft. She'll get nervous, make a mistake, and there goes your witness."

Bob and Elise entered the study as if on cue. Stone made them each a drink. "Now what's going on?" Stone asked.

"I think Rance Damien is onto me," Elise said. "He went through my personnel file and found that my mother's maiden name is D'Orio, and he questioned me closely about both her knowledge of Italian and mine. I think I held him off, but . . ."

"But suddenly, her apartment is bugged," Bob said.

"Since when?"

"I don't know, but I don't like coincidences."

"Who does?" Dino asked.

"Oh, God," Elise said suddenly.

"What's wrong?"

"I forgot to turn off the answering machine that my mother gave me. If my mother calls, she'll leave a message in Sicilian."

"And the bugs will pick it up," Bob said. "Give me your keys."

Elise handed them over.

"I'll be back in twenty minutes," Bob said. He took a swig of his drink and left.

"Did you hear anything new today, Elise?" Dino asked.

"No, not a word."

"I had a talk with the district attorney today," Dino said, "and he doesn't think we have enough to get a warrant for bugging the H. Thomas offices."

"If I don't show up for work tomorrow, Damien will know something's wrong," she said.

"We don't think you should go back to work in any case," Stone said. "It's getting too dangerous for you."

"That's a relief," she replied.

They drank and chatted for a few minutes, then Bob Cantor returned.

"Well?" Dino asked.

"There was a message on the machine: in Sicilian. They'll have a voice-activated recorder picking up any sound. Elise is blown."

"It doesn't matter," Stone said. "We were going to assume that she was, anyway."

The doorbell rang, and Fred came into the study. "The lady on the stretcher is here," he said. "Mrs. Doubtfire has taken charge upstairs."

"I believe her actual name is Miss Hartley," Stone said. "We'd all better get used to calling her that, or we'll slip up, and I don't want to be there when that happens."

"Nor do I, sir," Fred said.

"I'd better go up and see her," Bob said.

"Don't stay too long, Bob," Stone interjected. "Mrs. Dou . . . ah, Miss Hartley has nixed your sleeping in Sherry's room."

"What is she, a nun?" Bob asked. He didn't wait for an answer.

Stone called Dino into the living room for a moment, leaving Elise alone. "It occurs to me that we'd better get Elise's mother out of her apartment. She'll be in trouble the minute they hear her message in Sicilian."

"Do you have room here for anyone else?" Dino asked.

"She can bunk in with her daughter, but now that you mention it, the traffic is getting a little heavy around here."

"I'll see what I can do about moving them into a safe house," Dino said. "We keep a few places for witness protection, and I did hire her as a confidential informant."

"Good idea." They went back into the study. "Elise, we think we should bring your mother here tonight. I can send you and Fred downtown in my car to pick her up. Will you call her and explain everything?"

"Sure," Elise said, "and thanks for thinking of that." She picked up the study phone and dialed a number. "No answer," Elise said. "I'll try her cell." She dialed another number. "Mom?" she said, then lapsed into Sicilian. She stopped and covered the receiver. "Should she go back to her apartment?" she asked.

"No," Dino said firmly. "Where is she now?"

"She just got out of a movie on Sixth Avenue, at Eighth Street."

"I'll have an unmarked car pick her up. Tell her to stay near the box office."

Elise spoke to her mother in Sicilian at some length. Finally, she said goodbye and hung up. "She took some convincing," she said, "but she'll be there."

Dino got on the phone and gave the orders. "Tell them to call me when they've got her aboard." He accepted another drink from Stone.

"She'll be all right here for a day or two," Elise said. "She and I wear the same size of everything, so she can wear my clothes."

"Tomorrow, we'll send her to her apartment with a police-woman to escort her," Dino said, "so she can pick up some things."

Bob Cantor came back. "Sherry's already out," he said. "I think Mrs. . . . Miss Hartley gave her something."

"Bob," Elise said, "I just thought of something."

"What's that?"

"I forgot to turn off your bugs before I left the office today."

Dino brightened. "Maybe we'll hear something we can use, even if not in court."

"I've got the bugs on a recorder," Bob said.

"Something else," Elise said. "If we pick anything up, it could be in Sicilian, so you'll need either my mother or me to translate for you."

"Good," Dino said. "My Sicilian is pretty rusty." His cell phone rang. "Bacchetti." His brow furrowed. "Where exactly are you? Keep looking." He hung up and turned to Elise. "My cops can't find your mother at the theater."

41

Elise ran to the phone and dialed her mother's cell phone. "Mom, call me immediately, please." She hung up. "No answer. I left her a voice mail. I'll text her, too." She sent the text, then sat down to wait.

"Let's not get too excited," Stone said. "There may be a good reason she didn't answer."

"I have this awful feeling," Elise said. "This is all my fault; if I hadn't left my answering machine on . . ."

Dino's phone rang. "Bacchetti." He listened. "Your instructions are the same." He hung up.

Before he could speak, Elise's phone rang. "Mom?" She lapsed into Sicilian, then finally hung up. "She went back inside to use the ladies' room, and there was no signal in there. They're on the way here now."

Stone asked Fred to meet her in the garage and bring her up to the study. "All right," he said to the room, "everybody's safe now. We'll have some dinner when she gets here. Elise, what's your mother's name?"

"Elena Grant."

. . .

Shortly, Fred entered the study with Elena, and Elise introduced everybody. Elena recognized Dino and let loose with a stream of Sicilian, while Dino tried gamely to keep up.

"Mom," Elise said. "Let's speak English."

"Sure," Elena said. "His Sicilian is pretty spotty, anyway."

"It's been a long time," Dino said defensively.

Elise took her mother into the living room and spent several minutes explaining what was going on, then dinner was served, and they all sat down.

Dino put the phone down and picked up his after-dinner cognac. "Okay, I've nailed down a hotel suite for them over on Lex, not so far away. They can move in tomorrow morning."

"That's good news," Stone said.

"I had a call from the D.A.," Dino said, "but I didn't return it. I'll let the son of a bitch wait until tomorrow morning. There's nothing he can do tonight, anyway."

"Tell him we have a growing crowd of fugitives from Thomas justice," Stone said.

"I don't think that would move him."

"What would move him?"

"Maybe if the Thomases canceled their campaign contribution."

Stone laughed. "That sounds like our D.A."

. . .

Stone was in bed when Jamie called. "I was just wondering about you," he said.

"Wondering if I was dead or alive? Well, I'm alive, by the grace of God. No exploding flowers today. Maybe they've lost track of me."

"Don't count on that. Listen to your security people, they've done a great job so far."

"Well, I'm not in a coffin—not even in traction. I guess that's something."

"How are you handling the road?"

"It's wearing," she said. "I don't care how good the food is. You may find a little more of me to grab hold of when I get back."

"I won't complain."

"How about some phone sex?" she asked.

"I'll wait for the real thing."

"You just want me super-horny when I get home," she replied.

"That's a nice thought." He brought her up to date on the day's events.

"How many people is that staying at your house?"

"I've lost count. Two of them are moving into a police safe house tomorrow, that's a start."

"When I get home, can we go somewhere?"

"I thought you were homesick."

"I'll get over it. Didn't you say you have a house in L.A.?"

"I do."

"That might be fun."

"It would be. Let's see where this whole business goes before we make travel plans."

"Oh, okay. Well, if there's no phone sex in the offing, I'm going to sleep."

"Do it well." They hung up.

The following morning Stone woke later than usual. When he got to his office, Joan announced that Elise and her mother had just left, under the care of Fred.

"I'm moving Mrs. Doubtfire to Elise's room," she said.

"Don't call her that, or I'll start doing it."

"I've already called her that, and she loved it. First time I've seen her smile. She was going to sleep on a cot in Sherry's room, but Sherry drew the line there."

"I haven't been up to see her yet. How's she doing?"

"Sitting up in a chair and talking a blue streak. She's happiest when Bob is there."

"I expect he's happier, too."

Rance Damien went into Henry's office and found Hank already there. "I've got some bad news," he said in Sicilian.

"Now what?" Henry asked.

"I became suspicious of Elise, so I had her apartment wired yesterday. She came home from work, but apparently went out after that."

"So what's the bad news?" Hank asked.

"Her mother called and left a message—in Sicilian."

The Thomases let that sink in for a moment. "Can we talk here?" Henry asked.

Rance took Bob Cantor's bugs from his pocket and placed them on the desk. "We can now," he said. "My people found these in our offices last night."

Henry looked at the hardware as if it were a nest of poisonous spiders. "How long have they been here?"

"There's no way to tell," Rance replied. "The point is, Elise understands Sicilian. How many times have we used it when she was in the room?"

Everybody thought about it. "Only once, I think," Henry said. "She was waiting to take a letter."

"What did we talk about on that occasion?" Hank asked.

"Far too much," Rance said.

"Who was listening to these bugs?"

"My best guess is Cantor," Rance said, "but that's only a guess. Could be the police or the D.A."

"Maybe Barrington?"

"Maybe. If Barrington was listening, then Dino Bacchetti heard it, too."

"I had a call this morning," Hank said. "Bacchetti had a meeting with the D.A. yesterday."

"That may not have been about us," Rance pointed out.

"Let's assume that it was about us," Henry replied. "What's our next move?"

Hank looked at his grandfather. "Is that buyout offer we had still on the table?"

"Could be," Henry said.

"Then we should explore that possibility."

"I'll make a call," Henry said. "What if it isn't still on the table?"

"Then we'd better start thinking about our exit strategies," Rance said.

42

Stone went upstairs to see Sherry and found her doing the *Times* crossword. A good sign, he reckoned.

"You seem to be feeling better," he said.

"Thanks to you and Bob. I've got a new piece of bone in my skull, courtesy of my surgeon, and my ability to do the crossword seems to have improved. I recommend a bullet in the head to everybody."

Bob sat, dozing, in a chair in the corner.

"Can I borrow him for a minute?" he asked.

"Well," she said, looking at her sleeping boyfriend, "he isn't doing me much good right now. Go ahead, take him."

Stone shook Bob by the shoulder. He woke up, wide-eyed. "I thought you were a Thomas," he said.

"Let's go talk for a minute," Stone said, and Bob followed him into the hallway.

"What's up?"

"We don't seem to be getting anywhere. Sherry, Elise, and her mother are still in danger, and the D.A. doesn't buy Elise's testimony as sufficient for getting a warrant to bug the Thomases, let alone convict them."

"My bugs have gone dead, too," Bob said.

"I thought you might have something in mind," Stone said. "Something you might not want to share with me."

"Gotcha," Bob said. "I have dreams about machine-gunning them all."

"Something a little more subtle, perhaps."

"I'll give it some thought," Bob said.

"Don't get back to me," Stone replied, then sent Bob back in with Sherry.

When Stone was back at his desk, Joan buzzed. "Jamie on line one."

Stone picked up the phone. "You're up early," he said.

"I've been thinking."

"Tell me."

"If Dino's not getting anywhere with the D.A., why don't we plant a hand grenade under his ass?"

"That's an attractive thought. What do you have in mind?"

"Publishing the piece I wrote about what Elise Grant overheard the Thomases discussing. There's nothing the Thomases can do, except what they're already trying to do."

"Why don't I bring it up with Elise and see what she has to say?"

"You do that, then get back to me."

"Bye." Stone hung up the phone, then called Elise's throwaway cell.

"Good morning," she said.

"How are your new quarters?" he asked.

"Not bad. I mean, it's a hotel, not home. How long do you figure we might have to stay here?"

"I was just thinking about that," Stone said. "Dino isn't getting anywhere with the D.A. Jamie, however, called this morning and she has an idea that might shake things up."

"She wants to publish what I said, doesn't she?"

"She does, and she makes the point that doing so won't put you at any more risk than you are now."

"But it would rattle them to their core, wouldn't it? To see their own words in print?"

"That's the idea. Frightened people make mistakes."

"You tell Jamie to go ahead. I'm sure she took notes."

"She recorded you over the phone, and she's already written the piece."

"Tell her I'll look forward to reading it in tomorrow's *Times*."

"I'll do that. My best to your mother." He hung up and called Jamie.

"Yeah?"

"Elise is all for it. How do the paper's libel lawyers feel about it?"

"I've been on the phone with them and Scott for the past half hour. They're not happy, but they haven't vetoed it, either."

"Then go."

"I'm gone." She hung up.

Stone called Dino.

"Bacchetti."

"Just a heads-up for you."

"I'm listening."

"Jamie's piece on Elise is running in tomorrow's *Times*."

Dino laughed. "That should stick a firecracker up the D.A.'s ass."

"My thought is that the D.A. should hear about it when he reads it in the paper, not earlier."

"I haven't returned his call yet."

"Then don't."

"I have to. Anyway, I want to hear what he has to say."

"Let me know."

Dino put in the call to Ken Burrows.

"Yes, Dino?"

"I'm returning your call, Ken."

"Oh, yes. I wanted you to know: I'm not proceeding with a warrant for wiring the Thomases."

"What a shock," Dino said.

"Oh, don't be a smart-ass, Dino. I have to follow the law."

"Not asking for a warrant is not following the law," Dino pointed out. "If you ask for it, you might even get it."

"My best people think not."

"You ought to try listening to your conscience, instead of your 'best people,'" Dino said. "You might try making a decision all by yourself sometime."

"Good day," Burrows said, then hung up.

Dino called Stone back.

"Yes, Dino?"

"I spoke to Burrows. He says his best people have advised against getting a warrant."

"I'm shocked, *shocked*," Stone said.

"That's what I told him."

"Would you like to predict his actions when he reads tomorrow's *Times*?"

"I predict he'll call me and accuse me of giving the story to them."

"You have perfect deniability on that one."

"I guess I do, don't I?"

"Talk to you later." They hung up.

Bob Cantor was standing in Stone's doorway. He took a breath.

"Don't say it," Stone said. "Jamie is running her story on Elise in tomorrow's *Times*."

"I wish my bugs were still in place," Bob said. "I'd like to hear their reaction."

"So would I," Stone said.

43

Ari Kramer and Annie Lee sat on a bench in their Cambridge apartment, both naked, and watched Joe Box deliver a rousing speech to an audience of three thousand in Manchester, New Hampshire.

"You outdid yourself on this one," Annie said, stroking the inside of his thigh.

"I did, didn't I?" Ari replied, with his characteristic bluntness. "I believe the expression is, I knocked it out of the ball."

"That's ballpark," she corrected.

"You're becoming a pedant," Ari said.

"I am not. I'm just correcting a small error in your parlance that would damage your credibility if anyone but me heard it."

"I suppose I should be grateful," he said.

"I don't think you feel gratitude, Ari—not in the usual meaning of the word."

"I'd be grateful if you'd shut up about how I speak."

"No, you'd just get even angrier when I correct you."

"Why are you the arbiter of the quality of my speech?" he demanded.

"Because I'm all you've got," she said, moving her hand up farther.

Ari gave a little twitch as she neared home plate. "I'm grateful for what you just did," he said.

"That I can believe," Annie replied, continuing her exploration. They dived into the bed.

The Thomases and Damien sat in Henry's office and watched the Box speech on a large computer screen.

"I'm having trouble believing this," Henry said. "I've known the son of a bitch for a decade, and he's hardly ever missed an opportunity to say something awkward and turn people off. I was stunned when he was reelected."

"He's now got a nine-point lead over the incumbent in the Republican primary," Damien said.

"Yeah," Hank chimed in, "but that will disappear in the general election. Independents and young people are going to be harder to attract than your standard Republican voters."

"A good point," Damien said. "I'll see what I can do about it."

The couple had just come simultaneously for the first time, and they lay in each other's arms, panting.

"Oh my God," Annie said.

"If you're speaking to him, tell him I concur," Ari said.

His Skype ring nearly blasted them out of bed. Annie clutched a sheet over her breasts. "Can he see me?"

"He'll be able to, unless you get out of the bed," Ari said, "as soon as I answer."

She ran for the bathroom while Ari got into khakis and a polo shirt. "Yes, William?" he said, pressing a button.

"Good afternoon, Ari," the man said. The bandages that had been concealing his face were down to just one over his chin. Above that, his face was looking more normal.

"I hope you're well," Ari said, struggling to find a little sincerity.

"I'm very well, and so is Senator Box, if the speech I just watched is any measure."

"He's coming along very nicely," Ari said.

"I think we need to shift gears," Smith said.

"I'm sorry, I don't understand."

"It means we should take Senator Box to a higher level."

"What level do you mean? We have to get him nominated first."

"What I mean is: We've been appealing mostly to a Republican audience during the primary. Normally, we'd wait until after the primary, then begin appealing to independents, young people, and more conservative Democrats."

"I understand."

"But I don't think we should wait until after the primary, I think we should start now."

"I think that's a very good idea," Ari said.

"Perhaps he could say a kind word about Medicare," Smith said. "Perhaps even Obamacare."

"Health care is certainly going to be an important talking point in the general election," Ari agreed.

"He's speaking in Burlington tomorrow. That would be a good place to swing him more to the political center."

"I believe you're right," Ari replied. "I'll write him something tonight, and he can memorize it with his breakfast."

"Good, get right on it," Smith said. "I won't keep you any longer."

Ari signed off. He had already drafted a half dozen speeches of the kind Smith was asking for. He had only to touch up one for a Burlington audience.

Henry Thomas hung up the phone and grinned at his two companions. "They've made us a very good offer," he said. "I'll call them back in a few minutes and edge them up a little—less than they're expecting—and we'll be done."

"When do they want to close?"

"I haven't suggested a date; I don't want to sound anxious. I think they'll want to move quickly, though. We're at forty-two dollars a share. They think I'll come back with forty-eight, but I'll make it forty-six. I know we'd all like to have the extra two dollars, but if we get greedy we might delay or even blow the acquisition. After all, it's a cash offer. They've brought in a huge pile of overseas earnings, and they're itching to spend some of it."

"What are our personal obligations as managers of the company?" Hank asked. "How long do we have to stay? A year?"

"My guess is their final offer will come with a condition of our immediate departure."

"God, I'd love to be out from under," Hank said.

Henry's phone rang. "Yes? Hello, Harman. I'm listening." He listened, then said, "Hold the phone a minute, will you?" Henry covered the receiver. "The offer is $46.50 a share, closing within a week. He says they've already done their due diligence. And our duties end at closing."

Hank and Damien nodded.

"All right, Harman," Henry said. "Congratulations! You've got yourself the finest investment bank in the country. Just e-mail me a signed offer, I'll e-mail you back my signature, and we're done until closing." He said goodbye and hung up.

"Thanks for the extra fifty cents, Poppa," Hank said.

"Yes, sir," Damien echoed.

"So," Henry said, "what are you boys going to do?"

"I'm thinking Switzerland for a while," Hank said.

"It's someplace with no extradition treaty for me," Damien said. "I may hang around until the election."

"I'm staying right here," Henry said. "The house in the Hamptons in the summer, Aspen in the winter. I've got another season or two of skiing left in me."

44

tone, Dino, and Viv were at Brasserie Georgette, having just arrived.

"You'd better double the guard on the Grants," Stone said. "Jamie's story runs tomorrow in the *Times*."

"I have already done so," Dino replied.

"I'll double Jamie's guard, too," Viv said, reaching for her phone and making the call.

Stone's phone rang. "Hello?"

"It's Jamie."

"Viv, Dino, and I were just talking about you. All of it good."

"I'm delighted, but I have new news."

Stone looked around; nobody was too close. "I'll put you on speaker, to save me having to repeat it to Viv and Dino."

"Okay, ready?"

Stone pressed the button. "Ready."

"A reporter on our business page got a hot tip a few minutes ago. A preliminary agreement has been signed between H. Thomas & Son and DigiWorld, a hedge fund specializing in bank acquisitions."

"Who's buying whom?" Stone asked.

"DigiWorld is the buyer, at $46.50 a share, twenty-five percent over the stock price at closing."

"So the Thomases are getting richer," Stone said.

"The two remaining Thomases and a family member named Lawrance Damien own a majority of the shares."

"Well, your breaking story is going to put the fear of God into them, isn't it?"

"I can't imagine that it won't torpedo the acquisition, or at least lower the price significantly."

"It couldn't happen to a nicer bunch," Dino said.

"By the way," Viv chimed in, "I've already doubled your security. You'll have two outside men as well as the two inside women."

"Do you really think that's necessary, Viv?"

"It can't hurt," Viv replied.

"No, I guess it can't," Jamie agreed. "Well, I have some calls to make. Enjoy whatever dinner you're having wherever." She hung up.

"Well," Stone said, "if either of you has any H. Thomas shares, you'd better unload them on the foreign markets before bedtime."

"None here," Dino said.

"None here, either," Viv echoed.

"Have you got people on Huey, our computer whiz?" Stone asked Viv.

"Yes, and I'd better double that, too. I think Huey should know, too," Viv said.

Stone dialed the number.

"Huey here."

"Hi, Huey, it's Stone Barrington."

"Hey, Stone. You should see my new place. It's coming right along."

"Huey, have you been contemplating a vacation lately?"

"No, why do you ask?"

"Because this would be a good time to contemplate one. Two major stories about the Thomases are breaking tomorrow morning, and they are going to be very upset when they read them."

"Then they'll think I'm in my old place, not here," Huey said. "I'll lock the door."

"It's better if you assume they know exactly where you are."

"I'm staying right here," Huey said. "The cabinet work is being installed in the kitchen and the library tomorrow morning, and I have to be here for that."

"Well, you should know that Viv has doubled the security on your place."

"What security?"

"The security you didn't know about."

"Why didn't I know about it?"

"Because we thought you might object."

"I do object," Huey replied.

"To the first security or the doubling?"

"All of it."

"Well, that's tough because it's not going away. If you live through the next few days, then we can talk about it."

"*If* I live through the next few days?"

"Well, there's always the chance that the opposition might sneak through your defenses—if you insist on staying where you are."

"Where can I buy a gun at this hour?" Huey asked.

"You can't, but the people guarding your place will be armed. If you hear gunfire, hit the floor and tell the cabinet-makers to hit the floor, too. Good night, Huey. Get somebody to deliver a *Times* to you tomorrow morning; don't go out." Stone hung up.

"Huey protests," Stone said to Viv and Dino.

Their dinner arrived, and they set about dismantling roasted chicken.

45

enry Thomas rose at four AM, as was his wont, put on the coffee and made toast, and opened his front door to collect his daily newspaper. He was anxious to see what the *Times* had to say about the acquisition of H. Thomas & Son.

Before he could go to the business section, he caught a glimpse of the lower right-hand corner of the newspaper.

Secretary Roils the Waters at H. Thomas & Son

What secretary? he thought. It took a sip of his strong Italian coffee to snap his mind in place. Elise, who speaks Sicilian! He read the opening paragraphs of the story, which ascribed the planned murders of several people to himself, his grandson, and his cousin. The girl went to the papers! He checked the byline on the piece: Jamie Cox. The same reporter who had caused them all the trouble in the past! He called Hank and Rance and told them to go to the office immediately, and to read the *Times* on the way.

Before he got dressed he saw the other headline on the first page of the business section: *H. Thomas to be acquired by Digi-World.* He didn't have time to read the piece; he got dressed and went downstairs to his waiting car.

. . .

It was a grim meeting. "This has happened at the worst possible time," Henry said.

"Perhaps it has happened at the best possible time," Rance said.

"What the hell are you talking about?" Henry demanded.

"At the opening bell on Monday, the stock exchange will suspend trading in our stock because of the acquisition. That gives us two days to fix this."

Hank spoke up. "Fix it? How the fuck do we do that?"

"The first thing we do is to issue a very strong statement refuting the front-page story, and e-mail it to Harman Wills at DigiWorld. It should be the first thing he sees this morning. Also, one of you has to call him and talk him down."

"Poppa," Hank said, "that should be you. This acquisition is your doing, and you know Harman best."

"All right," Henry said, looking at his watch. "I'll wait until seven, then call him at home. Rance, you draft a statement for us."

Rance went to his office, typed fast for a few minutes, and returned with a sheet of paper.

To our shareholders, customers, and business associates:

An outrageous story has appeared in today's *New York Times*, calling into question the character and reputation of H. Thomas & Son. This story and all of its contentions are outright lies. The young woman in question, a previously trusted employee, clearly harbors a grudge against the company, following an injury to another previous employee, of which we were unaware until this morning.

The three H. Thomas executives mentioned, Henry Thomas, Hank Thomas, and Lawrance Damien, have been accused of plotting the murders of a number of people, while speaking in a Sicilian language that none of them speaks or understands. As far as we know, all the putative victims are alive and in good health.

Her story is a preposterous fabrication by a clearly disgruntled employee, who did not appear for work yesterday but later sent an e-mail, resigning her position. We suspect that her actions may be connected to the planned acquisition of H. Thomas & Son by DigiWorld, a fund specializing in bank acquisitions. The two companies have been in discussions for weeks and plan to announce it today. Apparently, she hopes to somehow stop or damage the acquisition, which has already been agreed to with a signing memo between the two parties. This seems to be an attempt to enable short sellers, who could reap large profits, should the story be believed.

H. Thomas & Son stands by its sterling reputation in the financial community, earned by more than fifty years of honest banking. We expect to clear the company's name in short order.

"It needs to be issued with your signature, Henry."

Henry grabbed the paper and a pen and signed it with a flourish. "Get it out to Harman Wills, the *Times*, the *Wall Street Journal*, and the Associated Press immediately," he said, checking his watch. "It's another couple of hours before I can call Harman."

Rance went to his office and e-mailed the statement to the list of publications they sent all releases to.

. . .

Stone was awakened at six-thirty by Dino, who was already at his office.

"Good morning, I think," Stone said.

"Are your hatches all battened down?" Dino asked, in an unexpectedly nautical mode.

"Aye, aye, sir," Stone replied sleepily. "I expect the folks at H. Thomas are scrambling to deny everything before the story can harm its acquisition."

"Hang on," Dino said, "I've got a call coming in from Ken Burrows's cell phone. I'll make it a conference call, so you shut up." He tapped in a code to join the three lines.

"Dino," Burrows said, "did you have something to do with this story in the *Times*?"

"What story, Ken? I haven't seen the *Times* yet."

"The story that you told me, which is now all over the paper."

"Oh, *that* story. This may come as a surprise to you, Ken, but I don't write for the *Times*, nor do I edit the paper." Dino made noise with the newspaper. "Ah, here it is. Give me a minute to read it."

"Hurry up," Burrows said.

Dino waited a moment. "Ah, it does seem to be the story I told you about. Remember, Ken, you had it first. In fact, on the inside page it says that I went to see you with the story, but that you did nothing. I can't deny that, can I?"

Burrows hung up without another word.

"I believe Ken is pissed off," Stone said.

"I agree, and I think that's wonderful," Dino said.

"The good thing about this," Stone said, "is that now the Thomases can't kill any of us."

"Not for a while, anyway," Dino agreed.

"Well, it's going to be interesting to see what happens to their merger, isn't it?"

"It sure is," Dino said, "and you'd better hope it goes off without a hitch and makes them a ton of money. That ought to buy you a year or two of good health."

"I feel better already," Stone said. "My heart has stopped making that funny noise."

"Now let's see what Ken Burrows has to say to the media," Dino said. "Talk to you later."

Stone turned on the TV to CNBC and watched for a few minutes. It gave him a warm, fuzzy feeling inside.

46

Rance Damien went to his desk, found the throwaway cell phone he used for these purposes, and called a number. All he got was a single beep. "You know who this is," he said. "All the picnics we discussed are canceled, because of rain. Confirm at once." He sent a text to the same effect.

Elise Grant was asleep after a fitful night when her mother, Elena, shook her awake.

"Wake up, baby!" she shouted. "We're off the hook."

The telephone rang, and Elise picked it up. "What?"

"It's Stone. The story has hit the *New York Times*, and as a result, we're all safe again. They wouldn't dare make a move against any of us now."

"Thank you, Stone," she said, then hung up. "Mother, why did you wake me up?"

"We're off the hook!" Elena repeated, holding up the front page of the *Times* and pointing at the story.

Elise read the whole story before responding. "We're off the hook," she said finally.

"I just told you that!" her mother yelled. "Now get up and get some clothes on. I want to have breakfast at the Plaza Hotel, then go to Bloomingdale's!"

Elise sat up on the edge of the bed. Something about that sentence didn't work. "We can't go to the Plaza or to Bloomingdale's," she said.

"Why not?" her mother demanded.

"Because I don't have a job anymore. I can't afford it."

"Well, *I* can afford it," Elena said. "It's autumn. You need some new clothes. Shake your ass!"

Elise shook her ass.

Joan knocked at Stone's door.

Something was wrong, Stone thought. Joan never bothered to knock unless she was about to try something on. "Come in," he said.

"I want to talk to you," Joan said.

"Oh, God. What is it now?"

"Just a little talk."

"A stand-up talk or a sit-down talk?"

"That depends on how hard you are to deal with."

"Didn't I just give you a raise?"

"Yes, and a very generous one."

"Well, what else would I be hard to deal with about?"

"I want to hire an assistant," Joan said.

"Have a seat." He looked at her closely to see if this was a joke. "Now, what are you talking about?"

"I want to hire an assistant."

"That's what I thought you said."

"Then my message is clear?"

"All right, give me the whole spiel," Stone said. "I know you've been rehearsing it."

"I want to hire Elise Grant. She's as smart as a whip and nice to be around. I'm getting on, and it's going to take years to train somebody to replace me, so we'd better start now. We have two empty offices next to mine; we can put the files in the small office and give her the larger one. We can get her for ten percent more than the Thomases were paying her, and that's a bargain. This way I can take a vacation without you going nuts. That's it. Oh, and in a way, you got her fired from H. Thomas, so you owe her a job."

"You just turned fifty last year," Stone said.

"Two years ago."

"Are you contemplating early retirement?"

"No."

"Do you have an incurable disease?"

"No."

"Have you come to hate me?"

"No more than usual. Did I mention that she speaks Sicilian?"

"No, and I was grateful for that. Hire her. She can have the apartment next door that got vacated when Fred and Helene got into bed together."

"Good idea. You're thinking unusually clearly," Joan said.

"Have you hired her yet?"

"Not yet."

"What are you waiting for?"

Joan jumped up and ran.

. . .

Elise and her mother had just sat down in the Plaza dining room when her cell phone rang—not the throwaway, her regular phone. It suddenly occurred to her that she could answer it.

"Yes? Hi. I'm listening." She sat back and listened for another two minutes. "Yes," she said. "Tomorrow. I have to let my mother shop herself out today. Goodbye." She put away the phone. "Mother?"

"Yes?"

"Breakfast is on me—so is Bloomie's."

"Did you get a job?"

"Yes, that was Stone's secretary. I'm to be her number two, and the money is even better than at H. Thomas, and I get a free apartment."

"Can I have your apartment? I want to be closer to Bloomingdale's, now that you're working again."

"Yes."

They each ordered the eggs Benedict and a glass of champagne.

Rance was at his desk when Henry called. "Get in here." He hung up.

Rance walked into Henry's office. Hank was already there. "I talked to Harman Wills," Henry said. "He had already read the piece, and he thought it was hilarious. The deal is still on."

Rance and Hank both shook his hand.

"Rance, did you cancel the arrangements you made earlier?"

"Yes, I did."

"Did you get an actual confirmation?"

"Not yet, but I'll hear from him soon."

"What were your instructions, if you canceled?"

Rance thought about that.

"It's my recollection," Henry said, "that such arrangements could not be canceled, except in person and upon payment in full for the work. Has that changed?"

"No, it hasn't," Rance said, and a film of sweat appeared on his upper lip. He checked his phone for messages. "Nothing yet."

"Go back to your office and call him again," Henry said. "And keep calling until you speak to him. Draw the cash, and be ready to pay him."

"Yes, sir," Rance said, rising.

"You understand, don't you, that if any one of those people mentioned in the *Times* is harmed, the deal will be blown, and we'll all be facing murder charges?"

"I understand," Rance said. He went back to his office and threw up into his wastebasket, then he made the call. No answer; just a beep. He threw up again.

47

Ari Kramer and Annie Lee went to New Hampshire for the primary election and, late in the day, followed Senator Box around, closely enough that they could hear him speaking to people.

Box was all smiles, and the words Ari had written for him spilled from his lips, without hesitation or errors.

Annie spoke up. "Has it occurred to you that you may have created a monster?"

"More than once," Ari replied, "but I haven't seen the thing operate up close before."

"Scary," Annie said.

"That's an excellent word for what I think. I'm tired of this. Why don't we go back to the motel, order a pizza, and watch the returns on TV?"

"Ari," Annie said, "I think you're developing a wit."

"How so?"

"That sometimes means when you make a remark that sounds perfectly ordinary, but it really means something else."

They went back to the motel and did something else.

. . .

At eleven o'clock, their pizza devoured and their other desires met, they switched on the news.

A young woman faced the camera. "Tonight's big news is that Senator Joseph Box has not only won New Hampshire's Republican nomination for president but has won by twelve points over his rival. His victory is making national news, and Republicans everywhere are beginning to think they have a new contender for the presidency.

"And, to no one's surprise, Secretary of State Holly Barker has won the Democratic primary by twenty-two points."

There followed several clips of comments from as far away as California.

"I guess Mr. Smith is going to be ecstatic," Annie said.

"William doesn't seem to get ecstatic," Ari said. "Nor does he get depressed. He just wants results for his money."

"And he's getting that in spades, isn't he?"

As if on cue, Ari's Skype alarm rang. He put a shirt on, turned the monitor away from the naked Annie, and logged on.

"Congratulations," Smith said, in his usual monotone. The bandages were gone from his face, and he looked fairly normal.

"Thank you," Ari replied. "Given the margin of his victory, we think he might do very well in other states, particularly Texas and Florida."

"Please see that he does," Smith replied. "Our group would be very pleased to see that happen. Good night." He went off the screen.

"There," Ari said. "That was William being enthusiastic."

. . .

Harod Avaya sat on a park bench at the base of the Fifty-ninth Street Bridge. During his two years in New York he had begun to think of this as his favorite spot in the city.

Harod had been born thirty years before in Paris, son of Palestinian parents who had spoken Arabic at home and had moved back to the Middle East when he was twelve. They found themselves herded into Gaza, and there Harod had joined a youth group and had risen through its ranks. By the time he was nineteen he had been performing assassinations of Israeli military and intelligence commanders, and his life had become luxurious. He was being very well paid and had secured a new apartment for his parents. Then the commander of his unit was murdered by a man on a motorcycle, and Harod had begun to think that life there was getting too dangerous.

He spoke with two of his compatriots, with whom he had worked on a dozen killings, and he suggested to them that they might lead an even more luxurious life, and a safer one, by becoming independent contractors.

They procured documents from a forger who equipped terrorists of every stripe, and within a couple of months they found themselves in New York removing an Israeli member of a United Nations delegation from the earth. Other assignments came along, then he met Rance Damien through a shadowy contact. Damien had heard of him and believed he could offer them work. At the moment, Harod had four active contracts with Damien.

His phone rang, and he picked it up.

"They're just leaving the Plaza Hotel, getting into a cab," his colleague Avin said.

"Follow them and find a way," Harod said.

"Yes," Avin said and hung up.

While on the phone Harod checked his messages and found one from Damien, canceling his four contracts. He knew they would be paid anyway, but it disturbed him that four people worthy of assassination had escaped his hand, especially since he had worked so hard to complete the contract. Their first victim, though shot in the head in a thoroughly professional manner, had somehow survived, and now the Grant woman and her mother, whom they had tracked to a police safe house, were suddenly available for elimination. He thought about it, but he did not respond to the cancellation message.

A few minutes later, Avin called again. "They are at Bloomingdale's," he said, "and it's very crowded. I can make it happen here."

Harod thought for a moment. "Then make it happen," he said.

Elena sat for a makeover in the cosmetics department, while Elise watched and took mental notes. Then her mother bought two hundred dollars' worth of cosmetics, and they moved on, up the escalator to the designer shops.

They strolled into the Ralph Lauren department, and both found things they liked. The dressing rooms were all full, so they sat down among other women who were waiting, their arms full of garments to try on. Finally, a compartment became available, and they moved in to try on things. As Elise closed the door, a man walked past, not seeming to notice her. What was a man doing in a dressing area of a women's department?

Elise called the store, asked for security, and reported the presence of the man.

"Don't leave your compartment," the officer said. "Someone is close by and on the way."

She hung up and, while waiting, slipped into a wool dress that looked just great on her. A moment later, she heard two odd popping noises and running feet in the corridor outside, then screams.

Someone was shouting at someone else to stop. She opened the door a crack and could see a uniformed security guard in the room just opposite hers. She could also see two women, lying on the floor of another compartment in a pool of blood.

Elise pushed her mother back into their room, leaned on the door, and called Joan Robertson. "Get dressed, Mother," she said as the phone rang.

"Hello, Elise," Joan said.

"Stone said we were in the clear, so we went shopping," Elise said.

"Yes, all is well."

"No, all is *not* well! We're at Bloomingdale's, in a dressing room at the Ralph Lauren shop upstairs, and two women across the hall from us have just been shot."

"Stay where you are," Joan said. "Don't move."

"Forget that. We're getting out of here, and *now*. Come on, Mother!"

48

E
lise and Elena hailed a cab on the Third Avenue side of Bloomingdale's and got into the rear seat just in time to see a policeman shoot a man on the sidewalk.

"You think that guy was after us?" Elena asked.

"Maybe," Elise replied, "but if he was, he isn't anymore." She gave the driver Stone's address and prayed for traffic to get out of the way.

Dino was on his way uptown in his car for lunch with Stone when his phone rang. "Bacchetti," he said.

"Dino, it's Joan," she said.

"Hi, Joan."

"There's trouble, and Stone isn't answering his phone."

"Tell me."

"This morning, after Jamie's story about the Thomases ran in the *Times*, Stone called Elise and gave her the all-clear— thinking they wouldn't dare go for her now."

"That seems reasonable."

"Elise and her mother went to Bloomingdale's. They were trying on clothes in the Ralph Lauren department when two women were shot in a dressing room opposite theirs. They're on their way here now."

"Shot in the middle of Bloomie's?"

"Exactly. Will you tell Stone about this and also tell him to watch his ass?"

"I'll do more than that," Dino said. He hung up and called the Nineteenth Precinct and found they were already on the job, and that a suspect had been shot by a street cop on Third Avenue, outside the store. He asked to be kept apprised of the details and hung up.

Stone was already at their table when Dino arrived and gave him the news.

"I'm flabbergasted," Stone said. "The Thomases have gone absolutely bonkers, and I've made a big mistake thinking they would behave sensibly now, in their own interests."

"Don't be too hard on yourself," Dino replied. "We haven't connected these killings to the Grants yet. At least we took out the assassin, though."

"Where?"

"On the street outside the store."

"Who was he?"

As if in answer to his question, Dino's phone rang, and he walked away from the dining room to answer it. He returned shortly.

"This is very interesting," Dino said, sitting down. "The killer had a notebook with the Grants' names in it and the Plaza was mentioned. Do you know if they had breakfast there?"

"No."

"Here's the other thing. The guy was carrying an American

passport in the name of Jonathan Morgan that, when checked, was valid, until our intelligence unit started running down the name. Turns out, Morgan doesn't exist, but the shooter entered the country on that passport, and the computer didn't kick back."

"What do you take that to mean?" Stone asked.

"It seems to mean that there's a foreign intelligence aspect to this thing. No street forger could make that passport. It requires a special kind of expert and a real number from the State Department or, abroad, an embassy or consulate. Our people are running prints and our facial recognition program now. We'll have to wait and see if they get a hit."

Harod Avaya was still sitting on his park bench when his telephone chimed loudly. That meant a news alert from the *New York Times* app. He pressed the alert and waited for the story to come up.

> Two women were fatally shot twenty minutes ago in the dressing room of a designer shop at Bloomingdale's. Shortly afterward, the alleged shooter was himself shot on the street outside the department store. No word yet on his identity or that of the victims.

Harod was stunned that Avin could have allowed himself to be chased down in the street and shot by the police. He began thinking ahead. Avin was carrying the passport by the same forger as that of his own. They would be tracking the ID down by now, but he had been assured that the document would hold up under scrutiny. He remembered that the three passports sold to Harod and his two compatriots did not have consecutive numbers; that was a relief.

His phone rang, and he recognized the number as that of a throwaway used by Rance Damien.

"Yes?"

"We have to meet right now," Damien said.

"Park bench on the East River, near the Fifty-ninth Street Bridge," he replied.

"Forty minutes," Damien said, then hung up.

Harod put away his phone and took a stroll, always keeping the bench in sight. Damien turned up on schedule and sat down, putting a briefcase between his legs. Harod went into his phone and deleted the voice mails and texts from Damien. Then, satisfied that the man had not been followed, he approached the bench and sat down. Damien was pretending to read the *Times*.

"Why didn't you return my calls?" Damien demanded.

"What calls?" Harod took out his iPhone, checked his e-mail and message pages. "Nothing here," he said. "Is something wrong?"

Damien put down the newspaper and slid it across the bench to Harod. "Front-page story on us," he said, "continued at length inside."

"I got that on my iPhone this morning. It's nothing to do with me."

"Did you send a man to Bloomingdale's to kill the Grants?"

"We located them at a police safe house this morning, and Avin followed them from there to the Plaza, where they had breakfast, and then to Bloomingdale's. I just got a flash from the *Times* that two women were shot in Bloomingdale's and the shooter was killed by police outside. I assume they are talking about the Grants and Avin, though no names have been released yet."

"Goddammit, I canceled the four contracts!" Damien shouted.

"Keep your voice down, or I will walk away." Harod looked around the area for threats. "I showed you my phone. I got no messages or texts."

"Don't you see what this means?" Damien asked. "As soon as they identify the women, they'll be coming for us. We may have to leave the country."

"There's no need to panic," Harod said. "They'll question you, and you were in your office at the time. They can't connect you to Avin or me. You're safe. Do you still want to cancel the other three contracts?"

"Yes, for now," Damien said.

"Then I'll have the money, as per our agreement."

"It's in the briefcase between my feet," Damien said. "Two hundred thousand dollars, as agreed."

"Then, when you reactivate the other contracts, there will be no further charge. Now go."

Damien rose and left, leaving the briefcase under the bench.

Harod's phone rang, and he checked the caller ID. Avin's phone; the police had found it. He switched off his iPhone, removed the data card, and ground it under his heel before kicking it into the grass. He then picked up the briefcase and laid it across his knees. It was beautiful, he thought, brand-new. He wanted to see the money. He placed his thumbs on the latches and pressed.

His world exploded in fire.

49

Rasheed Khan, the third member of Harod's team, sat and stared at his phone. He had called both Harod and Avin, and the calls had gone straight to voice mail. The TV was on, and a story came up about two killings at Bloomingdale's. Avin had called him earlier and said he was following the Grants there, so the women had to be them. But a man was dead, too, described as the assassin; that had to be Avin. But where was Harod?

Rasheed left the apartment and walked the three blocks to the East River, where Harod liked to go and sit. From a block away, it was clear that something was wrong. There was police tape across the street at the end of the block, and patrol cars and uniforms on foot were everywhere. He turned away and went into a coffee shop, where he ordered tomato soup and tea. Surreptitiously, he removed the data card from his iPhone and replaced it with another, then he dropped the old one into the remains of his soup. Harod and Avin had the new number, and he had their spares. He called them both and got nowhere.

He went back to the apartment, packed his things, and wiped it down. He dropped Harod's and Avin's clothes down the incinerator, then left the building. He walked four blocks to the backup safe apartment that was their last line of defense. From there, he would have to make his next move carefully.

Elise and Elena Grant entered Stone's building through the downstairs office and were greeted by Joan.

"Thank goodness you made it out safely," Joan said.

"It was a close call," Elise said, then told her their story.

"You're safe here," Joan said. "Would you like to see your new apartment?"

Stone and Dino left the club and rode downtown in Dino's SUV. They stopped at Bloomingdale's, where a big police operations van was parked on Third Avenue, partly obstructing traffic. Two EMTs were putting a body, hidden by a sheet, into their wagon.

Dino got out. "I want to see this guy," he said, hopping into the rear of the wagon and pulling the sheet back.

"Two in the chest, Commissioner," an EMT said.

Stone, who had no interest in the corpse, waited outside. A moment later Dino joined him. "Just a kid," he said, "no older than his mid-twenties." Dino went and conferred with the officer in charge, then he and Stone went back to Dino's car. "Below the Fifty-ninth Street Bridge," he said to his driver. "Ashore on the Manhattan side."

"What's under the Fifty-ninth Street Bridge?" Stone asked.

"The remains of what used to be a man," Dino said.

"Any connection to the shooter at Bloomingdale's?"

"Not yet," Dino said, "but I've got a feeling."

They drove as close as they could to the scene, then got out of the car. Dino sought out the detective in charge and collected a salute or two.

Stone looked around. A man's left arm, in a sleeve, lay on the grass, and on the wrist a Rolex was still ticking. Cops in cotton booties were searching every inch of the sidewalk and the lawn next to it.

"Got something!" a cop yelled, holding up a hand to identify himself.

A crime scene tech made his way carefully over to the cop and, as Stone watched, took out a pair of tweezers and picked up something. "Cell phone data card!" he yelled to his supervisor.

"Bring it home, and let's run it."

Stone walked up to where Dino was speaking with the on-scene supervisor.

"There must be a dozen security cameras round here trained on this scene," Dino said.

"Four, so far," the officer replied.

"I want to see the results, ASAP. E-mail them to me."

"Yes, sir."

Dino took Stone's arm and guided him back toward his car. "They found a piece of an American passport; they're running it by the State Department now."

"And a cell phone data card," Stone said. "I watched them pick it up, not far from the arm over there."

"That looks like the biggest piece of the guy remaining,"

Dino said. "We'll pick up prints and DNA from that. Nothing more we can do here."

They got back into the car and drove to Stone's house. "Too early for a drink?" Stone asked.

"What kind of question is that?" Dino asked, getting out of the car.

They entered through the office door and found Elise inside, sitting in her new office and looking around. Her mother was admiring it, too.

"Welcome aboard," Stone said, then led Dino upstairs to the study.

"Aboard?" Dino asked.

"We hired Elise as Joan's new assistant."

"Why does Joan need an assistant?"

"I asked the same question, but she was ready for me, had a barrage of answers. Elise is moving into Fred's old apartment."

Rance Damien got back to his office to find a note from Henry: *See me soonest.* He went directly to Henry's office.

Henry and Hank were waiting.

"Where have you been?" Henry asked.

"Confirming the cancellation of the contracts," Damien said.

"God, I hate paying those characters for doing nothing," Henry said.

"I didn't pay them," Rance said. "I made other arrangements."

"What arrangements?"

"You don't want to know."

"God, I hate being told that," Henry said.

"Poppa," Hank said. "Rance is right. You don't need to know, and neither do I."

"You heard about Bloomingdale's, I assume," Rance said.

"We did," Henry replied.

"My guy didn't get my phone messages. It was his colleague who took out the Grants and got shot on the street up there."

"So the contract wasn't canceled in time?"

"No, it wasn't."

"Whose fault is that?" Henry demanded.

"Nobody's," Rance said. "The messages didn't go through. If you need to blame somebody, try AT&T."

"Don't you get smart with me, boy," Henry said.

"Poppa!" Hank said. "He's just telling you the truth. At least, we won't have to worry about that girl now."

"Well, the police are going to make that connection pretty quick," Henry said. "I'm surprised they aren't already here."

"We've been in a meeting all morning, the three of us," Hank said. "I'll let the girls know." He left the office, then returned. "All square."

"Look," Henry said, pointing at the TV, which was muted. "Breaking news at Bloomingdale's." He turned up the volume.

"The man shot on the sidewalk, the assumed assassin, has not yet been identified by the police, but the two women shot in the changing room upstairs were Betty and Barbara Swearingen, of Greenwich, Connecticut. They were sisters, who were apparently in town for a day's shopping."

"What the fuck!" Henry shouted.

50

Stone and Dino were warming themselves by the fire and their innards with brown whiskey, when Dino's phone made a noise, and he turned it on. "Security-camera footage from the Fifty-ninth Street Bridge area."

Stone walked behind Dino's chair and looked over his shoulder, while the phone downloaded the footage.

"Here we go," Dino said. They stared intently at the screen; the shot was taken from upriver, apparently from a camera affixed to the bridge. "Long shot," Dino said.

A man wearing a windbreaker and a baseball cap walked over to the only bench in sight and sat down. Then he answered his phone and walked away. "These have already been edited for best use," Dino said.

Shortly, a figure appeared, walking up the river, a man in a black topcoat and a black hat, carrying a briefcase. "Who wears a hat these days?" Dino asked.

"Somebody who doesn't want to be seen by a security camera," Stone ventured. "It's the upper-class hoodie."

"Yeah."

The second man sat down on the bench, upriver side. He set

down his briefcase and turned to face the man in the baseball cap, who had walked toward him.

"No luck on the guy in the hat," Dino said. "But that's a clear shot of the guy in the baseball cap."

"They're a long way off from the camera, though," Stone said.

"We're already working on enhancing the face," Dino said.

The two men conversed for a short time, then the man in the hat rose and headed back the way he came.

"Did you see that?" Dino asked.

"See what? His back?"

"He left the briefcase under the bench when he got up."

"You're right," Stone said.

The man in black disappeared off screen, then the man in the baseball cap reached under the bench and brought out the briefcase.

"Here we go," Dino said.

The second man seemed to inspect the briefcase, then stroked it with one hand, then both his hands moved into position to open the case. The explosion was noiseless, since there was no audio, but the force of the blast was visible. The man in the baseball cap simply disappeared in a cloud of smoke.

They watched as debris began to fall around the bench.

"There's the arm we saw," Stone said, as it landed a few yards from the bench.

"Right," Dino replied. He quickly ran the three other camera views, but it was obvious that the shots from the first camera were the best. Dino set down his phone.

"It's not every day you see a guy blown to pieces," Dino said.

"Thank God for that," Stone replied.

Dino's phone made the noise again, and he picked it up. "Enhancement coming in," he said.

Stone stood behind him and watched as the shot from the first camera ran again in the enhanced mode. "Looks like a cashmere topcoat," he said.

"Yeah, but that's not going to help us."

"And a Yankees ball cap."

"Right again."

The motion stopped, a square was drawn around the head of the man in the Yankees cap. It was enlarged, then enhanced before their eyes.

"Hey, that's good!" Dino enthused. "Our facial recognition software ought to be able to do something with that." He turned off the phone, and Stone sat down.

"He looked sort of Mediterranean," Stone said.

"So did the guy at Bloomingdale's."

"So, a Middle Eastern terrorist shoots two women in Bloomingdale's and another Middle Eastern guy gets handed a briefcase with a surprise inside," Dino said.

"The guy at Bloomingdale's thought he was shooting Elise and Elena," Stone said, "but he got it wrong, then his cohort goes to accept payment for the job from a guy by the river, only the guy by the river didn't want to pay. That makes sense."

"It does," Dino said. Then his phone rang, and Dino put it on speaker and set it on the coffee table. "Bacchetti."

"Boss, it's Lieutenant Perdido, in intelligence tech services," a voice said.

"What have you got?"

"A connection between the guy at Bloomingdale's and the one from the bridge. Their passports, though their numbers were not consecutive, were both issued at the American embassy in Paris, and both on the same day."

"Bingo!" Dino said. "What home addresses were on the passport application?"

"The same address: a New York apartment."

"Well, get a warrant and get somebody over there," Dino said. "And send those shots to the D.A."

"Yes, sir!" The lieutenant hung up.

"I'd call that progress," Dino said. "Wouldn't you?"

"Not yet," Stone said. "All you've got are two corpses, one in pieces, and they got their passports from the same forger, probably in Paris. If you can find another guy in the cell, then that will be progress."

"That was going to be my next move," Dino said petulantly. "I'm calling the D.A." He picked up his phone. Someone answered, said the D.A. was unavailable, and took a message. "Probably not before tomorrow," she said.

Dino hung up in disgust.

51

In his study, Stone and Dino had a good dinner of roast lamb and potatoes au gratin, then Stone's phone rang.

"Hello?"

"Stone, it's Lance Cabot. I hope you're well." Lance was the director of the Central Intelligence Agency, and he had had dealings with Stone and Dino on many occasions.

"Hello, Lance, and yes, I am." He covered the mouthpiece. *It's Lance,* he mouthed.

"Why don't you put me on speaker, so Dino can hear me, too?" Lance asked. "It would save me a phone call."

Stone pressed the button and set the phone on the table. "You're on speaker, Lance."

"Good. I wanted you both to know that we've received a photograph, apparently of a suspect, shortly before he was blown to pieces. Your people, Dino, asked for our help in facial identification, since our software is, ah, somewhat better than yours."

"Thanks, Lance, we appreciate the condescension," Dino said.

"Not at all," Lance replied, unruffled. "We have identified your man as one Harod Avaya, born in Paris thirty years ago, last known residence, the Gaza Strip. I expect he was the gentleman who received the elegant briefcase over by the East River."

"Good guess, Lance," Dino replied.

"Mr. Avaya was a Palestinian activist from his late teens, and not much later, an assassin. About two years ago, he and a colleague, Avin, dropped out of sight and, apparently, took up assassination as a trade, not to say an art, along with a third youth, one Rasheed Khan. Mr. Avaya and Avin Kayam had American passports issued on the same day in Paris, same year. They both listed the same New York City apartment as their residence. Through a further search, we have determined that Mr. Khan may also have received such a passport—under another name, so far unknown—at the same address."

"It's being searched as we speak," Dino said, getting a little of his own back.

"My people, regrettably, assumed that the address was phony and did not bother to check it out."

"How very useless of them," Stone said.

"Quite."

"And, Lance," Dino interjected, "it was Mr. Kayam who was shot and killed by one of my officers this afternoon, outside Bloomingdale's."

"Ah," Lance said. "Good to know. Have you made any progress investigating the murders of the two Swearingen sisters?"

"Yes, Kayam shot the wrong two women," Dino said. "The real targets escaped and are now safe at Stone's house."

"That leaves our Mr. Rasheed Khan. What news of him?"

"We didn't know he existed until you called, Lance," Dino replied, "but you may rest assured we will turn our attention to him immediately."

"Ah, good," Lance said. "Have you anything on the person

or persons who hired Mr. Kayam to kill the two women? I leap to the conclusion that it might be the Thomases, since a rather unflattering piece about them was in this morning's *Times*."

"We hold that view, too," Dino said, "but I'm having trouble convincing the D.A."

"Would a call from me help?" Lance asked.

"It couldn't hurt," Dino replied. "It might be good for the D.A.'s spine, if he learned that others besides the NYPD like the Thomases for the crime. Might it be that you folks have something on them that we don't?"

"I very much doubt it," Lance said, "but I'll ask. I think that pretty much all of what we know of them—apart from what has appeared in the *Wall Street Journal* over the years—resides in the files that Stone procured from the Bianchi estate. We found those fascinating."

"Thank you, Lance," Stone said. "It's a pleasure to have fascinated you."

"You're very welcome. Dino, we would be most grateful if your intelligence division could pass along any other evidence of the last of the Palestinian trio."

"I promise to keep you informed," Dino said.

"Then I bid you good evening, gentlemen. Raise a glass for me." Lance hung up.

Dino was immediately on the phone to report the existence of a third member of the cell. He listened for quite a while, then hung up. "My people are combing through the trio's apartment right now," he said, "and they are finding absolutely zip. The place had been wiped down and vacuumed."

"Then," Stone said, "that must mean that the third member of the cell, Rasheed Khan, heard of the deaths of his two colleagues and abandoned the apartment."

"Makes sense, since both incidents were all over the news. Oh, they found fragments of male clothing in the apartment building's incinerator, all high-end designer stuff that could be bought on Madison Avenue."

"Then business must have been good," Stone said. "It might be interesting to ask your people to look into other recent homicides for a connection."

"Why would it do us any good to know about connections?"

"Perhaps the Thomases have used them in the recent past."

"Oh, all right," Dino said, and made the call.

Rasheed Khan, aka Timothy Tigner, let himself into the backup safe house, an apartment in a brownstone in the East 60s, and checked it carefully for any sign of recent attention from anyone except himself and his two dead colleagues. He did not waste time grieving for them—as he hadn't liked them much anyway—but he did hold a more professional grudge.

He had known that Harod would be meeting soon with Damien to receive the money due them, and he supposed Damien might have been reluctant to pay and, thus, found it more convenient to eliminate the contractees. That annoyed Tigner, down to his socks, and he resolved to do something about it.

It would have to be later, though, since he was exhausted from dealing with the threat of discovery, and he needed sleep.

He carefully put away his clothes, took a hot bath, and climbed gratefully into bed.

Tomorrow, he would find a way to deal with the Thomases.

As soon as Stone was in bed, he got a call from Dino.

"What's up?"

"That cell phone data card we found has yielded some results," Dino said, "and so has the one from Avin Kayam's phone."

"I'm happy to hear it."

"The three of them were talking to each other during the day."

"Not a big surprise," Stone said.

"I'm sorry to disappoint you," Dino said, then hung up.

52

Joan arrived in her office at eight AM sharp on Monday morning and heard noises from the adjoining office. She opened the door to find Elise Grant at her desk and the room spic-and-span, with everything in its place. "Good morning," Elise said brightly.

"And to you," Joan said. "This is the first time anyone has ever beaten me to the office."

"I can't work unless the space is in order," Elise said.

"I know the feeling," Joan replied.

"And what may I do with *that*?" she asked, pointing at an IBM Selectric typewriter on a stand in a corner of the room.

"Oh, I don't know," Joan replied. "Type on it, maybe?"

"I wouldn't know where to begin," Elise said. "I've never typed a word on anything that needed paper to work. May I put it in the file room?"

"Yes, until I can figure out a way to give it a Christian burial."

"I'm ready to move out of my apartment today, and my mother is moving out of hers and into mine. Can you recommend a mover?"

"I can," Joan said. "And since your putative assassins are dead, you should really be in the clear now."

"I'm still going to be careful, though," Elise said.

"Always a good idea. I've got some health insurance forms for you to fill out. I'll give you all that stuff later today."

Joan went back to her office, happy to have Elise as a backstop. Now she was going to have to think of something for her to do.

Damien met that morning with the Thomases.

Hank spoke up. "I understand that you have dispensed with the hired help."

"It became necessary," Damien said, surprised that Hank was taking an interest. "Saved us two hundred thousand dollars, too."

"That's all very well," Hank said, "but if we need that sort of help again, what are we to do?"

"Just leave it to me," Damien said. "It would be helpful if you could tell me now who the subject of the action would be."

"Someone we've kept at arm's length," Hank said. "Joe Box."

Damien's eyebrows shot up. "I've gone to some lengths to see that he does well in the primaries," he said, "and since he's done better than anyone expected, why would we want to unload him now? He might even go all the way."

"That's the problem," Hank said. "My private polling now favors him for the nomination, and if he gets that and something happens to Holly Barker, he might go all the way. It is not in my plan to have a buffoon like that in the White House. I have a party to build, and his presence on the scene would not be helpful."

"If it comes to that," Damien said, "I would like us to retain the services of the two young operatives who have shaped him into something like a viable candidate."

"By all means," Hank said. "Retain them and put them on salary, until I want them. There may be other candidates we might want to help along the way. We might also give some attention to the proper moment for Box to depart the scene—not too early or too late."

"I will leave the politics of that to you," Damien said, "but I'd like as much time as possible to arrange Box's departure. We don't want to rush something like that."

"I'll ponder his progress, then let you know," Hank said.

Henry Thomas had, uncharacteristically, held his peace, but now he spoke. "What exactly do you intend, Hank?"

"I have not yet given up the notion of moving into the White House next year. It will depend on how we get through the next couple of months. If the acquisition goes through, and the waters become smoother, and Box continues to do well, I think I might hear from the party that they would like me to resume my candidacy."

"As a Republican?" Henry asked.

"They are as frightened of Joe Box as I," Hank said, "and if he suddenly departs the scene, they have a paucity of replacements to choose from."

Henry smiled. "You know, my boy, I may have underestimated your guile."

"Poppa," Hank said with a smile, "that's the nicest thing you've ever said to me."

. . .

Damien was at his desk later in the day when a secretary came in. "Sir," she said, "there is a person on the phone who insists on speaking to you, but I don't know him."

"What is his name?"

"He says his name is Timothy Tigner," she said. "Oh, and he said to tell you that he is a friend of somebody called Harod, like the department store."

That news came like a bolt of lightning to Damien. He thought Harod had had only one cohort; now another was raising his head? And, perhaps, at just the right time.

"Thank you," he said. He waited until she had closed the door behind her before picking up the phone. "Mr. Tigner?"

"Yes, Mr. Damien," a smooth voice replied. He sounded younger than Harod.

"I understand we have a mutual friend?"

"No longer," Tigner replied. "He and my other colleague left town yesterday. I thought, perhaps, you might have heard about that."

"I have heard no such thing," Damien said. "I had a rendezvous with Harod set for yesterday, but as I approached the scene I saw policemen everywhere, so I retreated."

"Oh? What was the purpose of your meeting?"

"To confirm the cancellation of some contracts and to pay him the two hundred thousand dollars due. Now, could you tell me what is going on?"

"Have you heard about the shooting of two women at a department store? And the shooting of a man in the street there?"

"Yes, but the women were strangers to me. Was the man Harod?"

"No, he was our colleague, Rasheed. He had just shot the women, thinking they were the subjects of the contract."

"But I e-mailed and texted Harod about the cancellation. He did not answer his phone."

"Perhaps because he was already dead at your rendezvous point."

"If that is the case, I'm very sorry to hear it."

"Why? You canceled the contracts."

"Yes, but not permanently. Also, I have other work to be done."

"Before any work can be done," Tigner said, "there is the matter of the two hundred thousand dollars."

"I am certainly willing to pay that, as our agreement requires."

"Then you will have to pay it before we can discuss other work."

"How can I contact you?"

"Send an e-mail to the following address," he said, and then dictated the address. "Then I will call you on this number."

"No, not this number. I will give you another." Damien did so.

"Then we will be in touch as soon as the headlines change," Tigner said, then hung up.

Damien hung up, too, feeling both weak with relief that he had a solution to the Box problem and afraid of this man Tigner.

53

Tim Tigner, as he had begun to think of himself, began to feel very comfortable in his world. He had the amassed funds earned from assassinations by himself and his cohorts, amounting to nearly five hundred thousand dollars, and another two hundred thousand dollars on the way, when he requested it. He let his hair grow and began to shave his face every day; he bought some new, rather fashionable clothes; and to sharpen his English pronunciation, used as models television newspeople, all of whom seemed to be from the same place in the United States.

He attended lectures at the Metropolitan Museum of Art and went to the movies a lot. He was courteous and charming to his neighbors, who gathered at the cocktail hour in a lounge for tenants on the ground floor in his building, and in particular, a dark-haired, curvaceous young woman who seemed anxious to have someone to talk to.

"My name is Karen Landis," she said when asked.

"I'm Tim Tigner," he replied.

"Do I detect a slight accent?" she asked.

"I was born in Paris, to an American father and an Algerian mother, so my accent is a bit scrambled."

She switched to French, and he joined the conversation smoothly, French being one of his native languages.

"You have a beautiful accent," she said. "What do you do?"

"I am an investor," he said. "Or perhaps just unemployed."

She laughed. "I'm a registered nurse, at Lenox Hill Hospital," she said.

"Then you must care about others," he said.

"Yes, I do."

They talked on and agreed to have dinner, and by the end of that date, Tim felt that he had found his first girlfriend.

Damien was at his desk when a secretary knocked and entered. "Yes?"

"We have a request from our medical insurers for information about Elise Grant," she said, handing him a form. "They just want to know if she was employed here and if she had any medical problems at that time."

"Let me see that," Damien said, holding out his hand. She gave him the form, and he scanned it. Elise was now employed by the Barrington Practice, at a Turtle Bay address. "Ah, yes," he said, handing the form back to her, "give them the information they want."

"Bingo!" he said aloud to himself, when she had gone.

Bob Cantor sat on a bench in Central Park, with Sherry by his side. "It's so nice to be out of the house," Sherry said, "even if the house is awfully nice."

"Stone has been good to us," Bob said, "but now it's about time we move out. I'd like it to be together."

"I'd like that, too," Sherry replied, squeezing his hand. "I've grown accustomed to having you around, day and night, and I like it. Do you think we're safe now?"

"I think we're as safe as we can be until the Thomases are either out of the country or in prison, but I suppose that will take a while."

"The company has been acquired by that hedge fund," she said, "according to the *Times* business page. So I suppose there's nothing keeping them here."

"Not cell bars, anyway," Bob replied. "They haven't even been arrested."

Damien was feeling safer, too. The acquisition had gone smoothly, and he and the Thomases had been asked to stay on until the end of the year. He had begun to believe that Harman Wills liked him and might offer him something good soon.

The sound of a distant cell phone ringing could be heard and he opened his desk drawer and answered the throwaway inside.

"Good morning, this is Tim Tigner," that voice said.

"I hope you're well," Damien replied.

"I think it's time for us to meet," Tigner said.

"Where and when?"

"There is a restaurant called Patroon, on East Forty-sixth Street."

"I know the place."

"They have an outdoor bar and lounge upstairs. Let's meet there at six PM today."

"That will be satisfactory."

"And don't forget to bring payment," Tigner said, then hung up.

At six sharp, Damien got off the elevator at Patroon and, carrying a briefcase, walked onto the upstairs deck, which was busy with the after-work crowd. He looked around and saw no one who might be Tigner. Then, across the deck, sitting on a divan, a young man raised a single finger.

Damien crossed the deck and stood before the divan. "I can't quite remember the name," he said. "Mr. . . ."

"Tigner." He moved over to make room.

Damien sat down, and a waiter came over. "A very dry vodka martini," he said to the man.

"Two," Tigner added.

Damien set down his briefcase between them on the divan.

"Is that my payment?" Tigner asked.

"It is. Exactly two hundred thousand dollars in one-hundred-dollar bills."

Tigner reached for the briefcase, then stopped. "Open it, please," he said.

Damien noted that the dark, friendly eyes had hardened. "Of course," he replied. He rotated the case 180 degrees, reached out, released the locks, and, after a look around to be sure no one was watching them, opened the case.

Tigner reached out, riffled through each stack of notes, then nodded and closed the case. "Very good."

The waiter delivered their martinis and they raised their glasses to each other.

"To a useful and happy relationship," Damien said.

They clinked glasses and sipped.

"And now, I believe there is the matter of Miss Grant, Mr. Barrington, Robert Cantor, and Sherry Spector," Tigner said.

"There is, but that contract has been put on hold for a while. There is a new subject, however, one that will require a new contract."

"Please continue," Tigner said.

"His name is Joseph Box. He's a United States senator."

"Ah, yes," Tigner replied. "I have seen him on the news shows. He is very articulate."

"That he is," Damien replied.

"Where and when would you like the contract executed?"

"Senator Box is on the road at the moment," Damien said, withdrawing several sheets of paper from an inside pocket and handing them to Tigner. "This is his schedule. I would like you to follow him and discern his habits, particularly with women. It would be good if he were found dead with a woman, particularly if it were a married woman. That's something of a specialty of the senator."

"But no date?"

"To come—sometime during the next few weeks. When it does come, you'll be expected to execute within twenty-four hours."

"All right," Tigner said. "A hundred thousand for Box,

another fifty for the woman, and a thousand dollars a day for travel expenses."

"Done," Damien said. "You'll find another hundred thousand in the case, under a flap in the bottom, as a down payment; the rest, on execution."

"As you say," Tigner replied. "I will leave first, if that's all right."

"Of course."

Tigner handed him a throwaway cell phone. "This is to be used for all contacts."

"Right," Damien replied.

Both men rose, shook hands, then Tigner picked up the briefcase and walked to the elevator.

Damien poured the remains of Tigner's martini into his own glass, and made himself comfortable.

54

Tim Tigner took a one-week driving-school course, obtained a New York driver's license, and bought a five-year-old, low-mileage Mercedes station wagon from an online ad, paying the grateful seller in cash.

He rented garage space next door to his building, then removed the folding third-row seat from its compartment, installed a lock, and stowed his necessary weaponry, equipment, and cash there. He consulted a road map and Senator Box's schedule and selected Kansas City, Missouri, as an interception point.

Three days later, he checked into an old hotel across the street from Box's Kansas City, Missouri, campaign headquarters, then dropped in and collected some pamphlets and position papers, while casing the premises. Box's name was on a mezzanine office, overlooking a dozen desks, next to a plate-glass window. His hotel was in view, and the building next to it seemed a good point for a sniper, if the opportunity arose. He stopped at a desk and asked a young woman when the senator was due in town.

"He's already arrived," she said.

"Will he visit the headquarters?"

"Yes, about five o'clock, for the rally this evening," she said, "if you'd like to meet him."

"Thank you, I would," Tigner said. "I'm with *Nouveaux Temps* magazine, in Paris. We have a worldwide circulation, and I'd very much like to interview him."

She consulted a schedule—without asking for his credentials. "If you could be here at six-forty-five, he has fifteen minutes free then."

"Perfect," he replied. "Could you make a note of my name and publication for his schedule, so there won't be any mix-up?"

"Of course. We do that as a matter of routine."

He spelled everything for her, thanked her, and walked toward the front door.

Ari Kramer and Annie Lee were credentialed for the campaign aircraft, an elderly Boeing 727, with the words SENATOR JOE BOX FOR AMERICA emblazoned on the side, and arrived in the early afternoon. They were in the campaign headquarters when a young man in a business suit, wearing horn-rimmed glasses and carrying a briefcase, walked past them, gaining Ari's attention.

"Something wrong with that man?" Annie asked him.

"No, he's just about the only member of the public I've ever seen in a campaign headquarters wearing a suit and tie, that's all."

Annie took a good look at the young man. "It makes him more interesting," she said.

. . .

Tigner went back to his hotel, walked up the fire stairs to the third floor, and went out onto the fire escape, which hung slightly over the gap between the platform and the parapet of the building next door. He jumped down onto the roof, walked to the front of the neighboring building, and leaned on the parapet, which came up to his chest. There, just across the street, was the empty office of Senator Joseph Box, no more than fifty yards away.

It occurred to him that, after he had taken the shot, this was the first place the police would search. So he walked around the roof of the building looking for a way to dispose of his weapon and found a large ventilator shaft with a curved top, opening onto the roof. He put his hand inside and felt hot air blowing out. He then returned to the fire escape at a trot, found an empty wooden box near it, set the box next to the parapet, then with one step to the box and another to the parapet, jumped across the gap between the buildings and let himself into the hotel. A short walk down the hall, then he took the elevator to his room on the second floor.

He pulled away the velcroed inside flap of his suitcase and selected from a small array of forged documents a press pass issued by the Paris police with his photograph and name on it, giving him the title of U.S. correspondent and bearing an official-looking stamp. He also took out an international driver's license, then resealed the flap.

He got out his throwaway cell and called Damien.

"Yes?"

"Can you talk for a moment?"

"Yes."

"I have intersected in Kansas City with the gentleman you wanted me to say hello to. There will be an excellent opportunity for me to complete the introduction in a couple of hours."

"Let me check a few things, and I'll call you back," Damien said, then hung up.

Damien went to Hank's office. "This may be sooner than we expected, but there's an opportunity to take out Joe Box in Kansas City, in about two hours. What would you like to do?"

Hank sat back in his chair and thought about it, then he tapped a finger on the newspaper on his desk. "Box is still moving up in the polls," he said. "I think if we wait much longer he might become too big a thing, and they'll give him Secret Service protection, and we don't want to deal with that. I think this might be a good time."

"Then I will press the button," Damien said. He went back to his office and called the number.

"Yes?" Tigner asked

"This is a perfect time for you to meet the gentleman," he said.

"I'll be back in the city in a couple of days," Tigner said. "I'll call you then." He hung up.

Tigner walked down the stairs to the parking garage, where he unlocked and opened the rear of the station wagon. He put on a thin pair of driving gloves, took out a nylon carryall, and set inside it a military-style carbine, broken into two pieces, and a telescopic sight, along with a silencer/suppressor that was about eighteen inches long. He loaded the weapon with six rounds of ammunition, then he added a light black sweater and a ski mask and a pair of long latex gloves. He returned to his room and watched TV for a while, then he found a room service menu, picked up the phone, and ordered a strip steak, fries, beans, and half a bottle of cabernet.

"Yes, sir, Mr. Tigner. That will take about thirty or forty minutes."

"Fine," he replied. "I may be in the shower. Please ask the waiter just to let himself in and set up on the coffee table in my room and open the wine to breathe. Add a twenty-five percent tip to the check."

"Of course."

Tigner turned on the shower to a warm temperature, hung his suit jacket and tie in his closet, took the black bag, slipped on the light black sweater over his shirt, took the bag, and retraced his steps to the fire escape. He looked around and saw nobody watching, so he tossed the bag onto the roof, then jumped after it. Still looking for anyone who might see him, he walked to the parapet, put on the ski mask, pulled on the latex gloves over his sleeves. He assembled the rifle, affixed the scope, then took a peek over the parapet. Ten minutes passed before he heard a siren, and a police car pulled up at the campaign headquarters, followed by a short motorcade, which disgorged Senator Joseph Box and a dozen other people. They went inside, where the senator shook the hands of the campaign volunteers, then Box worked his way upstairs to his mezzanine office, and there he came into Tigner's view.

Tigner took one more look around, then rested the rifle on

the parapet, pulled back on the slide to move the first round into the chamber, and trained the sight's crosshairs on the plate-glass window.

Senator Box entered the office with two other people, one of whom closed the door behind them. Box sat down at the desk.

"Perfect," Tigner said, squeezing off the round. Box collapsed behind his desk. Tigner then disassembled the weapon, wiped it clean, and dropped it into the bag with the sweater, the ski mask, and, finally, the long latex gloves. Taking care not to touch anything but the handles, he trotted over to the ventilator, dropped it down the shaft, and turned toward the fire escape. He decided the box he had left there was too obvious, so he kicked it away a few feet, stood back, and ran at the parapet.

He got a foot on the parapet, then jumped for the fire escape. Once inside, he closed the door behind him and ran down the stairs to his floor, down the hall, and let himself into his room. His dinner rested on the coffee table.

He hung his clothes in the closet, got into the shower, and scrubbed his hands and body to remove any residue from the shots fired, then toweled down, got into a terrycloth robe, and went back into the living room. The TV was still on, and a news announcer was reporting, over a breaking news banner, that the presidential candidate, Senator Joseph Box, had been shot at his campaign headquarters; no word on his condition.

Tigner left it on and began to eat his steak and drink some of the wine. He was still eating his steak when there was a hammering on the door. "Police!" somebody shouted.

55

Ari and Annie met Senator Box as he came into the headquarters. "Let me shake some hands, and I'll be right with you," the senator said.

They watched him work the room, not missing a soul, and finally, he beckoned them to follow him up the stairs to his mezzanine office.

"You kids are doing a marvelous job!" Box enthused, waving them to seats and walking around the desk. "In fact, my private polling tells me—"

A loud noise and the sound of breaking glass interrupted the senator. He convulsed, and a spray of blood emanated from the back of his neck, then he collapsed like a felled ox behind the desk.

Annie dove for the floor, but Ari just stared at the bloody wall behind where the man had stood. He helped Annie to her feet. "There's the phone," he said, pointing to the desk. "Call nine-one-one." He calmly walked around the desk to where Senator Box lay facedown, bleeding copiously from the back of his neck. He turned, grabbed Annie by her shirtfront, and yanked it open, revealing a T-top. He turned her around, stripped her of the shirt, folded it, pressed it tightly to Box's neck, then sat down on the floor, holding firm pressure on the wound. "This is all we can do until emergency services arrive. You might put on your jacket."

Annie had already hung up the phone and just stood there, staring at Ari. "Now I know," she said, "that you are calm under every possible situation, or have I missed one?"

"I don't think so," Ari said. "Lock the office door until the EMTs arrive."

She did so, just in time to stop a half dozen people who had run up the stairs.

Tigner had halfway finished his steak when the hammering on his door began. He picked up his wineglass and, still chewing, opened it. Two plainclothes officers holding badges entered the room. "Let's see some ID," one of them barked.

Tigner took a sip of his wine, swallowed, set his glass on the coffee table, and went to the closet. He came back with his wallet and passport.

A cop read his documents. "What's your name?"

"Timothy Tigner," he replied. "I'm a correspondent for a Paris magazine. You have my press pass, there in my wallet."

"Where have you been for the past hour?" the cop asked.

"Here. I ordered some dinner—I missed lunch—and took a shower." He was still in his bathrobe, and his hair was wet.

"Has anyone else been in your room?"

"Just the room service waiter," he replied. "What's going on?"

The cop gestured at the TV, which was on, but with the volume turned down. A breaking-news banner and an alarmed-looking young news reader, moving his lips silently, were on-screen.

"Why are you in Kansas City?" the cop asked.

"I'm covering Senator Box's campaign for my magazine. I have a six-forty-five appointment with him for an interview."

"Well," the cop said, "he isn't going to make it."

"Why not?" Tigner asked.

"He's going into surgery, last we heard," the second cop said. "Gunshot wound. Mike, call over to campaign HQ and check this guy out." Then he turned back to Tigner. "Do you have any weapons in the room?"

Tigner pointed at the coffee table. "Just a steak knife."

"No firearms?"

"No."

The other cop hung up his phone. "He checks out," he said to his partner. "He's on Box's schedule for six-forty-five."

The first cop handed Tigner back his ID. "Don't leave town for the next twelve hours," he said.

"I wouldn't think of it," Tigner replied. "I have a different kind of story to cover now. What hospital is he in?"

The cop told him. "But let me give you some advice: In this country, you'll get the whole story faster by just watching that." He pointed at the TV.

"Good suggestion," Tigner said. "May I finish my dinner now?"

"Sure, go ahead, Mr. Tigner."

The cops left, and Tigner turned up the TV volume, then returned his attention to his steak.

. . .

A half hour later the police held a meeting in the hotel manager's conference room.

"What have we got in this hotel?" asked a uniformed captain wearing a lot of brass.

"Nothing unusual," somebody said. "Looks like half the rooms are taken by campaign people and journalists, and the other by traveling salesmen. Nobody smells funny."

"Another team found what appears to be the weapon in a furnace in the building next door," the captain said. "It's just a mess of melting metal, though. We won't get much from that."

In their hotel room, Ari and Annie had been thoroughly grilled by the police and FBI, and were taking police advice and skipping the hospital, watching TV instead.

"Let's order some dinner," Annie said, opening a room service menu.

"We may as well," Ari said. "If he dies, our jobs are over. Even if he makes it, he's not going to be campaigning anymore."

His Skype alarm went off, and he opened his laptop and signed on. Smith sat quietly, staring at him. "Good evening," he said.

"Good evening," Ari replied. "Have you heard the news?"

"I expect everybody has," Smith said. "Any news from the campaign on the senator's condition?"

"Last we heard, he was in surgery, but no outcome yet."

"Well, get a good night's sleep, then tomorrow, go home.

Even if Box recovers, I doubt if he'll stay in the race, but who knows? You'll still be paid. Just wait for news."

"Yes, sir," Ari said. "We'll be available." They both signed off.

"I want a steak, how about you?" Annie asked.

"Same here."

"I wonder what there is to do in Kansas City?"

"Less than in Boston, I imagine," Ari said.

She picked up the phone and ordered.

Annie hung up the phone. "We've got nearly an hour until dinner comes," she said. "Whatever will we do?" She made a dive for him across the bed.

56

Damien met with the Thomases the following morning, ready to defend himself.

"I see that Joe Box is recovering," Hank said.

"How did your man come to botch it?" Henry asked.

"No, Poppa," Hank said, holding up a hand. "It's better this way. He won't be a martyr, but he'll be out of the race, if his prognosis is accurate."

"That's right," Damien said. "Our man made the shot under difficult circumstances, through a plate-glass window, and still managed to disable the man."

"Oh, all right," Henry said, "I guess you're both right. When is your man coming back here?"

"A day or two," Damien said. "He's driving."

"Good," Henry said.

"Did you have something in mind, Poppa?" Hank asked.

"Stone Barrington," Henry said.

"You want him killed?"

"He's at the root of all our problems, going back to his discovery of the Tommassini files. If it weren't for him, we wouldn't be in this fix."

"What fix is that?" Hank asked. "We're richer than ever and on the brink of retirement to wherever we want to go."

"I spoke with our young D.A.'s daddy," Henry said. "His boy is thinking about indicting us."

"For what?" Hank asked.

"Manslaughter of the two women at Bloomingdale's."

"They can't connect us to that," Damien said.

"He's thinking about trying. There's been a lot of pressure on him since the *Times* piece."

"So, there's pressure," Hank said, "but there's no case."

"Even if it fails, it will bring humiliation upon us."

"We'll soon be gone," Hank pointed out. "Humiliation doesn't travel."

"He has a point," Damien said.

"Humiliation can be cured only by satisfaction," Henry said.

"Only by revenge, you mean?" Hank asked.

"Exactly. Revenge is in our blood. It has to be satisfied or we don't rest easy, not even in some tropical paradise."

"So you want Barrington taken out?" Damien asked.

"I do, and this time, I want it done right. Is that perfectly clear?"

"How about timing?"

"Before an indictment comes down."

"Do you have any indication of when that might be?" Hank asked.

"A couple of weeks," Henry replied.

"I'll speak to my man," Damien said.

Hank held up a hand. "There's another consideration," he said.

"What might that be?" Henry asked.

"I've been approached to speak at the Republican Convention."

"But you aren't a Republican anymore," his grandfather said.

"That would be repaired beforehand," Hank said. "The committee's best estimate, from private polling, is that with Joe Box out of the race, no candidate is going to win enough states in the primaries to come to the convention with a majority in the Electoral College. The thinking is: I give a barn burner of a speech on national television, I get nominated the same night, and I sweep the convention."

"That's not so far-fetched," Damien said.

"I guess not," Henry concurred.

"So," Hank said, "I'm going to need two things: a speech from those two consultants, Rance . . ."

"And Barrington dead," Henry said. "Plus, a campaign to smear Holly Barker over her sexual relationship with him. And he won't be around to deny anything." He was smiling.

"Maybe you'd better have another chat with the D.A.'s daddy," Hank said.

Back in their Cambridge apartment, Ari received another Skype call from William Smith.

"Yes, sir?" Ari asked, while Annie listened from the sidelines.

"Ari, the shooting of Senator Box has removed him from the race entirely, and that means we have a whole new playing field."

"I can see how that would be, William."

"That said, we're now going to back a new candidate, one who isn't in the race."

"He would have a very late start in the primaries, wouldn't he?"

"He won't be entering any primaries, and no one who is will come to the convention with a majority in the Electoral College."

"I've run the numbers," Ari said, "and I think that's likely."

"Our man will bet everything on one overwhelming speech at the convention."

Ari was nodding. "Then he'll be nominated from the floor and win the nomination."

"Exactly."

Annie held up six fingers and mouthed, *Six speeches.*

"May I make a suggestion, William?" Ari asked.

"Of course, that's what I expect from you."

"Why don't you have him make half a dozen speeches around the country in key states, with network television coverage, not backing any candidate but speaking to what the party can accomplish in office with the right man at the helm. In fact, I think that phrase, 'the right man,' might become almost a campaign slogan. After a while, a lot of people will be saying he is the right man."

"That's brilliant!" Smith said. "Those speeches could clear the way for him at the convention."

"Who is our man?" Ari asked.

"Former congressman Hank Thomas."

"But he's left the party, hasn't he?"

"Yes, but he hasn't registered as a Democrat or an Independent. The Republican Party leaders have let him know that they'd be thrilled to have him back."

"At some point in the series of speeches, he could begin hinting that he might return to the party, perhaps even make an announcement."

"Ari, start researching Hank's record, then draft a speech or two for his approval. You can polish them later."

"Yes, William, I think that's the right thing to do."

"I'll be in touch." William logged off.

Annie spoke up. "You heard that. We're not only back in business, but if we can pull this off and get this guy elected, we'll have a bright future as political consultants, with a reputation as geniuses!"

"I could stand that," Ari said.

57

Tim Tigner opened his bag, shook out the laundry into a pile on the floor, and threw himself on the bed. As he did, his throwaway rang.

"Yes?" he said wearily.

"We need to meet today," Damien said.

"It'll have to be tomorrow," Tigner replied. "I drove all the way back with no rest, and I need to sleep."

"Today," Damien said.

"I'll call you tomorrow. Don't call again today." Tigner hung up and went to sleep without undressing.

Bob and Sherry moved her things into his Brooklyn place in the dead of night, and began to settle in.

Sherry flopped onto the sofa. "My doctor says I can have an occasional drink," she said. "I'm feeling occasional."

Bob poured them both a drink and flopped down beside her. "What did he have to say about sex?" he asked.

"Oh, he said I had to avoid sex," she replied.

"*What?*"

"I'm just giving you a hard time," she said, laughing. "He said sex is okay, too, as long as I'm on top."

"Did he actually say that?"

"He did. He said it's better for my brain."

"Maybe no sex for a while is better for your brain."

"You're kidding."

"Yes, I am. How quickly can you get naked?"

"Shortly after I finish this drink," she said.

They both drank for a while without talking.

"You know," she said finally, "as tough as this has been, I think it's worked out well. I mean, getting shot in the head is no picnic, but I don't remember most of it, and as a result, I've met some very nice people, and I've gotten away from some very bad ones."

"On behalf of everyone you've met, I thank you," Bob said.

She jumped up and started shedding clothes. "Okay, I'm ready now."

Bob was ready, too.

Tigner slept through the night until early the following afternoon. After a shower and shave, he called Damien.

"It's about time," Damien said.

"Same place, five-thirty?"

"I'll be there." They both hung up.

Damien got there first and, for a moment, was afraid Tigner wasn't going to show.

Tigner sat down fifteen minutes later. "I've got to get a motorcycle," he said.

"Why?"

"The traffic in this city is too much. I need to be able to drive between lanes of traffic, the way I did in Paris."

"Makes sense," Damien said, "except for the head injuries."

"I always wear a helmet."

"Maybe a motorcycle is a good idea," Damien said.

"For work, you mean?"

"I mean that Barrington lives in a house that's a fortress. When he goes out, he leaves in an armored car from his own garage, and he doesn't take long walks. Not since we've been trying to kill him, anyway."

"So, I've got to catch him getting in or out of the car?"

"What a good idea!" Damien said.

"I've got to get a motorcycle, then."

"You're right."

"How much are you offering for the head of Stone Barrington?"

Damien almost mentioned that he and Harod had decided that another payment would not be made, then he caught himself. "What were you thinking?"

"I was thinking two hundred fifty thousand dollars," Tigner said.

"You were going to kill four people for two hundred thousand dollars," Damien said.

"That was before you told me how difficult and dangerous it was going to be. I can't sit in some comfortable perch and snipe at him; I have to be out on the street with no cover, and it's hard to make an escape in those conditions. You wouldn't want me to get caught, would you?"

"No," Damien said. "Two hundred thousand dollars."

"When?"

"It's in the briefcase," he said.

"Open it."

Damien opened it, gave him a peek at the money, and closed it again.

"Done," Tigner said. "But after this, we're not going to do any business for a while."

"I agree," Damien replied. "It would be too dangerous for both of us. This one, however, we need done in a hurry."

"There's no hurrying where assassination is concerned. There's too much planning and, in this case, on the street, too much can go wrong."

"I see your point," Damien said, "but . . ."

"I'll try to make it happen soon," Tigner said, "but no promises. If that doesn't work for you, you can have your money back." He set the briefcase in front of Damien.

Damien moved it back to him. "Do the best you can," he said.

"I always do the best I can."

"There was some question about your last job being incomplete."

"The man is out of the race," Tigner said, getting to his feet. "We won't be meeting again for a long while." He walked out of the restaurant carrying the briefcase.

Damien finished his drink. He had a good feeling about this one.

. . .

Joan buzzed Stone. "Dino on one."

"Good morning," Stone said.

"Not really," Dino replied.

"What's the problem?"

"Ken Burrows has become a problem."

"Ken has always been a problem."

"He's backsliding on indicting the Thomases for *anything*."

"Maybe that's not a terrible thing," Stone said.

"How is it not a terrible thing?"

"Three ways," Stone said. "First, the Thomases have sold up and will soon scatter to the four winds." He paused.

"And what are the other two ways?"

"I forget," Stone said. "But trust me, they're no longer a problem."

"So, you're going to start leaving the house like a normal human being?"

"I'm not going to let the bastards turn me into a turtle."

"Okay, how about dinner tonight?"

"Patroon, at seven-thirty?" Stone said.

"Done. Just me. Viv is somewhere in South America."

58

Tigner got on the Internet, and before bedtime he had bought himself a light motorcycle and tucked it into the garage, next to the Mercedes station wagon. He would not register it, since he didn't plan to own it for long.

The following morning, he read a long piece in the *Times* by Jamie Cox, the reporter who had written the original piece, and now the book about the Thomas family. She also outlined the political career of Hank Thomas, and she seemed to think he might become a candidate for president again, with Senator Joseph Box out of the way. His interest was piqued, since he was working for the Thomas family—if what Harod had told him about their employer was true, and he had no reason to think it wasn't.

He had breakfast, then went out, found a bookstore, and bought a copy of Cox's book about the Thomases. He went home and started reading, and didn't stop until he had finished it, at bedtime.

After that, he went to his computer and googled Stone Barrington. He began to feel he knew the man he was reading about. The Thomases wanted him dead as revenge for taking the Tommassini files to the district attorney and the *Times*, all of which had caused them so much trouble.

Tigner didn't sleep well that night. The following morning he went shopping and bought some new throwaway cell phones, then he made a phone call.

Jamie Cox rose at the Bel-Air Hotel, in Los Angeles, where she had spoken to a group the previous evening, the last stop on her book tour. She was packing her bags for the trip back to New York when her phone rang. She checked the number before answering; it was her secretary at the *Times*. She called back.

"Jamie Cox's office," she said.

"June, it's Jamie. What's up?"

"I went through your phone messages first thing this morning. It was the usual stuff—they loved your book, they hated your book, like that. Except for one, from somebody called Rasheed." She spelled it.

"What did the message say?"

"I'll play it back for you," June said. "Hang on a sec."

Jamie got out her recorder and pressed record when she heard the message. "Good day," a young man's voice said. "My name is . . . Well, you may call me Rasheed. I have read your book and many of your pieces in the newspaper. You seem to think your story is over now, but it is not. I have further information for you about the Thomases and their connection to a recent assassination attempt. Also, concerning your friend, Stone Barrington, who is in danger. If you wish to hear this information, go and buy a throwaway cell phone and call me on the following number." He spoke the digits twice. "Leave a message containing your new number, and I will call you and give you the information."

"That's all," June said. "Got it?"

"Yes, thank you, June." Jamie played the message again, then used her throwaway to call Rasheed's number. She heard only a beep. "This is Jamie Cox," she said. "I am very much interested in your information. I am flying to New York this morning, and I will call you again after I'm in the city, late in the afternoon." She hung up and called Stone Barrington.

"Hi, there," Stone said. "Is your book tour over?"

"Yes, thank God. I'm leaving L.A. this morning, and I'll be home late this afternoon."

"I hope by 'home' you mean my house."

"I accept the invitation."

"Dinner tonight, then."

"May we have it at home? I'll probably be very tired."

"Certainly."

"By the way, I received an interesting phone message on my *Times* line. I'll play it for you now. Can you record it?"

"Sure, give me a second. All right, I'm recording."

Jamie played her message back.

"That certainly *is* interesting," Stone said.

"It sounds like you'd better watch your ass," she said.

"I've made a habit of that lately," Stone replied. "Have you called him?"

"Yes, but only to leave a message that I'll be back later today. We'll call him together."

"Good. See you when I see you."

They both hung up.

Stone called Dino and played the message for him.

"That's pretty vague," Dino said.

"What did you think of the voice?"

"Young man, in his twenties, probably. A slight accent of some sort—educated, well-spoken."

"I'll buy all of that."

"Has she returned the call?"

"She'll do that when she's back in New York."

"I'd be interested to hear what he has to say."

"I'll record it for you," Stone said. "Later."

"Later. Watch your ass," Dino said, then hung up.

59

Stone welcomed Jamie back to New York, then, while Fred took her luggage up to the master suite, he made her a drink in the study.

"Is everything all right with you?" he asked, handing her the drink.

"I'll know more about that after I've talked to this Rasheed," she replied. They clinked glasses and drank. "Are you ready for me to call him?"

"Let's wait a few minutes. Dino is on his way, and I want him to hear what this guy has to say."

"All right, I suppose it's better to have another witness."

"What do you think this guy has on the Thomases?" he asked.

"Maybe the shooting of Joe Box?" she suggested. "By the way, one of our reporters has learned that he's walking and talking."

"Anything of any importance?"

"Not yet. He doesn't know who shot him or why anyone would try. He let slip that the Thomases have been paying a speechwriter for him, though."

"Now, why would they do that?" Stone asked.

"Maybe to offer some competition to the rest of the field?"

"That makes sense."

"Sort of, but only if Hank is planning to run himself. We've heard that the Republican National Committee has been putting out feelers for him to come home."

"And save them from Joe Box?"

She laughed. "Maybe the Thomases did too good a job of remaking Joe, and now they're having second thoughts."

Stone laughed. "That's an amusing idea," he said. "I expect that Joe is pretty much unhandleable. He could say or do anything."

"And has," Jamie echoed.

Dino had let himself into the house and now joined them in the study; he poured his own scotch. "Okay," he said. "What now?"

"Now Jamie calls her new friend, Rasheed," Stone said.

She got out some wiring and a microphone and plugged them into her throwaway. "Here we go," she said.

They listened as the phone emitted a beep. "This is Jamie Cox," she said. "It's a little after seven, and I'm in a quiet place, ready to talk. Please call me on the following number." She left the number, then hung up.

"Now what?" Dino asked.

"Now he's supposed to call back," Jamie said.

"See if you can get him to come here," Dino said.

"Do you think he's that dumb?" Stone asked.

"Maybe. It's worth a try."

"All right," Jamie said, "if he gives me an opportunity, I'll invite him."

They chatted on for a few minutes, then the throwaway rang. Jamie held her hands up for silence, then picked up the phone. "This is Jamie."

"And this is Rasheed," he replied.

"Are you from the Middle East?" she asked.

"I am born in Paris, of an American father and an Algerian mother."

"Where were you educated?" she asked.

"I was tutored. What you call homeschooled."

"University?"

"Two years, in Paris."

"How did you come to be in your current business?"

"I was recruited by a friend," he said. "He's now dead."

"Have you lost a lot of friends in your business?"

"All of them," he replied. "Which, in a way, is why I'm talking to you."

"You must be very lonely."

"I was, but not so much lately; I've met someone."

"Girl? Guy?"

He paused before replying. "I am not a poofter," he said firmly.

"Girl, then."

"Yes, a very nice one."

"Does that mean you are thinking of changing professions?"

"I am, as a matter of fact. I have one more job to do, then I'm a free man."

"And what, or *who*, is the job?"

"I would rather not say. You will know soon enough."

"Are you afraid I'll turn you in?"

"You don't have enough information to turn me in," he replied smoothly. "And remember, you have no idea whether anything I've told you is true."

"That is correct, but why would you establish contact with me, only to lie to me? I think you are telling the truth."

"You are very perceptive."

"You referred to a recent attempt on someone's life: Could that have been Senator Joseph Box?"

"It could have been."

"Why did you miss?"

"I didn't miss. The glass deflected the round slightly, and he fell behind a desk where I couldn't see him."

"Did the Thomases hire you to assassinate Senator Box?"

"One of them did. I have dealt only with him."

"Would that be Mr. Damien?"

"Again, you are very perceptive."

"Did Damien ask you to kill Stone Barrington?"

"Perhaps. But he is safe."

"Safe because you decided not to kill him?"

"Perhaps. I have talked too long now. Perhaps we will chat again sometime. Goodbye."

"Wait . . ."

"Yes?"

"There are some friends I'd like you to meet. One of them is Stone Barrington."

"Then the other must be his policeman friend, Mr. Bacchetti."

"Now it's you who are perceptive."

"Perhaps some other day," he said, then hung up.

"Okay," Jamie said, "I gave it my best shot."

"He's very talkative," Dino said, "but what did we learn?"

"Only what he wanted us to learn," Stone said.

"Well," Jamie said, "at least you're off the griddle."

"At least, that's what he said," Dino said. "True or not. Maybe he wants Stone to relax a little, so he'll be an easier target."

"You're a real comfort, Dino," Stone said.

"I'm just being realistic."

"I believe him," Jamie said.

"Why?"

"I don't know. He just feels credible. I think that, in his way, he's an honest man."

"But still an assassin," Stone said.

"Ah, yes," Jamie replied. "He said he has one more job to do."

"I wonder who that could be?" Stone asked.

60

im Tigner took his new girlfriend, Karen Landis, to dinner at the new Four Seasons restaurant.

"This is very special," Karen said. "What's the occasion?"

"I don't know yet," Tim replied, sipping his champagne and tasting his foie gras. "Perhaps you will make it special."

"It's up to me, is it?" She laughed. "This is some seduction."

"Is it not polite these days to leave the decision to the woman?"

"I suppose that's one way to do it," she said. "Perhaps it's not a bad idea."

"Well?"

"I'll let you know," she said.

They continued through their lavish dinner and expensive wine.

"Well," she said finally, "I'm off tomorrow."

"May I take that as an acceptance?" Tim asked.

"You may," she said.

His phone vibrated on his belt. "Will you excuse me for a moment?" he asked, then headed for the men's room. "Yes?"

"Good evening, I hope I'm not disturbing your dinner."

"Yes, you are, so please be brief."

"We'd like the contract completed tomorrow, as early as possible."

"I will, if I can," Tim said.

"There's one other thing we'd like, though I know it may not be possible."

"What is that?"

"We—my senior partner, in particular—would like to have a word with Mr. B. before you are finished."

"That's bizarre."

"Only if it's manageable and doesn't jeopardize the enterprise."

"If it is, I'll call you," Tim said, then hung up. He went back to his table, nursing a new idea.

"I'm ready," Karen said.

"Then we're both ready," Tim replied. He paid the bill, and they left.

The following morning, Tim awoke very early. Karen was snoring lightly next to him in bed. He got up, dressed in light clothing, then put on a gray jumpsuit over them. He went to his secret cache of weapons and supplies and chose a few things, tucked them into the commodious pockets of the jumpsuit, and went to the garage. He got the motorcycle started, put on his helmet, and drove downtown.

He drove around slowly for a half hour, then found the perfect vehicle: an elderly but serviceable Honda van with a homemade, stick-on household repairs sign on the rear. He drove around the corner, parked the motorcycle, then returned to the van, and jump-started it. He drove around the corner, past the motorcycle, and into the parking garage of H. Thomas & Son, taking a ticket from the automated machine.

Once inside, he found a parking place, tucked away behind an elevator shaft, looked around to be sure he wouldn't be observed, then went to work. He got out of the van, walked to the rear, and made sure the doors there were unlocked, then he opened them, got inside, and closed them behind him.

Once inside, he took an object the size of a piece of fruit—say a pear—taped it to the rear of the passenger seat, then secured a thin strand of wire from a ring on the object to the rear door of the van, the one that had to be opened first. He tightened it slightly, clipped the end, and put it in his pocket. Then he went forward and got out of the van.

He left the garage and walked around the corner to where the motorcycle was parked, started it, and sat on it as it idled. He took his throwaway cell phone from a pocket and speed-dialed Damien.

Damien sat in Henry's office, with Hank next to him, sipping a cup of mid-morning coffee. He glance at the cell phone, recognized the number, and picked it up. "Just a moment," he said to his companions, "this may be news." He pressed a button. "Yes?"

"You know who this is?"

"Of course."

"You made a request last evening?"

"I did."

"That has been accomplished. Would you like to visit, briefly, with the gentleman?"

"Of course. Where are you?"

"Downstairs in your garage."

"Just a moment." Damien covered the phone. "My man has taken Mr. Barrington," he said. "Would you like to see him for a moment?"

"I certainly would," Henry said.

"Why not?" Hank asked. "Where is he?"

"Conveniently located," Damien replied. "Downstairs, in our garage. We should go now." Everybody got to their feet.

He spoke into the phone again. "We're on our way down. Where, exactly, in the garage?"

"Take the elevator down, get off, turn right, and there's a white van parked in the corner. Don't speak to me. Open the rear door, and you'll find the gentleman waiting for you. Remove the tape over his mouth, if you wish him to speak, then replace it when you are done, close the door, and return to your office."

"Fine," Damien said.

"We will not speak again for a while," Tigner said, then hung up.

"Let's go downstairs," Damien said to his companions. They went to the elevator and rode down to the garage. Damien led the way. "It should be right around the corner," he said.

The van was there, and the three gathered around the rear door. "Henry," Damien said, "would you like the honors?"

Henry reached out, worked the handles, and opened both doors. There was nothing inside.

Damien heard the tiny noise of a metal ring striking the floor of the van. "Grenade . . ." he began to say.

Tigner sat on the motorcycle around the corner and heard the sound of the explosion through the garage ventilator next to him. He put the motorcycle in gear, kicked up the stand, and drove slowly away. "There we go," he said aloud, "all accounts settled." He drove a few blocks away to a small wharf he knew on the East River, got out of his jumpsuit, took a length of duct tape from a roll, then stuffed it, along with the jumpsuit, into a saddlebag. He revved the engine to about fifty percent, kicked up the stand, kicked the engine into gear, and released the clutch. The machine shot straight ahead along the little wharf, then sailed out over the water and plunged into its depths.

Tigner found a cab, and when he got back to his apartment, armed with a bag of hot bagels, Karen was still asleep. He kissed her on the ear, and she stirred.

"Wake up, love," he said. "Breakfast is ready, and the day is ours."

Stone was having lunch with Dino at their club when his phone buzzed. He saw that it was Jamie, so he got up from the table, walked through a door, and answered it.

"Hi, there," Jamie said. "I hope I'm not interrupting your lunch."

"You are, but not unpleasantly," he replied.

"Somebody on the police desk just got a report that sounds like a message from Rasheed."

"Yes?"

"There has just been an explosion in the parking garage of H. Thomas & Son. Three men are dead."

"And this is a message from Rasheed?"

"The three have been identified as Henry Thomas, Hank Thomas, and Lawrance Damien."

"That sounds more like a gift," Stone said.

"And a perfect ending to my story," Jamie said, "which I have to go and write now. See you later." She hung up.

Stone walked back to his table and sat down.

"Why do you look so happy?" Dino asked.

"We just got a gift from Jamie's contact, Rasheed." Stone told him what she had said.

Dino smiled.

AUTHOR'S NOTE

I am happy to hear from readers, but you should know that if you write to me in care of my publisher, three to six months will pass before I receive your letter, and when it finally arrives it will be one among many, and I will not be able to reply.

However, if you have access to the Internet, you may visit my website at www.stuartwoods.com, where there is a button for sending me an e-mail. So far, I have been able to reply to all of my e-mail, and I will continue to try to do so.

If you send me an e-mail and do not receive a reply, it is probably because you are among an alarming number of people who have entered their e-mail address incorrectly in their mail software. I have many of my replies returned as undeliverable.

Remember: e-mail, reply; snail mail, no reply.

When you e-mail, please do not send attachments, as I never open these. They can take twenty minutes to download, and they often contain viruses.

Please do not place me on your mailing lists for funny stories, prayers, political causes, charitable fund-raising, petitions, or sentimental claptrap. I get enough of that from people I already know. Generally speaking, when I get e-mail addressed to a large number of people, I immediately delete it without reading it.

Please do not send me your ideas for a book, as I have a policy of writing only what I myself invent. If you send me story ideas, I will immediately delete them without reading them. If you have a good idea for a book, write it yourself, but I will not be able to advise you on how to get it published. Buy a copy of *Writer's Market* at any bookstore; that will tell you how.

Anyone with a request concerning events or appearances may e-mail it to me or send it to: Publicity Department, Penguin Random House LLC, 1745 Broadway, New York, NY 10019.

Those ambitious folk who wish to buy film, dramatic, or television rights to my books should contact Matthew Snyder, Creative Artists Agency, 9830 Wilshire Boulevard, Beverly Hills, CA 98212-1825.

Those who wish to make offers for rights of a literary nature should contact Anne Sibbald, Janklow & Nesbit, 445 Park Avenue, New York, NY 10022. (Note: This is not an invitation for you to send her your manuscript or to solicit her to be your agent.)

If you want to know if I will be signing books in your city, please visit my website, www.stuartwoods.com, where the tour schedule will be published a month or so in advance. If you wish me to do a book signing in your locality, ask your favorite bookseller to contact his Penguin representative or the Penguin publicity department with the request.

If you find typographical or editorial errors in my book and feel an irresistible urge to tell someone, please write to Sara Minnich at Penguin's address above. Do not e-mail your discoveries to me, as I will already have learned about them from others.

A list of my published works appears in the front of this book and on my website. All the novels are still in print in paperback and can be found at or ordered from any bookstore. If you wish to obtain hardcover copies of earlier novels or of the two nonfiction books, a good used-book store or one of the online bookstores can help you find them. Otherwise, you will have to go to a great many garage sales.